'If poetry was the supreme literary form of the First World War then, as if in riposte, in the Second World War, the English novel came of age. This wonderful series is an exemplary reminder of that fact. Great novels were written about the Second World War and we should not forget them.'

WILLIAM BOYD

'It's wonderful to see these four books given a new lease of life because all of them are classic novels from the Second World War written by those who were there, experienced the fear, anguish, pain and excitement first-hand and whose writings really do shine an incredibly vivid light onto what it was like to live and fight through that terrible conflict.'

JAMES HOLLAND, Historian, author and TV presenter

'The Imperial War Museum has performed a valuable public service by reissuing these four absolutely superb novels covering four very different aspects of the Second World War. I defy you to choose which is best: I keep changing my mind!'

ANDREW ROBERTS, author of *Churchill: Walking with Destiny*

T0019687

'*Eight Hours from England* is much more than a novel. Its author may be remembered today as a distinguished actor on stage and screen, but during the Second World War he had served gallantly as an officer in Britain's elite Special Operations Executive, and this book, which first appeared in 1945, is a faithful evocation of his searing experiences in Nazi-occupied Albania after he was sent there to assist the Resistance. One of the earliest accounts to be published by any ex-SOE officer, it remains a powerful study not only of the desperate dilemmas faced by occupied populations but also of the challenges faced by outsiders inclined to help.'

RODERICK BAILEY

'I loved this book, and felt I was really there.'

LOUIS de BERNIÈRES

'As well as being one of our greatest actors, Anthony Quayle was an intrepid war hero and his autobiographical novel is one of the greatest adventure stories of the Second World War. Beautifully written and full of pathos and authenticity, it brings alive the terrible moral decisions that have to be taken by soldiers under unimaginable pressures in wartime.'

ANDREW ROBERTS, author of *Churchill: Walking with Destiny*

EIGHT HOURS FROM ENGLAND

Anthony Quayle

IMPERIAL WAR MUSEUMS

First published in Great Britain by William Heinemann Ltd 1945

First published in this format in 2019 by
IWM, Lambeth Road, London SE1 6HZ
iwm.org.uk

ISBN 978-1-912423-10-1

A catalogue record for this book is available from the
British Library.

Printed and bound by CPI Group (UK) Ltd, Croydon CR0 4YY

Every effort has been made to contact all copyright holders.
The publishers will be glad to make good in future editions
any error or omissions brought to their attention.

Cover illustration by Bill Bragg
Design and art direction by Clare Skeats

About the Author

Anthony Quayle (1913–1989)

ANTHONY QUAYLE was a successful British actor and theatre director, well known for his roles in classic plays on the stage as well as his film career. After appearing in music hall he joined the Old Vic in 1932, touring in various productions before the outbreak of the Second World War.

During the war Quayle served in the Royal Artillery, and later joined the Special Operations Executive (SOE), whence he was deployed to Albania. *Eight Hours from England* is a fictionalised account of Quayle's time behind enemy lines there. He also wrote a later novel, *On Such a Night*, about his time with the British Army in Gibraltar.

After the war Quayle returned to the stage. From 1948 to 1956 he was the director of the Shakespeare Memorial Theatre, laying the foundations for the creation of the Royal Shakespeare Company and helping to establish Stratford-on-Avon as a major centre of British theatre.

Quayle's screen career began in 1938 and he appeared in many classic films such as *Ice Cold in Alex* (1958), *The Guns of Navarone* (1961), and *Lawrence of Arabia* (1962). Quayle received both Academy Award and Golden Globe nominations for his role in *Anne of the Thousand Days* (1969), and his towering stage career took him around the world to both popular and critical acclaim. He was knighted in 1985.

Introduction

War novels are often associated with the First World War, with an explosion of the genre in the late 1920s. Erich Maria Remarque's *All Quiet on the Western Front* was a bestseller and was later made into a Hollywood film in 1930. In the same year Siegfried Sassoon's *Memoirs of an Infantry Officer* sold 24,000 copies (and remains in print), with generations of school children growing up on a diet of the poetry of Wilfred Owen and the novels of Sassoon. The novels of the Second World War are often forgotten, and the aim of this series is to bring some classic titles of that later war back into print. While there are in fact many (unjustly) forgotten Second World War novels based on frontline experience both in Europe and beyond, *Eight Hours from England*, written by the famed Shakespearian actor Anthony Quayle, provides an interesting contrast. First published in 1945, it concerns the exploits of SOE operative John Overton (read – the author himself) behind enemy lines in Nazi-occupied Albania. Here then is a 'secret' front line; there is no huge supporting cast where Overton is going.

The Special Operations Executive (SOE) was established as a secret service in July 1940 with the aim of infiltrating enemy-occupied countries and, in the words of the Prime Minister Winston Churchill, to 'set Europe ablaze'. Tasked with work such as sabotage and liaising with local resistance movements, the missions were extremely dangerous, with many now-famous operatives such as Violette Szabo meeting their fate at the hands of the enemy. At its largest, SOE employed some 10,000 men and 3,000 women, many of whom worked as secret agents. The largest branch headquarters in the Mediterranean and Middle East theatre was in Cairo, and this is where the novel's protagonist Major John Overton is initially sent, before being posted to Albania. When queried regarding his understanding of the country, his knowledge is negligible, the Lieutenant Colonel in turn remarking: 'All the better: you won't have a political bias. It's the least developed of all the Balkan sections, and so possibly the best fun. It looks as though civil war is going to break out there any day now – but never mind, it hasn't started yet.'

Albania was invaded by Italy on 7 April 1939 and was swiftly conquered; the reigning King Zog escaped to the UK, where the Royal family stayed for the duration of the war. Communist partisans under Enver Hoxha and the more traditional Balli Kombetar were both supported by SOE initially. After the overthrow of Benito Mussolini – the Italian fascist leader – in July 1943, some Italian forces in Albania sided with the partisans, whilst others went over to the Germans. The resulting chaos was quickly quelled by German forces, who installed a government led by Mehdi Frasheri. However the government had little control outside the main towns, with the rest of the country ruled by rival guerrilla leaders. It is against this backdrop that Overton is sent to Albania in December 1943.

* * *

Anthony Quayle was originally commissioned into the Royal Artillery in 1940. In Gibraltar, he served with the coastal artillery and was Aid-de-Camp to the Governor (furthermore, having been an accomplished actor, he was involved in various productions on the island). In June 1941 he returned to England and spent a few months with the Auxiliary Units in Northumberland – Home Guard units training to fight a guerrilla war – before returning once again to Gibraltar. Yet after three and half years in the army Quayle had still not seen any combat. This caused him significant frustration; in his autobiography *A Time to Speak*, he said of that period: 'I was becoming restless and self-accusatory'. One of his friends suggested joining the SOE, proclaiming 'for heaven's sake – come and join us in SOE. It's an independent sort of life, and as a bonus there is the parachuting. You'd enjoy it'. The author subsequently applied to join SOE in October 1943.

Quayle was sent to Albania on 31st December that year, exactly the same date that Overton is sent in the novel. Indeed, his time in

Albania is so closely reflected in *Eight Hours from England* that the book almost acts as a memoir, merely with the names altered. Tom Keith, for example, whom Overton is sent to replace as the man in charge of the Valona area at the start of the novel, is based on Major Jerry Field. When Overton first meets Keith, he is disillusioned with the partisans; similarly, he has a low opinion of the Ballists who 'won't fight the Germans. They won't even let me blow the road near their precious village'. He is more complimentary about the Italians, remarking that 'their spirit's all right, but physically they're broken… malaria, starvation… Some gave themselves up to the Germans in September, quite a few joined the Partisans, and a whole lot just took to the mountains'. Like the fictional Keith, Field was also disillusioned with the partisans; in *A Time to Speak*, Quayle noted that Field 'could not understand that his war and their war was different'. Field also nicknamed his base in a cave as 'Sea View' (as in the novel) and, like Tom Keith, he also blew himself up. In an interview held in the IWM archives, Lieutenant Commander Alexander 'Sandy' Glen (who thought Field was mad, contrastingly describing Quayle as 'delightful'), described Field fishing with explosives. When one went off in his face, he then fell thirty feet off the rocks, became unconscious, sustained a number of broken bones and a dislodged eyeball – which Glen 'put back in with a spoon'.

Another character directly drawn from life is Skender Mucho. In the real events, this was Skender Muco of the Balli Kombetar, who admitted to Quayle that the Ballists had aligned themselves with the Germans in order to defeat the Communist Partisans. Muco had been willing to work with the British but wanted representation in London and assurances for Albania's independence after the war. The British authorities, however, were only concerned with those groups who attacked the German occupying forces, and were fundamentally disinterested in Albanian politics. Muco later lost his life to the Germans – something Overton predicts for his counterpart Mucho in the novel:

Mucho could go running all over the mountains, hiding, scheming, intriguing, but he was doomed. He would never make another trip to Paris. Somewhere here in these mountains a German or an Albanian bullet would put an end to his fevered life. I felt quite sure of it.

* * *

The novel focuses much on Overton's attempts as a liaison officer to meet with the Partisans and the Ballists, as his mission is always clear: support those who attack the Germans (in the words of Lieutenant-Colonel Cleaver, 'your main task is to kill Germans'). Nothing is quite what it seems, however, even relations amongst the allies. Overton is sent out with 'sole operational responsibility' but the actual command structure is unclear, with two other officers inhabiting 'Sea View', namely Commander Trent – responsible for coastal reconnaissance and intelligence – as well as an American intelligence officer, Macavoy Benson. These two characters were based on Sandy Glen, a naval commander in MI6 (quoted above), and Major Dale McAdoo from the Office of Strategic Services – an American wartime intelligence agency. Overton comments that after his arrival:

> *Breakfast in the cave was the best I had eaten since peacetime and very international: English porridge, American bacon, Albanian eggs, and warm bread freshly baked by an Italian. As we ate and talked, each was sending out feelers, trying to assess the other two, like three wrestlers together in a ring. Trent talked a lot, Benson was rather quiet. Once or twice I caught him looking at me watchfully through expressionless brown eyes.*

This passage aptly encapsulates the international flavour of those Overton faces: British and American intelligence officers, the competing Albanian factions and the worn out remaining Italian forces, all behind enemy lines, which were dominated by the occupying German forces. Overton is obliged to placate them all, often under dangerous and precarious conditions. Quayle himself found working with the Balli and the Partisans very difficult, and the reader has a real sense of the problems Quayle/Overton and his allies face, and the dislike for many of those they are forced to deal with (modern readers may indeed find some of the language of the period used about the locals rather jarring). Ostensibly this is an 'exciting' set up (in the fictional sense, at least), but the logistics of operating in enemy territory, their precarious position and the feeling of isolation is challenging for all the men. One of the few positives, Overton finds, is his friendship with Munzi.

* * *

Quayle was eventually extracted from Albania on the night of 3 April 1944 and the stress of the last few months had evidently caught up with him, as he remarked in his autobiography: 'The joy to be back amongst my own was so great that it was almost pain. I jolted along in the back of the truck sobbing with happiness'. He was taken to hospital in Brindisi only to be diagnosed with malaria and jaundice. He commented that these illnesses were 'nothing serious, but sufficient to lay me flat for several weeks: time enough to lie and contemplate the total failure of my mission'. He went back briefly to pick up the men he left behind, as does Overton at the end of the novel. Quayle later told Harold Macmillan, British Minister Resident in North Africa and future Prime Minister, that the dilemma was immense for liaison officers, 'whose task was to urge Balkan peasants into attacking the enemy, but knowing perfectly well the price those peasants would pay in death and the destruction of their villages'. Indeed at the end of the war Albania under Enver Hoxha, who had eliminated his wartime colleagues, fell out first with the Western Allies and later the Communist Bloc, going on to function as a nation in isolation.

This eloquent, engaging novel of life behind the lines in Albania rightly deserves to be brought back into print. Originally published in 1945, Quayle later wrote that 'it was well enough received to make me wonder if I might not turn to writing instead of acting. But although I could write, I knew I did not have enough experience of life to be a writer: no, I was an actor'. Quayle did go on to enjoy a glittering acting career, including a number of war movies such as *Ice Cold in Alex* (1958) and *The Guns of Navarone* (1961), his performances no doubt based on his wartime experiences. This remarkable career has indeed rather overshadowed Quayle's time as an author, but despite his perceivable pessimism, his novel surpasses both his and the reader's expectations alike.

Alan Jeffreys
2019

ONE

THE WIRELESS SET was cheap and rather old; certain tones would set in vibration a screw that had come loose in its mysterious interior. There were five or six of us standing round it that Sunday morning, and all the time the Prime Minister spoke the little screw kept vibrating. When he reached the words: 'A state of war now exists between this country and Germany,' Ann walked quickly out of the cottage through the open door. I followed her outside when Chamberlain's speech was ended and found her in the orchard, her head golden beneath the apple trees. She was weeping silently, her arms limp by her sides, the tears running unchecked down her cheeks. As she heard my feet in the long grass she raised her head and looked at me.

In that moment I saw Ann, as it were, for the first time, and my whole being was filled with a sudden, almost intolerable yearning for her.

Two months later I was sent abroad, not to return to England till the autumn of forty-three. I left the country knowing well that Ann was not in love with me, yet, though at first I tried, nothing I could do was able to exorcise her image from my mind. For four years I thought, breathed and lived Ann till in the end I could only yield to the belief that here was something more than natural and that no feeling so strong could be without fruition.

Harry Matthews was one of the first friends I met when I got back. Harry had been in Intelligence since before the war; he had chronic arthritis and a thin face warped with pain.

'I've a wonderful job for you,' he said.

'What is it?'

'How would you like to go into the Balkans?'

'Not at all at this time of year, thanks. Too much snow.'

'I'm serious. Greece, Albania, Jugoslavia – you can choose.'

'When would it mean going?'

'Almost at once.'

'No, thank you, Harry,' I said. 'I've got two months' leave coming to me, and I'm going to need every minute of it.'

By a miracle Ann was living in London. She was glad to see me and gave me a lot of her time. They were strange days, passed in a kind of tortured happiness, for I soon discovered that she was fond of another man – how fond I could not tell; I don't think she knew herself. I felt knotted with frustration; my mind beat round and round seeking some sign, some magic word that in a flash could make clear to her what was in my heart. I could not find it.

After ten days I phoned Harry.

'I'll take that job of yours if it's still going.'

'You're too late.'

'Try, will you,' I said. 'I want it badly.'

It was midnight when he phoned me back.

'You're in luck,' he said. 'I've fixed it. You'll leave for Cairo by air tomorrow evening.'

Ann was late arriving for lunch that last day. I sat against the wall in the entrance to the restaurant watching the people push through the glass doors. Each taxi that stopped outside I thought must be hers; but it wasn't.

I began to panic. Something had gone wrong; she'd gone to a different place; she hadn't heard me properly on the phone; now I wouldn't be able to find her at all. I looked at my watch and told myself not to be a fool; she was only ten minutes late.

Then, suddenly, she was there. She came in quickly and stopped in the centre of the hall looking round, not seeing me. I let her stand there for a moment, pretending to myself that I was seeing her as a stranger for the first time. She was wearing a black coat and dress, her hair uncovered, and there was a pathos about such extreme beauty that caught at my heart.

I had ordered a good lunch and one of the last bottles of the Bollinger '28.

'John!' she cried when she saw it. 'This is wonderful. But it will be disastrous – I never drink at all nowadays.'

'I'll drink it alone then.'

2

'Oh no, you won't!' she said. 'But what do you mean by all this extravagance?'

'Because it's my last meal in London, and I thought we'd do it properly.'

Ann put down her knife and fork.

'What do you mean, your last meal?' she asked.

'I'm off this afternoon.'

'This afternoon! But I thought you were here for several weeks.'

'I know,' I said. 'It's all very sudden. Anyhow I've got to be at Paddington by three-thirty. My luggage is there now.'

And I told her that I had taken on a new job in the Middle East, and that I had been ordered to fly out to Cairo at once.

'You're extraordinary,' she said. 'You've only this minute got back to England. Why do you want to go rushing into a new job?'

'Because.'

There was a little silence. Then she said: 'Well, I'm sorry.'

She lifted her glass. 'Anyway, here's to the new job.'

I wanted to try and make her say more, but I stopped myself.

During my few days in England, Ann had seemed full of laughter, but that day she was quiet and ill at ease: perhaps she had caught something from my own mood. After a glass of champagne, though, she began to talk. She spoke about her life during the war – about air-raids, and coupons, and standing in queues, and darkness – not complainingly, rather with a kind of affection. As she talked I watched her face; it might be a long time before I saw it again. She had grown to look older in these four years, and even more beautiful. There were fine lines round her eyes and the modelling of the cheek-bones was firmer, but her mouth was soft as ever and still her laughter seemed somehow near the brink of tears.

When lunch was over and we stood outside in Piccadilly, I said: 'Walk with me across the Park.'

'But that's going away from Paddington.'

'Never mind. I've just time, and I'd like to walk through the Green Park with you. Look at the sun. It's like a great blood-orange.'

There was a jostle of people moving in and out of the park gate.

'I'm jealous of them,' I said.

'Why?'

'Because they can go on living in this wonderful city, and every day walk in and out of London parks, and every day watch London buses go roaring down the slope there, and every day see you if they have eyes in their heads. And I must go away again without hardly seeing you.'

'The war can't go on much longer,' she said.

'I'm afraid it can,' I answered. 'And, anyway, it's not only the present that I'm jealous of; I'm jealous of all the years when I never knew you – the years when you were a little girl and I didn't even know that you existed.'

'I was an awful child,' she said, with a smile.

Under a clump of damp trees some children were playing with a black dog, jumping through the smoke of a bonfire which an old gardener was making. Ann put her arm into mine and made me stop. We stood looking at him as he shuffled about, raking his leaves together.

I said:

> 'Only an old man harrowing clods
>   In a slow, silent walk
> With an old horse that stumbles and nods
>   Half asleep as they stalk;

'Do you know it?'

'Yes,' she said. 'Go on.'

> 'Only thin smoke without flame
>   From the heaps of couch grass,
> Yet these shall continue the same
>   Though dynasties pass.
> Yonder a maid and her wight
>   Go whispering by:
> War's annals shall cloud into night
>   Ere their story die.'

4

'Let's move,' Ann said. 'It's too cold to stand.'

I was glad she still kept her arm through mine.

We were getting near Buckingham Palace; I hadn't much longer.

'Ann,' I said. 'I've something to say which I find hard to put into words, and even if I find them they'll be inadequate. Will you try and understand what's beyond the words?'

She looked up at me for a moment, quickly, then away again.

'I'll try,' she said.

'If I were to ask you to marry me I know what your answer would be, and since I don't like getting 'no' for an answer, I shan't ask you. That's why in these years I've never asked you. But, as I'm off now and don't quite know when I'll be back, and as letters will probably be a bit difficult, I want you to know that I cannot think of life without you. I know that you're not in love with me, but I cannot go away again leaving this thing unsaid. It's important to me that you should know how much I want to marry you. And I... it's...' I began to flounder. 'It's no good,' I said. 'I can't say it.'

'You say it very well,' Ann said quietly, 'and I understand.'

'You see what I mean?' I asked.

She gave me a half-mocking, half-rueful smile. 'Oh yes,' she said.

'I may add,' I went on, 'that should you elect on anyone else, you had better choose very well indeed, or you will have me to answer to when I come back.'

We had reached the Mall. I had to go, or miss my train. I signalled a taxi that was passing; it pulled in by the kerb just beyond us, and there was a 'ting' as the driver put his flag down. The sound was like a punctuation stop.

'You get into this one,' I said. 'I'll find another.'

Ann smiled. 'You'll be lucky if you do.'

We stood, looking at each other.

'Well...'

'Well... good-bye, John darling. I wish that... I wish I could...' Her face was puzzled and unhappy.

'You can't help it,' I said. 'Neither can I.'

When she had climbed in I slammed the taxi door and told the man to drive off. I heard the sound of the gears and I knew the car was moving, but I was walking away by then, and I could not bear to turn back and look.

It was a long flight to Cairo, tedious and cold. Through a night and two days the plane drew an aerial furrow half-way round a continent smoking with war, but no sound of the fury reached us in the sky. There, detached and sealed in our flying cylinder, life was aseptic, commonplace, an alternation of waking, sleeping and joyless eating of sandwiches. In the night great cities passed below, but they were only a cluster of lights to help navigation or a significant darkness where lights should have been.

For a while I enjoyed the suspension of life, the freedom from the necessity of thinking, but by the last afternoon I had reached a point where memory, motive, purpose were all obliterated by an aching and peevish desire for the flight to end. I wriggled inside my clothes to gain some warmth.

Of the dozen passengers none spoke. One or two men read magazines, others dozed – or tried to, but most sat still, combating their boredom. From a socket in the wing oozed a confident trickle of oil; then the wind ribbed and flattened it till it cringed and splayed across the smooth metal surface. Hour after hour it never altered.

Two thousand feet below lay the Western Desert. I gazed down at it as it crawled away beneath the wing, but there was little to be seen; in a year the tracks and scars of battle had almost gone. Most of the men in the plane, I judged, had fought either in the desert or in the skies above it, but not one spoke or commented as he peered down through his small window; each sat compressed into himself by the unvarying and violent self-assertion of the engines, forced into isolation, uncurious of the past or future of his fellows, indifferent almost to his own.

In the forward part of the plane an American Air Corp pilot had made a bed on a clumsy pile of mail-bags and sprawled across them, half-asleep. Once the letters had held a life of their own, had lain warm and open beneath the writer's hand; soon they would have a rebirth as men eagerly sought in them a longed-for word of love;

but now pilot and letters were alike in their loss of individuality; both had become mere flying bundles of freight – though there was something more definite about the letters than the man in that they at least bore clearly the mark of their destination.

Swiftly the night fell and in the plane it became quite dark. Another hour to be endured.

Suddenly the engine note changes; the plane loses height. The passengers sit up and stir expectantly, unwilling to believe that anything can be amiss and yet incredulous that we can have arrived.

'*C'est le Caire.*' The French captain has his face pressed to the window. It is the first time I have heard him speak.

Another voice in the darkness says tonelessly: 'This is it all right.'

As the wheels go down the plane checks in the air; then the long wings bank and wheel; another check as the wing-flaps drop; then there is a rushing sound, and a bump as we hit the ground.

We're there. The knowledge brings no immediate quickening to the numbed mind; thought and feeling seep slowly back like blood returning to a limb that has gone to sleep. Now we are on earth again. Now we must again take up our lives and move forward. Already the mail-bags are being unloaded. We're there.

Cairo was quite unchanged, I thought, as next morning my gharri drove towards G.H.Q. True, the streets were thronged with khaki, but the soldiers had no look of permanence; before long they would be gone, they and their trucks, their brothels, and their welfare clubs, and soon the *fellahin* – as poor as ever – would drive their strings of camels past the deserted and silent barracks, while Suleiman Pasha – richer than he had ever dreamed of being – would roll fatly in his car towards the Bank of Egypt buildings. Nothing was really changed, least of all the smell.

Outside the building that was my destination a students' fight was in progress. I paid the gharri-driver and advanced on foot. It was the traditional Egyptian fight, with the opposing sides hurling stones and insults at each other from fifty paces' distance. The door which was my objective lay in the centre of no-man's land and such a rain of stones was falling round it that I was tempted to delay my entrance till the battle had moved on. On second thoughts this seemed too ignoble a course; I advanced with as much display of calm as I could muster, and miraculously reached the doorway unscathed.

Inside an office labelled 'Personnel' sat an amiable lieutenant. To him I reported my arrival, but he had never heard of me.

'Try the D.A.A.G., sir,' he suggested. 'He might have some dope on you.'

The D.A.A.G. was very tall and rather sleepy; he wore a Guard's hat perched on top of curly, red hair.

'Never heard of you, old boy,' he said. 'What country do you think you're booked for?'

'I hoped *you'd* tell *me*.' I replied.

'But I tell you we've never heard of you.'

'London has signalled.'

The D.A.A.G. smiled at me with intent to charm. 'My dear old boy, they've probably done nothing of the sort. Or if they have,' he added, 'it's ten to one that the signal is lost in the message centre of this great institution.'

He fell silent and sat looking at me blandly.

'Well,' I asked, 'what do you suggest I do?'

He raised his eyebrows. 'Would you care to go back where you came from?'

I replied at some length and to the point.

'No,' he conceded. 'I see. That doesn't seem a very good idea.'

Suddenly his face lit up. 'You'd better go and have a chat with John Lester. Delightful fellow; you'll like him. Perhaps he'll be able to fix you up in Greece.'

Three hours later I ran down Major Lester. He looked like a more vital Charles Boyer, and wore a Military Cross below parachute wings. He walked with difficulty, having just broken his leg while engaged, apparently, in some desperate mission.

He had no idea what to do with me.

'I can't send you to Greece,' he apologised. 'We're sending no more bodies in for the time being. How would you like to go to the Far East?'

'What as?'

'Parachutist. Working behind the Jap lines.'

I had a sneaking feeling that I was being quite brave enough as it was, but I was ashamed to say so to a man who obviously took extreme courage as a matter of course, so I merely said: 'Well, I had thought I was going to be used in Europe, but... er...' and the sentence died away.

The major thought for a moment, then suddenly asked: 'Care for a plain-clothes job?'

The conversation, I felt, was going awry.

'Where?' I asked.

'Hungary or Roumania.'

'But I don't speak either Hungarian or Roumanian.'

'H'm,' said Major Lester, 'that certainly makes it a little difficult. Well, frankly, I don't know what to do with you. I can't make out why you ever came here.'

'I was sent,' I said apologetically.

The major brightened. 'I know! You'd better go and do some courses till something turns up.'

'What courses?'

'Oh!...' He cast about in his mind. 'Parachute course first; that'll take several days. Then we'll send you on a para-military course to rub up your demolitions: that'll take another fortnight or so; and by that time something is sure to have turned up.'

I thanked the major and left his office in a fog of gloom.

Outside the door I ran into Darrel Johnson disguised as a lieutenant-colonel. I did not know him well, but we had been at school together, and as he seemed both to have authority and be disposed to listen, I told him my tale of woe.

'It's no use waiting for Greece,' he said when I had finished. 'Things are in a frightful mess over there. At the moment we're pulling chaps out, not sending them in. Is there anywhere you particularly want to go, or is it all the same to you?'

'I don't mind where I go,' I replied, 'so long as I can get on with it quickly.'

'You'd better come along with me and see the fellow who runs the Albanian section. Know anything about Albania? ...No? All the better: you won't have a political bias. It's the least developed of all the Balkan sections, and so possibly the best fun. It looks as though civil war is going to break out there any day now – but never mind, it hasn't started yet.'

And so, with little more ado, it was arranged that I should go into Albania as agent, saboteur, and general fanner of the flames of revolt.

Before leaving Cairo for Italy, where I was to report to the Albanian Section's headquarters in Bari; I went to the bazaar to buy some silk for Ann. After long searching I found the materials I wanted: one piece was white and the other palest blue, and both were exquisite. The little Levantine spread them out on the counter, and as the brocade fell in soft, heavy folds across my hands I thought: now I am touching it – soon she will be wearing it. It was a happy afternoon.

The parachute course at Bari was both terrifying and exhilarating. There was a moment as you left the plane that was like Annihilation – when the slip-stream caught your body and the 'chute had not yet opened, when the wind gripped you like a solid element, like the flowing tissues of God's beard.

On the same course were several others destined for different parts of Albania. One of them, Corporal Drake, a market gardener before the war and now a radio operator, came close behind me on our first jump. From the ground I watched the last fifty feet or so of his descent. He hit the ground a tremendous crash, flat on his back. I ran to help him, as I thought he must be injured, but by the time I got to him, he was already folding his sprawling parachute.

'How did it feel?' I asked.

Drake was almost speechless with excitement and desire to express the inexpressible. 'It's like... it's like... Christ! it's just like falling out of a bloody aeroplane.'

When the parachute course was over there followed a week of vaccinations, inoculations, visits to the dentist, overhaul by the doctor, instruction in enciphering and deciphering, instruction in how to escape if captured, drawing of kit and choosing of weapons, nailing of boots and packing of everything up. In the middle of it, Tom Keith made his appearance.

Keith was in charge of the area surrounding the Albanian port of Valona, and had established a sea base on the mountainous coast a few miles south of the town. 'Sea View' he had named his base, with perverted humour, and the name had stuck. He had come out one night by boat so as to explain personally to H.Q. his need to obtain a dozen commando men.

'Only way I'll ever kill any Germans,' he explained. 'The Albs are worse than useless.'

Keith and I lunched together at the local *albergo*. He drank a good deal and talked a lot. He was a regular soldier, very dry and forthright, and, it also struck me, slightly mad.

'I don't know why you want to come to Albania,' he said. 'It's the filthiest, lousiest country I've ever been in.'

He enquired for what part of the country I was destined.

'The interior,' I told him. 'I'm dropping in as second in command to Linley in a fortnight's time. We want to see if it's possible to land seaplanes on Lake Ochrida.'

'Well,' said Keith, 'Hope for your sake that the natives in those parts are better than the lot I have round me.'

'You don't much like them?' I asked.

'Like 'em? I won't have the bastards near me. I keep 'em off.'

'How do you do that?'

'I shoot at them.'

'And what do they do while you're shooting at them?'

'Shoot back.'

For a moment I thought he was joking, but then I saw he was completely serious.

'Listen,' said Keith. 'I'll tell you a story about those Albs. I was with the Partisans a month ago, and we were expecting a plane sortie. We were up on the mountain-top, myself and a dozen Partisans, to collect the stores when they dropped. Well, the plane came all right – but it crashed. Everyone in it was killed. It was a frightful mess. Bits of bodies spread all over the dropping ground. And do you know what those beasts did?... They ran around pulling the boots off the dead men; I found one with a spare arm trying to take the wrist-watch off it. They wouldn't help collect the bits: oh no! But when I'd done it alone, working all night – and I had to keep them off with my revolver or they'd have robbed every single body – do you know what they wanted to do?... Build a fire and burn them. Beasts, animals, that's what the Albanians are.'

He emptied his wine-glass. The orchestra struck up its eternal 'Lilli Marlene' and a few half-drunken officers started shouting the tune. The noise in the khaki-crowded restaurant was terrific.

Keith went on: 'Then I got orders to open a sea base on the coast. I was damn glad to leave the Partisans after that experience: couldn't bear the sight of 'em any more. I came down to the coast and found me a fine cave to live in. It's a splendid cave, except that the roof's full of scorpions.'

'Scorpions!'

'Yes. We kill a few occasionally to keep the numbers down, but they seem quite friendly fellows. At any rate they haven't bitten anyone yet.'

Keith had a trick of coming out with some surprising statements without in the least giving the impression that he was talking for effect.

'I'm with the Balli now,' he went on. 'You know – the Right Wing boys; but they're no better. They won't fight the Germans. They won't even let me blow the road near their precious village. There's only one way to do anything – with British troops. With a dozen tough men I could play hell with the Germans, but without them it's a waste of time going back.'

'What about Italians?' I asked. 'Haven't some joined you since the armistice? Can't you use them?'

He gave a shrug. 'I've managed to send a number back to Italy, and I've kept a few to work in the camp, but they're not much good. Their spirit's all right, but physically they're broken... malaria, starvation... Some gave themselves up to the Germans in September, quite a few joined the Partisans, and a whole lot just took to the mountains.'

'And how have the Albanians treated them?'

'Like cattle. They feed them for as long as they can work, then when their strength fails, they turn them out to die.'

'Do you mean to say,' I said, 'that they just wander off... and...'

'And slowly die,' said Keith. 'Just that. Unless the dogs get at them,' he added, 'and then they die quickly.'

'How long have you been in Albania?' I asked.

'Five months,' he replied. 'Five months too long.'

The orchestra had finished playing 'Lilli Marlene' as a march; they were now playing it in waltz-time; next they would play it as a tango, and finally they would play 'Santa Lucia' with half the restaurant joining in. Someone wanted our table; we paid and walked out past the queue of officers waiting to eat.

A few days later Keith returned to Sea View, having failed to obtain his commandos. He took with him Corporal Drake as a replacement for his own wireless operator whom he had brought out sick.

He went back as he had come out, by sea and at night.

A week elapsed and then, late one evening, Cleaver sent for me to come to the office. Cleaver was the young lieutenant-colonel, painfully intense, who ran the Albanian section. That night he looked even more intense than usual.

'Keith's had an accident,' he announced. 'Blown himself up or something.'

I didn't speak, so he went on: 'John, I want you to go in at once and take his place. Valona's an important area and we can't leave it uncovered. I'm afraid this means a change in your plans, but this way you'll have your own area to run. Do you like the idea?'

'Very much.'

'Good. I'm trying to get a sea-sortie laid on for tomorrow. I hope we'll be in time to save Tom's life. You'll have to leave at crack of dawn and join the *Sea Maid* at Brindisi. Rawlinson is the name of the captain.'

'It's rather a pity,' I said, 'that I don't know a thing about this Valona area.'

'I know,' Cleaver agreed. 'But you'll find two excellent officers in Sea View: they'll help you.'

'Who are they?' I asked.

'Commander Trent is one – Royal Navy; he's there primarily to help you with coastal reconnaissance, but he does straight Intelligence as well. The other's an American major called Benson; he works for the American Intelligence.'

'And who's in charge?' I asked.

'The definition is very clear,' Cleaver replied. 'You have the sole operational responsibility. The Americans are only there for Intelligence.'

'But if there's a question of moving the base or something like that, and we differ – then who is in charge? Someone must be.'

Cleaver smiled. 'You're all intelligent and understanding men. You won't differ.'

'In other words none of us is in command?' I wouldn't let him squirm out of it.

Cleaver put on his most engaging smile. 'No,' he conceded, ' – no.'

I had a strong feeling that the colonel was playing a part, the part of the 'man behind the scenes' in a spy film, the man in the darkened room who at the end of the interview says: 'You have an important mission ahead of you, young man, a dangerous mission.' (Here the character usually rises to his feet and holds out his hand.) 'Good-bye to you...' (a pregnant pause) '...and good luck!' It was so much a performance that I found myself watching it in a detached way.

'Keep us fully informed,' said Cleaver, 'of everything that goes on. Remember always that we're right behind you, and that if there's anything you want or any support which you need we'll do our utmost to bring it to you.'

'Thanks.'

'Above all, John, don't forget – ' and here Cleaver contrived to make his face unbelievably ferocious, ' – don't forget that your main task is to kill Germans.'

I didn't know how to reply, for his performance had suddenly stepped outside all bounds. No doubt I was intended to take fire at his words and, with teeth bared like his own, declare: 'I will. I will.'

The image made me want to laugh, but that would have only disconcerted him, so I managed not to.

Instead I said: 'O.K.'

Cleaver rose to his feet and held out his hand.

'Good-bye to you,' he said. A pregnant pause. 'And good luck!'

TWO

IN THE LATE EVENING of the last day in 1943, the hundred-foot *Sea Maid* bucketed her way eastwards across the Adriatic.

The sea was rough.

Down in the hold I lay jammed between a tub of grease and a sackful of boots. With every roll of the ship I slid across the floor with the tub, the boots, and all the other confused tackle with which the tiny space was crammed. I was too weak and sick to resist; I simply lay and sweated.

Water was cascading all round the deck; a lot of it was finding its way down into the hold. From the galley above my head came a terrible din; the ship's puppy had been locked in to prevent him being washed overboard, and now every pot, pan and ladle had come loose and were crashing all around him. He was yelling his head off, but no one paid attention; he was safer in the galley than in the scuppers.

Gradually the sea seemed to grow calmer, and I judged we must be in the lee of the mountains. Soon there was no mistake about it; we were rolling much less and the pandemonium of breaking crockery had ceased. Even the dog was silent; perhaps a mug had hit him on the head. My nausea ebbed away and desire to live returned.

We must be getting near, I thought; perhaps the mountains were visible. I crawled over the piles of tumbled gear till I reached the foot of the companion ladder. Before I climbed up it I said a word to Ann:

'I would like to keep you in my mind during this landing, but I am going to be busy now. If for a few hours I forget you, forgive me.'

Then I climbed up on deck.

A living wind smote me in the face, and from the tarry confinement of the hold my mind spun out into the star-filled, immeasurable distance. I steadied myself against the halyards. The *Sea Maid* was breaking through a rolling swell, whirls and glints of phosphorus slipping away beneath us. The moon had not yet risen, and despite the frosty stars it was very dark. Motionless and silent the crew stood about the deck, stretching their senses into the night to detect an enemy patrol. They spoke in whispers as though their caution could compensate for the din of our Diesel engine or for the showers of sparks which flew from our smoke-stack and trailed away into the night. I hoped no E-boat was about; it could hardly fail to see us.

I made out the captain's form standing on the hatch in front of the wheel-house, and went and joined him.

'What's that?' I said suddenly. I had seen a light on the starboard bow.

'Just a village.' Rawlinson kept his voice low. 'South of our pin-point. You'll see it better soon.'

Ten minutes passed, and the light had become a cluster.

'That's it – Vuno,' said Rawlinson. 'Keep a good look-out for their signal; we should be seeing it any time now. They'll be flashing K.'

He stamped on the thin hatch, our only form of engine-room telegraph, and we dropped to half-speed. It was a relief, for the firework display ceased and the motor ran so quietly that I could hear the swish and ripple of the bow-wave. By contrast men were emboldened to speak louder.

Close to me the doctor said: 'Do you think they'll have Keith down on the beach?'

'I don't know,' I replied.

There was a pause, then he asked: 'How much longer now?'

'I've no idea,' I answered.

Rawlinson gave a quiet order through the open window of the wheel-house, and the steering-cable rattled slightly as the helmsman, eyes fixed on his red-glowing compass, altered course a point or two.

Minutes went by, then the doctor said excitedly: 'There it is!'

Sure enough a light was twinkling ahead of us, but Rawlinson dismissed it. 'Too high up,' he said. 'They signal from nearer sea-level. Besides, that's not Morse. Probably a shepherd's fire.'

Suddenly I became aware that the darkness ahead had taken on a different hue, and almost at the same moment I could hear a noise like a giant hoarsely letting out his breath. It was the sound of breakers. A cold excitement took hold of me. Each instant the land mass ahead became more certain, the skyline, high above our heads, more clearly defined.

'Is this the place?' I asked Rawlinson.

'This is it. Can't think why they don't flash. It's past eight.'

He stamped on the engine-room roof, and the screw stopped turning, the motor idling free. Now the breathing sound came clearer, and I fancied I could see the froth of waves.

'We'll lie here for a bit,' said Rawlinson, 'and wait for them to start flashing. Perhaps they've got the time wrong.'

We lay, strained and silent, for half an hour.

The moon had been behind the mountains, throwing them into silhouette; now she rose in the heavens and as she poured a pale of light on the coast before us, I had my first view of Albania. Cold and grey, mammoth-ribbed, the mountain rose up out of the fret of white water round its base. So bare the hill-side looked, so utterly devoid of life, that it might itself have been one of the mountains of the moon.

The doctor said in my ear: 'Is this the place?'

'I gather so,' I said.

'Then why don't they flash?'

'I don't know.'

'Perhaps they're captured... Perhaps they're killed.'

'Perhaps,' I said.

'But if we don't get Keith out tonight he may die.'

'I know that.'

'Then...'

'Listen, doctor,' I said, 'I'm just as nervous as you are, and I don't know anything. So it's no good asking me. Just keep quiet and wait.'

I walked away from him; I had to.

Rawlinson was uneasy. 'I know this is the place,' he said when I stood by him. 'I know it well even in the dark but with this moonlight...' He made a sound of exasperation then gave a stamp on the engine-room roof.

'We'll take a turn down the coast,' he said. 'I suppose I might have made a mistake.'

At half-speed we turned south and crept along not three hundred yards from the coast. Once a shepherd's fire glowed high on the hill-side and twice I could have sworn I saw a flash – but it was only the phosphorus in the breaking waves. After half an hour we turned about and steered northwards till we were back at our starting point.

Rawlinson stamped, and once again we lay rolling in the swell. 'Dammit!' he said, 'I'm not going to patrol the enemy's coast for him when I *know* this is the place.'

A breeze struck us from the south. If the wind shifted to that quarter we would lose the protection of the hills and it might be hard to make a landing.

'I'm going to risk signalling,' said the captain. 'D'you mind?'

'No,' I answered. 'Go ahead. W is our letter for the night, isn't it?'

With a flashlight Rawlinson sent 'W' towards the coast. Though he screened the beam with his hand he could not prevent the light from spilling on to the bulwarks, the rigging, the still figures on the deck.

There was no reply.

He steadied himself against the wheel-house, ready to signal again, when suddenly an answering flash leapt out of the hillside.

'There it is!' we all cried.

'Long-short-long. That's them all right!'

Again it came, stabbing out across the water, unfaltering, linking us upon the dark sea to our countrymen ashore in a hostile land. There were tears of excitement in my eyes as the *Sea Maid* moved slowly forward and I plunged down into the hold to collect my scattered gear.

When I regained the deck the *Sea Maid* was close in under the cliffs, and the weight of the mountain above seemed to be crushing down on us. Rawlinson was at the wheel himself, heading us straight for the narrow entrance to a bay; he had judged it carefully, swinging his clumsy boat in a wide arc to get the right angle of approach. Nearer we came – nearer; now I could hear the slap and boom of each separate wave as it hit the rocks and burst into spray above our heads. Tensely we stood as the *Sea Maid* slipped through the entrance without a dozen yards to spare on either side.

Orders were given; quickly the engine went into reverse, and our makeshift anchor of weights was dropped over the stern. From the side of the ship came the sound of splashing and a confused shouting in foreign tongues. Torchlights were turned towards the noise; for a moment the beams wavered across empty, tossing water, then fastened on a small canvas boat in which crouched half a dozen men, paddling furiously and all shouting unintelligible directions.

Suddenly, there rang out a voice – unmistakably, blessedly, authoritatively English – a voice with an edge of exasperation.

'For God's sake catch that rope and make it fast!'

I saw the speaker a moment later as the plunging canvas boat came alongside, a soaking-wet figure with a naval cap perched above a bearded face. It must be Trent, I thought – the naval commander.

'Is there a doctor on board?' he shouted up.

'Yes,' I answered. 'And I'm Overton – come to take over from Keith.'

'Good! You two had better come ashore at once. Mind how you jump down.'

We fell down the ship's side into the boat, and as we pushed off Rawlinson called: 'I'll launch the dinghy and start unloading at once.'

As we bobbed across the bay Trent told the doctor about Keith's wounds. They were bad, it seemed, but the sailor thought he would live.

'Where do we land?' I asked. 'I can't see any beach.'

'There's no beach in the bay itself,' Trent explained. 'The beach is at the end of a creek. You'll see.'

Sharply we turned into a gulley between narrow cliffs and were at once in calm water. As we glided forward I could see upon the wall of rock ahead the reflection of firelight coming from somewhere that was as yet out of sight. The steep walls narrowed still further, and, as we turned again, I saw before me an unforgettable scene.

Ahead was a narrow beach, hemmed in by precipitous cliffs and overhanging trees, lit by the crackling flames of four enormous fires. Groups of brigand-like figures stood waiting to receive us, and as the boat drew nearer I saw that ringed round by the fires, like a chieftain on his funeral pyre, and beneath a great pile of blankets, lay a man.

Trent led the doctor and myself across the sliding pebbles. 'We did our best to keep him warm,' he said. 'He complains all the time of being cold.'

Only Keith's head emerged from the blankets; the top part was covered with bloody bandages, but his jaw was free.

'Here's the doctor, Tom,' said Trent. 'Only a few more hours and you'll be in Italy.'

There was a grunt from Keith.

The doctor was a changed man. His querulousness was gone; rapidly and deftly he examined the wounded man, and when he spoke it was with authority.

'I'm going to give him a shot of morphia,' he said. 'If you've anything to say to him, will you please say it quickly.'

I moved close to the bandaged head. 'I have come to take over the area from you,' I said. 'Don't bother to talk unless there's anything you particularly want to tell me.'

For a moment Keith did not speak and I thought he had not heard me, then the lips moved and he said slowly, and very clearly:

'I wish you joy of the damned place.'

That was all he said. Ten minutes later we carried him down the beach and stowed him in the ship's dinghy. He didn't make a sound; the morphia had worked quickly.

When the dinghy had disappeared down the creek into the darkness I had time to take in my surroundings. The tiny beach was crowded with men wearing a strange assortment of clothes and weapons. There were many in battle-dress, but speaking Italian; at one side huddled a wretched-looking group still wearing the remains of Italian uniform. These last, Trent explained to me, were sick men who would return that night to Italy on the *Sea Maid*.

The Commander himself was a surprising figure. He was short and smiling, with a prematurely bald head and slanting eyes that gave him the appearance of a genial mandarin.

It was not long before the stores began to arrive. Sea View possessed two canvas boats, and soon every man able to walk was working on the unloading of these and of the ship's dinghy as they plied to and fro between the *Sea Maid* and the beach. In the firelight we stumbled across the stones with cases of ammunition, machine-guns, boxes of rations, mines, explosives, stacking them high up the beach where the sea could not damage them.

A familiar, stocky figure in a white duffie-coat came up and saluted. 'Corporal Drake!' I cried.

The wireless operator was grinning from ear to ear, and nearly shook my hand off.

'I'm very glad you've come, sir – very glad indeed.'

There was a splash from the water's edge as someone dropped a case into the sea, and Drake shot off to deal with the culprit. In the fortnight since I had last seen him, he seemed to have acquired a surprising command of Italian invective.

At length the Italians had been ferried out to the ship, and with the last boatload of stores Rawlinson himself came ashore to say good-bye. He had clapped a naval cap on his grizzled head – in honour of his first landing on Albanian soil, he explained.

'Nice place you've got here,' he said, looking round the beach.

Trent invited him to spend the weekend with us and Rawlinson smiled in his quiet way. 'No, thanks,' he said. 'This is no life for me. Besides, I've a date in Brindisi tomorrow night that I don't want to miss.'

It seemed strange to hear him speak of tomorrow night in Brindisi. Already the outside world seemed utterly remote.

'Well, cheerio!' said Rawlinson. 'Time I was off. If I'm not well on my way by dawn I'll be having a dirty Boche plane drop his bombs on me.'

The dinghy vanished round the bend in the creek. The last thread attaching me to the outside world snapped. Here I was now in Albania, an enemy-occupied country, and nothing could alter it. I had a feeling of exhilaration at having committed myself to an irrevocable course.

I turned to Trent. 'What now?' I asked.

'Now we climb up to the cave,' he said. 'And you carry with you anything you want for the night. We'll fetch all the rest of the stuff by mule in the morning.'

As we toiled up the mountain-side, Trent questioned me on the happenings in the world from which I had come; the Russian advance? The campaign in Italy? London?... How long was it since I had left London?

'A month ago,' I answered.

He stopped in the track and shone his torch onto me.

'My God!' He exclaimed. 'I look upon you with awe – a man who only four weeks ago was in London.'

When I was not answering his questions Trent talked volubly himself. He seemed to be spilling over with energy and enthusiasm.

'What happened to your signalling to-night?' I asked. 'You never signalled at all until we flashed to you.'

Trent explained that the signal announcing the sortie had been corrupt and that they had therefore not known what time to expect the boat. 'We heard your engines,' he explained, 'but we felt it was safer to wait till you gave the call-sign, in case you were an enemy patrol-boat.'

The track we followed wound through a wood then climbed steeply over bare, rocky hill-side. I found it a struggle, and I was glad when Trent said: 'Look! You can see the firelight from the caves now. That's where we live.'

I looked up and saw lights twinkling on the hill-side a hundred feet or so above our heads.

'Aren't you afraid to show so much light?' I asked.

'Lord! no,' Trent laughed. 'The nearest Germans are four hours away on the other side of the mountain. We can do what we want here. It's like Coney Island!'

Soon I could smell wood-smoke and in a few more minutes I could tell that we were in a narrow place inhabited by men. Here and there lights glimmered and there was a muffled sound of talking.

'That's our home,' said the Commander, indicating a small cave-mouth from which shone the glow of firelight. Mind your head,' he warned as we reached the entrance; then: 'Tank!' He called.

'Hallo there!' from within – an American voice.

'Have you got a hot drink for us?'

'I certainly have. Yes, *sir*!'

A moment later I was in the cave and shaking hands with a

man who, incongruously, wore an enormous, bushy beard and a completely shaven head.

'You'll excuse my not getting up,' said the American, but there's not much head-room.'

He was right; the ceiling was little more than five feet high.

'You'd best sit down too,' he went on. My name's Benson. I'm glad to know you.' He held out his hand. Welcome to Sea View boarding-house. Have some cocoa.'

'Take a look round the house,' said Trent who had followed me in. 'You can do it from where you're sitting.'

The cave was very small indeed, and what little space existed was taken up by a table made of machine-gun boxes. Sleeping-bags and blankets lay on the floor, and every cranny and ledge in the walls held papers, ink-bottles, revolvers, maps, and ammunition magazines. In a rough hearth blazed a wood fire and by this and a few home-made oil-lamps the place was lit.

'Well, is it anything like you'd imagined?' Benson spoke in a slow, even tone.

'Yes,' I said, 'this is just about how I'd pictured it.'

'They'd told you about us?' asked Trent.

'Oh, yes,' I nodded. 'I hadn't imagined though that you'd look like this.'

'How did you think we'd look?'

'Less...' I searched for the word, '...less bizarre.'

Trent laughed as though conscious of his odd appearance and delighting in it.

'Bizarre, eh?' said Benson. He turned to Trent; 'I hope that's a polite way of saying original, but I'm afraid he just means screwy.'

'We probably are too,' Trent admitted. 'And you'll be just the same after a month or two,' he warned me. 'You'll likely end as mad as Tom Keith.'

'I wish you'd tell me,' I asked, 'how Keith was wounded? You didn't say in your signal how it happened.'

Trent pulled a face. 'Just blew himself up.'

'But how?'

'Oh! nothing heroic. He was testing some explosive and struck a faulty detonator. Poor fellow, it made an awful mess of him. Thank goodness you came at once or he'd certainly have died on us.'

'Just a moment!' said Benson suddenly. 'Quiet!' He was looking at his watch. 'Fifteen seconds... ten seconds... five seconds...' He looked up. 'Gentlemen,' he said, 'I have the honour to inform you that we are now in next year. A happy New Year to you both... I wish I had someone to kiss,' he added.

New Year's Eve! I had completely forgotten it. Trent jumped to his feet; he was short enough to stand in the cave without stooping. 'A happy New Year,' he said. 'We must celebrate it somehow... I know!' he exclaimed. 'We'll kill a scorpion.'

'What?' I cried.

'The roof's full of them,' he explained enthusiastically. 'Come on now a torch – and where's a knife?'

In a moment we were all three peering intently at the pockmarked roof as Trent slowly shone his torch over it.

'There's one!' he said excitedly. 'Confound the brute. Look at him! Taking the evening air.'

I could make out a small, crab-like creature that was sitting in one of the fissures – an evil-looking thing.

We manoeuvred for the kill. Benson shone the torch; I got an empty wooden box and held it so as to catch the beast in case it fell. Trent poised his pen-knife.

'Now!' he cried, and stabbed.

'Got it!' we all three shouted.

There was a grating noise as Trent wriggled the knife about, then scraped out into the box all that was left of the scorpion. We threw it on the fire.

'An excellent omen!' declared Trent in triumph. 'Overton arrives – and we kill a scorpion! The year begins well.'

The excitement died down; there was a feeling of anti-climax.

'I think I shall turn in,' said Benson. 'There's a lot to talk about, but we can do it in the morning.'

They showed me my place on the floor. As my own sleeping-bag was still down on the beach I was to use Keith's, which he had left behind. For an instant I wondered if that, too, was an omen.

While the others got ready for sleep I stepped out of the cave to be alone for a minute. I walked a few paces till I could no longer hear the murmur of voices. The lights of the camp had gone; it was utterly silent. Far below, so far below that I could not hear it, the sea wrinkled in the moonlight.

'A happy New Year, my love,' I said aloud. Perhaps my wish would reach Ann.

Ponderous beyond thought the world spun on its ordained way through space and time, moving precisely to the millionth, millionth part of a second; and mankind, crawling on its ancient crust, fighting, loving, hating, striving, scratched off another year of its history.

Of a sudden I was intensely conscious of myself standing on this remote spit of land, of my loneliness under the stars.

'Ann,' I said. 'In four years I have not been able to show you how I love you, but I pray that you will understand this. You must understand it. *This is for you.* All that happens to me here, anything that I succeed in doing, is for you. This is where it begins – *now.*'

I said it with all my strength, then I turned and went back into the cave.

THREE

FROM THE VERY DAY when I had known that I was to go into Albania I had deliberately shut my ears to much of the talk at Headquarters. Such information as we had came in the form of signals from officers already in the country, and it appeared to me that these took considerable colour from the opinions of the Albanians with whom they lived and fought. An officer attached to the Partisans was very apt to regard the Balli, as the Right Wing party was called, as a gang of neo-Fascists; the officer who had connections with the Balli saw in the Partisans nothing but the cunning and bloody agents of world bolshevism. During December had come many reports of armed clashes between the two parties, and at Headquarters sides were being taken and favours worn.

My resolve to arrive unbiased in the country succeeded so well that I awoke on New Year's Day not only unbiased but almost completely ignorant of the problems that faced me. But this pleased rather than dismayed me. It was the first day of a new year, the first day of my gift to Ann; I was beginning it free of any prejudice. If I succeeded it would be by my own efforts; if I failed I should have only myself to blame. But I was quite confident that I should not fail.

Before the other two sleepers in the cave were stirring I pulled on my clothes and went outside to view my inheritance.

The camp was at the head of a steep and narrow gorge, where in addition to several natural caves, a number of rough dwellings had been made by adding to the overhanging rock face another wall of stones or brushwood. Although on the previous night a large party of Italians had been sent off on the *Sea Maid*, there were still plenty about. Food was being cooked, wood chopped; in a big oven bread was baking, and below me I could see some mules being whacked up the hill, carrying the stores and kit which had been left on the beach.

I think Corporal Drake must have been on the look-out for me for I had not been standing there a minute when he came up. He could find no words to begin with, but stood grinning at me, turning his head from side to side and clicking his tongue.

'Were you surprised to see me last night? I asked.

'Surprised?' His voice had a slight West Country burr. 'Sir, when I saw you come ashore last night, I was so surprised I – well, I nearly fell into the water. Goodness gracious! I never thought I'd see you here.' He clicked his tongue again.

'It certainly happened quickly,' I admitted. 'I was sitting there in Bari, all ready to drop inland, when your signal arrived. By a stroke of good luck the old *Sea Maid* was ready to sail – and here I am. At least,' I added, 'I suppose I am. I can hardly believe it yet.'

'Sir,' said Corporal Drake, 'may I speak freely?

'Go ahead,' I said.

Drake looked around and, though no one was near, lowered his voice. 'From the day I landed, two weeks ago, I knew something would happen to Major Keith.'

'How do you mean?' I asked.

'He was queer, sir. Been in the country too long, I reckon.'

'How d'you mean – queer?'

'Look, sir,' said Drake. 'We're supposed to get these Albanians to fight, aren't we?'

'That's right,' I said.

'Well,' the corporal went on, 'Major Keith had reached a point where he so hated Albanians that he wouldn't let none of them come near this camp.'

'I gathered as much in Bari.'

'And look at this place.' He jerked his head toward the cluster of huts and caves. 'I don't like to say it, but it's a mess. That's what it is – a proper mess. Well, sir, you'll see how it is for yourself. Excuse me if I've talked too much.'

'That's all right,' I said. 'You'd better go and have your breakfast now. We'll see each other later.'

Breakfast in the cave was the best I had eaten since peace-time and very international: English porridge, American bacon, Albanian eggs, and warm bread freshly baked by an Italian. As we ate and talked, each was sending out feelers, trying to assess the other two, like three wrestlers put together in a ring. Trent talked a lot;

Benson was rather quiet. Once or twice I caught him looking at me watchfully through expressionless brown eyes.

'You'll have to tell me what the position is here,' I said 'I know there's a civil war going on, but little else; I left Bari in too much of a hurry to be briefed properly. I gather we're not in Partisan territory?'

'No, indeed!' Trent gave a wriggle of enjoyment.

All things appeared to amuse the Commander, and every remark he made seemed to be prompted by a suppressed glee.

'All the people in this area,' he went on, 'are strongly anti-communist – therefore anti-Partisan. To hear them talk you'd think they were dyed-in-the-wool reactionaries, and certainly they're considered as such by the Partisans. In point of fact, they're nothing but a poverty-stricken bunch of goatherds and smallholders.'

'Alpino!'

At Benson's call there appeared the Italian soldier who had served the breakfast, a sturdy fellow with a bedraggled feather still stuck in his hat. In fluent Italian Benson told him to clear away the breakfast things, and, when this was done, he spread a map over the machine-gun boxes.

'We're better here in the office,' he explained. 'The dining room's too cramped. Now, this is the position. Firstly, Albanians: on the inland side of the mountain we're on now is a big village called Dukat. Dukat is the village Sailor has been talking about. It controls the whole valley northwards as far as the Bay of Valona. Inland again of Dukat valley are more mountains, and they, more or less, are Partisan-land.'

'And the Germans?'

'There's a big German garrison in Valona, and they constantly use the main road that runs through Dukat valley.'

'I see,' I said. 'Thanks. And now for our three selves. You are both here, I take it, for Intelligence?'

'Right,' said Benson. 'And you're here to fight?'

I nodded. 'Also to collect Intelligence and to keep open a sea base, but primarily to fight – or at least to encourage the sport.'

A smile passed between the other two.

'Far be it from me to sound a discordant note,' said Trent, 'but our interests are therefore slightly opposed.'

'I don't see that,' I said.

'It's simple,' he replied. 'The only way for Secret Agent X to bring me information is across a certain bridge – a bridge which the Germans also use. You, therefore, want to blow it up. I, on the other hand, do not want it blown up – as Agent X, poor chap, can't swim.'

'But surely the two things go hand in hand,' I said. 'On the information provided by your non-aquatic X I might decide to go and blow up a different bridge altogether.'

Grudgingly they both agreed that this might be so.

'If you're afraid,' I went on, 'that I shall immediately go running round the area accompanied by explosions and bursts of machine-gun-fire, you needn't worry. I shan't ruin your nice game of 'I Spy'. Before I do a thing I want to get inland and find out for myself what the local picture is.'

An undercurrent of antagonism had crept into our talk and I thought it best to change the conversation.

'What news of the nurses whose plane crashed? Bari was expecting them to arrive here at Sea View any day now.'

'We reckon they'll take another week yet,' Benson answered. 'We've heard that some of them are pretty sick. I'm not surprised after they've been tramping six weeks across these mountains. Say, Sailor.' He turned to Trent. 'Won't it be amazing to see women in this cave? Maybe,' he went on ruminatively, 'maybe I can pick myself a little mouse who'll want to stay behind with me – like a Hemingway novel.'

'In my experience,' said Trent, 'all nurses look like hell, and these will probably be no exception.'

'Now there you're wrong,' Benson objected, and launched into some detailed reminiscences of a little nurse he had known intimately in Philadelphia.

I could see that if his hair were grown and his beard shaved he would be a strikingly good-looking man.

The rest of the morning I took going round the camp with Drake; Benson and Trent had signals and reports on which to work.

The corporal had been right about Sea View; it was in a state of chaos. Dirty rags of discarded Italian uniform lay about, together with empty tins of food and old cigarette packages. Depressingly near the living quarters was the grave of an Italian soldier who had died of pneumonia; the site had been chosen of necessity, as being the only place on the rocky hill-side where there was sufficient depth of soil to protect the body from being dug up by wolves.

By the end of the morning I had arrived at the decision that my very first task was to leave Sea View and establish a new base of my own elsewhere. Sea View was too far gone to think of cleaning it up, too sunk in an atmosphere of stale death. Keith's legacy was not a happy one, and for my own sake and for the good of the whole mission, I felt the need to make a fresh start.

Yet this was a decision which I could not put bluntly to Trent and Benson, who for weeks had been living quite contentedly in the place. I was not in command of them, and therefore could not give an order, nor could I afford to run entirely counter to their wishes, for though our interests differed, yet necessity bound us together – the necessity for companionship, for the sharing of knowledge, for the sharing of the very food that came to us across the Adriatic. I would have to approach my point obliquely.

As we talked in the cave over lunch the wrestling-match had taken a step forward; now we were feinting, dodging, never quite coming to grips, quick to notice any tendency in the other two to form alliances.

'Tell me,' I said, 'what was Keith's policy towards the Italians? Isn't there a danger of becoming inundated with them?'

'I don't think Tom ever worked out a policy,' Trent replied. 'He never encouraged Italians to come to 'Sea View', but on the other hand, there's no way of stopping them. The sick he repatriated whenever there was a boat; the healthy he kept back to help run the base.'

'And have they an officer of their own in charge of them?' I asked.

'They had until today,' said Trent. 'Manzitti his name was; but he went down with bad malaria. I sent him out last night.'

I remembered the man now; we had met for a moment on the beach. He wore thick spectacles.

'Yeah, it's a pity Manzitti's gone,' said Benson. 'He was a fine guy.'

I had obtained the opening that I wanted: I stepped into it.

'Since, then, we must inevitably have large numbers here isn't it very dangerous,' I said, 'to base our whole organisation on this one pin-point? What if we get chased out of it? Surely there ought to be an alternative base. What are the possibilities of making a second base either to the north or to the south?'

'I wouldn't recommend the north,' said Trent. 'Three miles up the coast there's a horrid lot of Germans manning the coastal defences. I made a trip up there a week ago to have a look at them.'

'What about the south?'

'There's a good bay about two hours' walk south of here; Grama Bay it's called. But the best man to ask is Chela,' Trent went on. 'He'll tell you all about the country round here. He should be back in camp this evening.'

'And who is Chela?' I asked.

'Who is Chela?' they repeated, staring at me incredulously. 'Didn't Cleaver tell you about Chela?'

'He told me very little,' I said.

'Chela is our main prop and stay,' said, Trent. 'We couldn't do a thing here without him. Now that Manzitti's gone, it's through Chela that we get all our information from Valona.'

'Not only information,' Benson murmured. 'Vermouth as well.'

'Why do you say,' I asked, 'now that Manzitti's gone? Did he do Intelligence work for you?'

'Manzitti,' said Benson, 'was once the Intelligence Officer of the Italian Divisional Headquarters in Valona. He joined Tom Keith immediately after the armistice in September. Tom had no good contacts in Valona at that time, so he used to send Manzitti into the town, in plain clothes, to get various bits of information. It was a hell of a risk for Manzitti as he was well known in the place – but he took it. In fact, Manzitti is one of my many reasons for being pro-Italian.'

'The other reasons, I take it,' said Trent, 'being of the opposite sex?'

Benson smiled. 'You see,' he said to me, 'this Italian question is a pretty vexed one between Sailor and me.'

'It's not vexed in the least,' replied Trent. 'I simply adhere to my old father's maxim... "___ begin at Calais".'

Chela came as dusk was falling, a sub-machine-gun across his back and leading two heavily-laden mules. He came and sat down in the cave, smiling deferentially, and showing, as he did so, a mouthful of silver teeth. He was a strange-looking young man, very soft-spoken, whose wide-set eyes held a gentleness that was altogether at variance with the ferocity of his mouth. A week-old beard fringed his lean jaws.

Oh yes, he said in answer to my questions, Grama Bay would be a very good place for a base – in fact, when Major Keith had first come to the area, that was where he wanted him to go. He spoke good English, though with an accent that would have defied imitation.

'I would like to see it,' I said. 'Would you show me the way?'

The eyes smiled and there was an accompanying flash of metal from the mouth. 'As you wish,' he said. 'I am soldier of the Allies.'

Other than Drake I had only two British soldiers in the mission, and when I left for Grama next day I took them both with me, Black because I trusted him, Adams because I didn't and wished to know him better.

Black was a tall, handsome lad who had only been a short time in the country; he had been a slaughterer in private life, he told me. The revolver and commando knife which he wore in his belt, together with the beret stuck at a dashing angle on the back of his head, combined to give him a very war-like appearance. I had the feeling, too, that he was probably as tough as he looked.

Adams was a puffy-faced little Cockney from whose eyes I could draw not the slightest response when I spoke to him.

There were two routes to Grama; the quicker lay through the ravines that scored the lower slopes of the mountain, but this way was only passable to men on foot. Mules had to take an easier but longer track that ran high up the mountain. As Adams claimed to know the lower path, I sent Chela to guide the Italian muleteers along the upper one. The two parties were to meet at Grama.

It did not take Adams long to show some of his character. He would walk on ahead at a pace with which neither Black nor I could keep up, and disappear from sight. When at last we caught him up he would be sitting on the rocks, smoking a cigarette, and affecting an air of bored resignation.

'Adams,' I said to him on one of these occasions, 'you'll have no difficulty in getting to Grama before me. At present I can only go very slowly. Will you kindly stick around and keep us on the path; you're no good either to Black or me as a guide if we can't see you.'

'Yessir,' he replied, but his face remained buttoned up, and for the rest of the walk he managed to keep just far enough ahead to be useless, yet not far enough to warrant my calling him back.

I could not understand the man's behaviour; he had scarcely had time to take a personal dislike to me. Perhaps he resented me as a newcomer; perhaps he naturally resented all officers. Whatever the reason was, it depressed me.

At the end of two and a half hours we had not reached halfway, so Adams sententiously informed me. Our slow progress was due partly to my inability to go fast, and partly to Adams, who was continually losing the way and causing us to go back on our tracks.

It was at one of these times, as we stood gazing miserably at a particularly bad mixture of chasm, boulders and overhanging rock, undecided which way to tackle it, that I heard a man's shout. I looked up, but could see nothing; nor could the other two. Again the shout came, and this time we saw the man as he detached himself from the background of rock and scrub against which he had been hidden and moved down the hillside towards us. He moved fast over the rough ground, yet gave an impression of leisureliness.

As he drew near, I could see that he was an elderly man with fine features and a weathered face. He wore a rough black coat over a velvet waistcoat, dark breeches, with his shins and calves bound round with coarse, light-coloured cloth. A fine, silver chain hung round his neck, and the slippers into which his horny, bare feet were thrust were of Turkish design but fashioned out of old car tyres. I was intrigued with him; he was the first real Albanian I had met. There had been Chela, to be sure, but in him the edge of racial originality had been dulled by his association with the little group of Allied officers.

The old shepherd greeted us with great dignity and seriousness, and when by means of indifferent Italian he had been made to understand that we were having some difficulty in finding our way to Grama Bay, he at once undertook to guide us there. He set off at an easy pace, his rubber shoes gripping the rocks, while I struggled along behind, my nails slipping and sliding all the time. Adams, to show his independence, walked at some distance from us, picking his own path.

By five o'clock we had reached the valley where our guide lived. With great solemnity he invited us to enter his house, and, though it was late and we still had far to go, it was impossible to refuse. One after another we stooped low through the narrow doorway and, when our eyes could get used to the darkness, found that we were in a one-roomed hut with floor and walls of stone. Rugs, some sacks of brown flour, and a quantity of raw wool were stacked at one end of the hut; at the other end, near the door, burnt an open wood fire, its smoke escaping through the roof, which was made of crude wooden planks.

The old man kicked off his shoes, though he kept his round cap on his head, and squatted down by the fire, cross-legged. Remembering what I had been told about removing my boots in Moslem houses, I made a move to undo my laces, but the old man saw me and made a regal gesture signifying that it was unnecessary.

Two serious-eyed girls appeared bringing a large, flat loaf of maize-bread and a wooden bowl of goat's milk. The bread was crumbled into the milk, and the bowl set between us. The milk was rich and very cold, and as we sat dipping into it with wooden spoons, the solemn family watched us in silence, the girls standing at a respectful distance. They wore richly embroidered bodices and big, baggy trousers like the girls in the advertisements for Balkan Sobranies.

When we had finished all the milk and thanked our host, we went out into the evening sunlight. The valley was the most fertile we had crossed, and there were several huts scattered up and down.

'What is the name of your valley?' we asked. The name we were told was unpronounceable.

It looked very green, and under the trees moved large flocks of goats and baby kids, filling the air with their bleating. The whole scene had an ancient and Biblical serenity.

'We will call it Shepherd's Valley,' I said. And so it was always called.

Another hour of painful climbing and we were looking down on a small bay; cupped round with high cliffs, the mountain rising steep behind it. It was Grama Bay at last, and very lovely it looked in the setting sun; though as I stumbled down the hill towards it I was less concerned with its beauty than that the sun should not fail me entirely before my bruised and tender feet had groped their way down into the valley.

That night, in the bivouac which we made, I told the two soldiers and Chela of my plan to leave Sea View. I had taken a liking to Chela, and I was glad that he approved the scheme. Black, too, was delighted; I think he felt, as I did, the need to start afresh, unhampered by the legacy of the past. Only Adams was unresponsive; he was silent and supercilious, and even when we had lain down together, keeping close for warmth under our few blankets, I could feel his hostility and was troubled by it.

The next morning we found a perfect site for the new camp in a grove of oak-trees that topped the cliff above the bay. A solitary goatherd who stood watching us was convinced that the grove was haunted, and warned me of dire results if we did damage to the trees. It was not hard to believe him, for there was a pagan beauty about the place – the firm, green turf, the grey stones that lay tumbled in the grass, and the leaves which, though on the turn, still clung to the boughs; and, at one edge of the wood, a tiny outpost of Christianity, stood a dilapidated shrine. Untended and unvisited, its ruined walls held little to be seen except a battered picture of St. George doing to death a pasteboard dragon, yet they sung their story with a martyr's tongue – the story of unseen, silent battle through the years against the old, strong gods, and every fallen stone cried its protest against the hairy hands that had flung it down and the hooves that had drummed gleefully away.

In the evening the new camp had visitors. From the surrounding hills came the local goatherds, half a dozen of them, bringing gifts of goats' milk; small, strong-looking men in black coats, each with a rifle across his shoulder. Through Chela I spoke to them. I said that I had come as their friend to help them rid their country of the

Germans; that as yet I did not want them to fight, but only to bring us goats, and eggs, and milk; for which we would pay. Above all, as they wandered with their flocks through the day, I wanted them to keep a keen look-out for German patrols. Chela, too, gave them a speech – a fiery and emotional affair it sounded. When he had finished, the goatherds conferred together and one addressed me. He was a villainous-looking fellow, but he spoke with dignity.

'They say that you are their guest,' said Chela. 'They say that they must die before you die, and that now they will think only to serve you. They will think no more for their wives, or for their children, or even for their goats.'

I could only hope that more sincerity lay in their words than in the usual exchange of diplomatic courtesies.

In the days that followed, I grew to have an understanding of Chela. He had never been outside Albania, but, as a boy, he had received a good education at the American school in Tirana. Many of his class-mates were now prominent in the Partisan movement.

'They learnt how to fight during the war in Spain,' Chela said. 'Yes, there they commanded companies and battalions, but now they have promotion. They have returned to Albania to command brigades.'

He was a painful mixture of extreme pride and sudden humility, deeply conscious that we Allies were his guests and that he was responsible for our safety; above all, tormented by doubt as to his own proper course of action in the crisis of civil war that was immediately facing not only his country in general, but his valley, his very family.

For a week I shuttled to and fro establishing the new base, growing daily more and more impatient of the mountain barrier that kept me on the country's rim, pinning me against the sea. But at last Grama was in a fit state to leave in Drake's care and I felt free to start inland.

The last night before I crossed the mountain I spent in the cave in Sea View. Both Trent and Benson had welcomed Grama as a secondary base, and I felt that I had extricated my men from Sea View with commendable diplomacy.

In honour of my departure we opened a bottle of vermouth,

the vermouth which Chela had brought from Valona. Helped by the wine, our talk slipped away into Intelligence gossip – the bomb explosion in Istanbul... Of course, my dear fellow, you know what really happened?... Old Stuffy Whatnot, who was doing such a splendid job in Bulgaria till he was captured...

'I once knew a cute little Bulgarian girl in Athens,' said Benson reminiscently.

'As a matter of interest,' I asked, 'what happens to us if we are captured at this game? Are we treated as spies?'

'Ah!' said Trent. 'A nice point! But one on which I'm afraid there is little evidence. There's a pertinent remark in *Hamlet* which covers it... 'That unknown country...' How does it go?'

I said: "That undiscovered country from whose bourne no traveller returns."

'That's it. Anyhow, by far the best plan is to avoid putting it to the test.'

The talk went on, and all the time Chela sat with a puzzled look on his face, quietly listening to it, quick to jump to his feet if anything was needed – a cigarette, a match, more wood for the fire. We spoke about the war, about women, about politics, just the sort of conversation that comes readily over dinner-tables and which in any sophisticated country would pass as quite normal – indeed, possibly intelligent and even amusing; but as I thought of how we were situated – in the midst of a small, wild country occupied by the enemy, the sea below us, the desolate mountain above – and as I looked at Chela's lean, bearded face, the talk suddenly sounded glib and utterly cynical, and I wished with all my heart that he could not understand it.

FOUR

THREE HOURS' CLIMBING in hot sunshine had brought Chela and me almost to the summit of the mountain. Both the sweat running down my face and dripping rhythmically from my chin, together with the knowledge that I was leaving the base at Grama well-founded, gave me a feeling of satisfaction, and Moses himself could not have been more eager to reach the summit of Pisgah and survey the land of his people's destiny than I was to look down upon the valley of Dukat.

Another minute now and I should be at the top; another twenty paces and I should see my own Gilead, my own Ephraim and Manasseh; yet I hesitated, savouring the moment of anticipation, while there still was nothing before my eyes but the mountain ridge cutting the empty sky; then I walked forward, and as I did so a tremendous panorama blossomed out beneath me.

From the mass of mountains to the south, the valley of Dukat flowed northward like a river, steep and narrow at its start, broadening out till it poured into the great sweep of Valona Bay. Fifteen miles away to the north, and clearly visible, lay Valona itself, while from the valley below a series of foot-hills rose, piling one upon another, building up into the main massif that enclosed the valley on its eastern side. Behind this again, peak after mountain peak melted into the distance.

A bitter wind striking through our sweat-soaked clothes soon drove us from the summit, and we set off down-hill through woods and undergrowth which, though sparse, were in contrast to the bare desolation of the seaward slopes. The light was beginning to fail as we reached the last ridge from which the mountain dropped precipitously into the valley, and here we rested, drinking from the rain-water pools in the rocks, watching through my field-glasses the scene below. The whole valley was full of sound, and a hubbub of goats bleating, people crying, dogs barking, rose up on the still evening air.

Chela pointed to the distant road along which moved a few cars. 'German trucks,' he said.

'Where is the meeting tonight?' I asked.

'In my house,' he replied. 'There.' And he proudly indicated a rough farm-house, the biggest I could see in the valley.

I felt it was my cue for flattery. 'Is *that* your house?' I asked, with astonishment.

Chela's face assumed an expression of self-conscious pride.

'It's a very fine, large house,' I said.

'I am a rich man,' replied Chela simply.

'But aren't you afraid of being raided during this meeting? It looks dangerously near the road.'

'My shepherds will be on guard round the house,' Chela answered. 'If the Germans come to catch us we shall have time to run away.'

As we drew near to the house a figure came to meet us across the fields.

'It is Zechir,' said Chela. 'He is my man.'

He was a slight, fair-headed lad with a face that hunger or sickness had thinned painfully. He saluted me, touching heart, lips and forehead, then with a quick gesture seized my hand and kissed it.

We passed through a heavy stone archway, across the courtyard, up a flight of stone steps. As we turned into a corridor, there was a scuffle behind me, and I turned in time to catch a glimpse of women's and children's faces peeping out through a half-opened door before it was swiftly shut. As I was in a Moslem house I made no comment.

The guest-room into which I was shown surprised me; I had expected to find a native Albanian atmosphere, but instead there were two iron beds, a white-wood desk, and some chairs of the type that furnish village halls in England.

Chela must have seen my surprise, for he said: 'It is the custom of Albania to sleep on the floor, but for me...' And he made an expression of ineffable superiority.

I saw which way the wind lay, and said quickly: 'What a nice room. I like your curtains very much.'

They were hideous things made of cheap blue lace and clashed horribly with the pink walls, but Chela flashed a metallic smile of pride.

'Yes,' he said. 'I bought them in Valona last year. They were very expensive.'

Dinner consisted of a bitter soup, roast turkey and a kind of junket. Obviously the house had produced its best; the only pity was that the food was half spoilt by being served cold and congealed. Chela ate ravenously, all the while plying me with tit-bits. I was hungry enough myself, not having eaten since breakfast.

We were waited on throughout the meal by Zechir and another of Chela's henchmen, whose name was Old Ali. This was a ceremonious and sly-looking old rascal with an air of faded splendour, who seemed to scorn to wear his jacket in the manner of common mortals, but carried it slung raffishly over one shoulder like a hussar's pelisse. His long moustaches, too, would have been the pride of any old-fashioned hussar.

After dinner my host excused himself. The leaders of the village, he explained, were assembling in another room and he must greet them.

There was no fireplace in the cold little room; the only warmth came from a charcoal brazier over which I huddled, waiting for the entrance of the elders and scribbling some notes for the speech that I was to make to them. They were so long in coming that, left alone, I began to grow self-conscious. How should they find me, I wondered, when they first came in? Sitting or standing? With my beret on or off? Standing, I decided; it was more impressive. And hat on – according to the custom of the country. I was going to need all my skill to persuade these men of Dukat that their interests lay in fighting with the Allies; I couldn't afford to miss a single trick. I heard their voices outside the door and rose to my feet.

There were about a dozen of them, all armed and wearing elaborate cartridge-belts. A few were in Albanian costume, but most wore ordinary European clothes, breeches and cloth caps. They came silently into the room in stockinged feet, and, when the punctilious introductions were all done and they were seated, I began my speech to them. They watched me intently as I spoke, and while Chela translated, some of them took notes. It was not an easy speech, since I had little immediately to offer in return for what I wanted of them, and my object was to gain their confidence and find out their attitude without disclosing either the strength or weakness of my own hand.

I told them that I had come to take the place of Major Keith, and that I was there that night to find out in what way we could be of mutual assistance; that I had come to fight the Germans and to help the Albanians to fight them. I said that I realised that a tragic impasse had arisen between the Balli and the Partisans, and that I would do my utmost to heal this breach. I promised them that I would do my utmost to bring no further unhappiness on a country that already had its full share. I finished with some soft-sugar about Albania being a small country and that her contribution had already been great, but that the final stage of the war, which we were now entering, demanded the last extreme effort from every country, great or small, etc., etc.... Finally, I asked them for a statement of their position and views.

There was a lot of discussion among them, and eventually their spokesman, a keen, precise little man in a knitted white cap, began his reply. Till Chela translated to me, I could not understand a word he said, but I could at least see that White Cap was a skilful speaker and that he presented his case with considerable force and humour. In fact, if I had been expecting a collection of boors and bumpkins I was very wrong; there was an astonishing level of education among these representatives of a village that numbered no more than four thousand. All spoke Italian, several spoke French, and besides Chela, there were two or three with a good command of English.

The Major must realise, said White Cap, that the men of Dukat were in a very difficult position. Their patriotism was undeniable; this was proved by their numerous actions against the invader during the Italian occupation. But now they were faced with the threat of civil war. Only last month the Partisans, had attacked their village, and, though they had no intention of taking retaliatory action, yet day and night the men of Dukat were now on guard against a second attack. The spokesman did not deny that fine ideals motivated many Partisans, but he begged me to believe that the leaders for the most part were unscrupulous and ambitious young men who were out to gain power. It was for this reason, he said, that Dukat could never side with the Partisans, and instead had decided on a course of neutrality.

I tried my next line of approach. Being so newly arrived in Albania, I said, I did not as yet presume to argue against the decisions which they had taken, but, since we were exploring possibilities, what would be their reaction if I were to attack the Germans myself, with my own men, in Dukat valley?

This question caused much shaking of heads and pulling down of mouths... To take aggressive action against the Germans was very dangerous, since the main coast road passed directly through the village, and if the Germans were even to suspect Dukat hostility they could, and would, destroy the place with one blow. If the action were taken by British soldiers it would make no difference: Dukat would be accused of complicity and its fate would be the same. In short, they would be definitely opposed to my making any attack upon the Germans in their area.

I tried my last tack. Since they found themselves unable to take offensive action, and since for geographical reasons my base had to be in their territory, what would be their attitude to the passage of arms across their valley to the Partisans?

This question provoked a long discussion which ended with the reply that though highly dangerous, for if the Balli leaders in Valona got to hear of it Dukat would certainly be attacked by both Balli and Germans together, yet it might be considered if the Partisans in return would leave the village unmolested. Here, at last, was some hope.

'Tell them,' I said to Chela, 'that I hope shortly to meet the leaders of the local Partisan Brigade, and that I will sound them along the lines of this proposal.'

The talk was ended. They rose, shook hands, picked up their weapons, and went out into the night to take their places in the village guard.

I felt depressed when they had gone. Here was a situation of more complexity than I had anticipated. Only self-interest or a choice between two evils drags a great nation into war; in my optimism I had forgotten that the same rule might hold good for a mountain village in Albania, and at present I did not see how on a basis of self-interest I was to sell the war against the Germans to the surprisingly level-headed men of Dukat.

It was too cold to undress. I lay down on one of the beds and pulled round me the coarse, heavy blanket which Zechir brought in. In the other bed Chela lay, propped on his elbow, smoking cigarette after cigarette. I fell asleep.

...There was confusion in the house; doors crashed; voices; a trampling outside... I struggled through sleep and sat up in bed. Chela was just coming into the room. Why was he coming into the room? He ought to be in bed.

'The nurses are here,' he said.

Nurses? What nurses? What's he talking about? Slowly my brain cleared. Nurses. Yes! The American nurses who had crashed in the plane...

There were girls' voices in the corridor. 'Oh, Jean darling! Say, Jean, where are you?'

Men were coming into the room, American officers.

'Stone's my name. Glad to know you,' said one. He was bearded and chunky. 'I'll give you girls twenty minutes,' he called out through the door. 'It's now ten past five. We'll leave at five-thirty sharp.'

'That's tough on the girls,' said another officer, wearing Air Corps insignia. 'They've been walking all night.'

'Can't help it,' said Stone. 'If we give them any longer they'll stiffen up, and we'll never get them to move again.' He turned to Chela. 'Two of these girls are in pretty poor shape. Can you lend me any mules?'

'I think I can find two.'

'Good. Have them saddled right away.'

The girls were all in another room. I would have liked to have said a word to them, but I thought it best to keep out of the way.

'Six weeks!' The aviator was talking. 'Six weeks in this flaming country, and always walking. Jesus grant I never see Albania again!'

A new figure came into the room; he wore a small beard and had parachute wings sewn into a fur cap; two pips on his shoulder.

'Hallo,' I said.

'Good Lord! Are you English?'

'Yes,' I said.

'What on earth are you doing here? Never mind, skip it. There's no time for explanations. Got an English cigarette?'

Stone began to round up his flock.

'Come on, girls. You've got to be well up the mountain by dawn. We don't want you caught by Jerry at this stage.'

I stood by the door as the girls went clumping down the corridor.

'Good luck!' I called. 'You're really on the last lap now.'

They turned at the sound of my voice and I had a glimpse of round faces, unexpectedly feminine, framed in their parka hoods.

'Oh, thanks! Good night!'

'Good night!'

'Say, darling! You haven't lost that lipstick, have you?'

Gay, American voices.

'Good night! Good night!'

For a while there was a clattering in the yard outside then all was still again. They were gone.

Lipstick!... I turned back into the room and lay down again on the bed – not yet to sleep, but to smoke a cigarette and wonder a little at the unconscious, heart-breaking courage of women.

'Major, we are now in the hills of Trajas, and Trajas is Partisan.' Chela spoke apologetically. 'It is not safe for me to go any farther with you. Zechir will guide you now. The Partisans will not hurt him; he is only a poor one.'

'Thank you for your help, Chela.' I handed back to him the civilian greatcoat which he had given me to wear over my uniform as we crossed over the road inland. 'I hope the Partisans will not be too hard to find.'

'I will wait for you at my house till you come back. Good-bye, Major. Remember at Trajas to ask for Doctor Georgie; he will surely be able to help you.'

Two hours brought us to Trajas. It was the first Albanian village I had entered, and it was a desolate sight. Out of some six hundred little houses, not more than fifty were inhabited. Walls gaped, roofs had fallen in, stones cascaded into the narrow paths that served for streets. At a spring, some women were washing clothes, but without soap. A few men sat about. There was no sign of food; neither crops, vegetables, fruits, fowls – just nothing.

Zechir left me at a corner while he went to find the man who, Chela had said, would know where I could find the leaders of the Partisan Brigade. Four or five people gathered round, staring at me.

'*Inglese?*' asked one.

'*Si*,' I replied.

Some words were spoken in Albanian, and a boy who was there went running off. The others continued to stare, neither with gaiety nor yet with hostility.

The boy returned, leading a scarecrow of a man in tattered, Western clothes. He was pushed in front of me and stood there looking me up and down. All the faces in the group were turned to him expectantly.

'English?'

His voice was like a rusty hinge.

'My name Hassan. Speak good English. This goddam country she no good.'

He held out a filthy claw.

The combination of American accent and unexpected vehemence took me by surprise.

'You've been in America?' I asked.

'Me... janitor... Detroit... Twelve years.'

I could see the words come painfully into his head. His face was set with concentration. Then he blurted: 'This country son-of-a-bitch. All finished.' He pointed to the ruined houses. 'Italians... Germans... Balli.'

With the last word his gummy eyes lit up and the little crowd murmured. For how much of this desolation, I wondered, were my Balli friends of last night responsible, together with the Italians and Germans?

'Where will I find the Partisans?' I asked.

The prophet's face remained blank, so I repeated the question slowly; but he couldn't understand. His English was at an end, and so was his strength.

As the boy led him off I could see an expression of doubt on the faces of the little crowd. Had their champion acquitted himself well? I felt that I could not fail him.

'*Parla benissimo Inglese*,' I said. '*Benissimo*.'

They seemed reassured.

Of Zechir, or of this Doctor Georgie whom I should meet, there was no sign, so I sat on the wall in the sun watching some children playing in the distance. Children make the same noise in any language, and the sound of those squeaking voices was the only thing that linked the stricken village with any normal form of life.

A whole hour had gone by before Zechir returned, bringing with him the elusive doctor. The latter came up smiling all over his face.

'My name is Doctor Georgie. I sure am pretty pleased to see you.' The newcomer's accent was more strongly American than that of my first interlocutor.

He was a little man, quite young, with a pleasant, sensitive face. His clothes hung about him, as though he had shrunk inside them, and he wore a curious tweed cap with ear-flaps that tied together on the top of his head.

'And mine's Overton. I'm a British officer just arrived in this area. I'm told you can help me get in touch with the local Partisan leaders. Is that true?'

'Sure. I'll do all I can to help.' He was nearly stammering with eagerness. 'Two days ago the Commissar was in Gjormi; I think maybe we still find him there.'

'And where is Gjormi?'

'It's on the other side of the mountain. Farther inland.'

I looked up at the monster that hung above our heads.

'Well, I'm very anxious to meet them.'

'Gee! They'll be anxious to meet you too, Major.' He looked like an earnest and intelligent guinea-pig.

'How long will it take to cross?'

'Five hours, I guess. We could make Gumenitza tonight and go on to Gjormi in the morning.'

'Will you come with me?'

I liked the little fellow, and it was a relief to find someone who spoke English.

'Sure. I guess I'd better. And we'll take three good boys as guards.' He gave a deprecatory laugh. 'I don't know the way so good.'

He spoke to the men who stood round us, then turned back to me. 'Well, let's go.'

'But haven't you anything to collect before you leave?' I asked.

He laughed.

'No, I got nothing. Nor have they.' And he indicated the men who were to guide us. 'Let's go. We've not got too much daylight left.'

Four hours' steady climbing brought us to the top of the mountain, and by then night was falling.

Of our three guards, one had been a schoolmaster and the other two were father and son. The boy had a thick, black scab all round his mouth – caused by fever, I was told. We were too busy climbing to speak much, but when we reached the plateau on the top the boy started to sing quietly. He had a pleasant voice, and he sang one after another of the Partisan songs. They were in a minor key and sad, like Russian tunes.

The moon came up, and it was evident that we had lost our way. I was feeling rather weak, as I had had nothing to eat since breakfast. I made a note to carry my own food with me on these walks in future.

We were going along in single file, the old man leading and I next, when he slipped on a rock and fell. The rifle he carried went off in my face, but luckily the bullet missed me. The others thought it was an ambush and flung themselves on their faces. When they realised what had happened, they thought it was a very funny joke.

Once, as we floundered along through the dark, we heard a shrill whooping, and the next moment stones started to fall among us. We halted and the old man called aloud. Out of the darkness emerged a small boy; though very sturdy, he could not have been more than eight years old. They spoke together and something he said made the men laugh.

'He's telling us that he's up here alone guarding the goats,' the doctor explained. 'When he heard us coming he thought we must be either wolves or robbers, so he threw stones at us to scare us away.'

I looked at the little creature pattering along bare-foot beside us.

'And he is left up here in the mountain all alone?' I asked.

Georgie nodded.

'Yes, all alone.'

An hour later, thanks to the directions of our diminutive guide, we were coming into Gumenitza. As far as I could tell in the darkness, it was much like Trajas. It was quite silent till, suddenly, every dog in the place began to bark; one huge beast ran at us and had to be driven off with a rifle-shot.

The ex-schoolmaster had been sent on ahead to announce our coming, and when we arrived a room was already prepared for us in the house of the village commissar. It was a high, whitewashed room, and although empty of furniture save for two great chests which stood one on each side of the door, it did not look bare; it was filled with the glow of a crackling wood fire, and with the warmth of the brightly coloured rugs and cushions that were strewn about the floor.

The leaders of the Fifth Brigade, it seemed, were still in Gjormi – the next village on – and already a messenger had been sent through the night to warn them of my coming. I felt rather pleased; it was the first time my presence had aroused any enthusiasm since I had arrived in Albania.

A bottle of raki was brought in – a clear, colourless spirit that would have tasted disgusting if I had not been in such need of a drink. It was very strong.

My clothes were sodden with sweat and the doctor's were the same, so we dried our vests and shirts in rotation, wearing one for warmth while the steam rose from the other. The boy with the scabby mouth took off his top coat and revealed his only upper garment as an Italian sailor's white blouse, complete with big, blue collar. I wondered how he had come by it, but decided not to enquire. The boy was ready enough to go into gory details without being prompted.

Food came, a mush of sodden bread and entrails; we gobbled it down, scrabbling in the bowl with our fingers, and when it was all gone I leaned back against the wall, my belly like a drum and my head buzzing with the raki, staring bemusedly at the fire.

'Say, Major.'

'Yes, Georgie?'

'These boys you'll meet tomorrow – I'd like to tell you something about them.'

He started off, a long story about Partisans and Balli and Albania and the Allies, but I couldn't concentrate, and I didn't hear the end of it; I had fallen asleep.

I heard about the leaders of the Fifth Brigade, though, as we walked towards Gjormi next morning in the cold, clear sunlight.

'Petchi, the Commander, used to be an officer in the Albanian Army.'

'And the Commissar?'

'He's called Besnik.'

Georgie pronounced the name with a kind of awe.

'You'll like him, Major. He's tough, but he's a pretty swell boy.'

The doctor was not a good walker. There was something pathetic about him as he flopped along in his loose clothes. His Alpine boots were so worn and battered that the nails round the edge, instead of pointing down, stuck out sideways like a ragged moustache.

'I take it they're both communists?'

At once the doctor was on the defensive.

'Maybe they are; they fight well against the Huns.'

I hadn't heard the word 'Hun' since I arrived in Albania.

'Where did you learn your English?' I asked.

'I spent three years in America. I took a degree in bacteriology at Collingwood University. That's why these folks call me "doctor". I'm not a doctor really: I just do what I can.'

His face lit up when he spoke of America, and he prattled on about its wonders till we arrived at Gjormi.

The place was nothing but a heap of ruins, but it swarmed with Partisans waiting for my arrival. They came clustering round me, shaking hands, giving the communist salute with the clenched fist. They were young men for the most part, with hard, thin faces, most of them wearing a red star in their caps.

Besnik and Petchi were expected any moment, I was told. While I waited they bombarded me with questions. How was the war going? When would it end? How were the armies doing in Italy? Would the Russians break through in the spring? I answered their questions as best I could, with an appropriate mixture of tact and enthusiasm, but it was a slight ordeal and I was glad to be rescued from it by the arrival of a messenger.

'Death to Fascism!' he shouted.

The men round me vied with each other in the ferocity of their tone as they replied: 'The Freedom of the People!'

'They are coming!' said the messenger, and stamped off.

Another seven or eight minutes went by before another courier came walking quickly towards us.

'They are coming!' he said, and disappeared after the first.

'They are coming!' said the Partisans around me, and they began to lead me away.

'...To the meeting-place,' Doctor Georgie informed me as we approached one of the three hovels that were still standing.

In the yard a large goat was being done to death, its blood running over the stones. So, I thought, the talk was to be followed by a lunch-party. Three wretched-looking women eyed us as we trooped into the little house.

The room inside was better than I had expected – clean, whitewashed walls, the fire burning, and on the floor a few rugs and cushions of bright red.

'What's the matter, Georgie?' I asked.

The little man was a picture of dejection as he pulled his boots off.

'They're going to use me as interpreter.' He sighed and gave a frightened smile. 'It makes me kind of nervous.'

The entrance, when at last it came, justified the build-up, there was no denying it was good. There was a noise of voices in the yard and the crash of heavy boots in the corridor outside, then the door flung open and: 'Death to Fascism!'... 'Death to Fascism!' rang out simultaneously from the Commander and the Commissar of the Fifth Partisan Brigade.

I came to attention and gave my best 'King's Regulations' salute; I had purposely kept on my beret so that I could do so. They were hung about with all the implements of war – automatic rifles, revolvers, field-glasses, map-cases, and, in the commissar's belt, a hand-grenade. I was glad to see him discard it, for it looked very precarious. Quickly the accoutrements were shed, boots removed, and in a very short time we were sitting on the floor round the fire, ready for business. I had expected that this was going to be a tough interview, and as I looked at the two men opposite me I knew that I had been right. Two purposeful faces looked back at me. I braced myself.

'Ask them if they will speak first, or if they want me to.'

Georgie translated.

'They say will you please begin.'

Again I glanced at the two Partisans. Fair words would butter no parsnips here.

'First of all, I wish to state clearly the purpose of my mission here in Albania.'

I spoke slowly, picking my words with care.

'I have been sent here to give assistance to all who are fighting the common enemy. I am, therefore, here to help you. How that help is to be brought, and in what quantity, is for us to discuss today.'

That, I thought, should set the ball rolling.

'Will you give me your comments so far.'

When Georgie had translated my words, the two leaders spoke together for a minute, and I had time to study them. Petchi was a short man of perhaps forty. Curly black hair topped an animal face, deeply seamed in the cheeks, with a full, aggressive, lower lip. Besnik was ten years younger, I judged, and considerably the taller of the two. He had fair, straight hair and a pointed face that might have been over-subtle had it not been so weathered and toughened by his life. Both were clean-shaven.

Though I could not understand a word they spoke, I guessed that Besnik was asking in effect: 'Shall I give him the works?' and that Petchi agreed. At any rate, he proceeded to do so. For a long time he spoke quietly in Albanian while the doctor, with a worried face, made notes. When he had ceased speaking, Georgie turned to me.

'These guys are pretty sore. They've suffered pretty bad and...'

'Come on,' I cut in. 'I want to know exactly what he said – exactly.'

'This is what he says,' began Georgie miserably. 'The words "to give assistance" are very welcome, especially as after many fair promises we have received absolutely nothing.'

The little man looked at me with frightened eyes. 'Don't get me wrong, Major. I'm only translating what he said.'

I nodded. 'Go on.'

'Major Keith dropped by parachute into our area and we took care of him. He made us many promises of help, but instead of fulfilling them he left us and moved his base into Balli territory. He gave to Dukat the help that he had promised to us. Major Keith was not for the war. And so, though we are glad to hear the word "help", we do not believe you, for we have been too often betrayed. That's what Besnik says,' the doctor finished lamely.

The attack on Tom was both absurd and irritating.

'Major Keith was a regular officer for ten years before ever this war began,' I replied. 'His profession was to fight for his country. To say, therefore, that he was not "for" the war is ridiculous. The reason for his moving to Balli territory is simple; he was ordered to. He was ordered to open a base on the coast, and he obeyed his orders. It was a geographical accident that the perfect place for a sea base was in Balli hands. As to help, you do not tell the truth; to my knowledge you received four planeloads of material while the major was with you, while Dukat has been given only some clothing – as payment for the protection of the base. To conclude, I do not wish to discuss what Major Keith did, or did not do. I am here now; and I do not care to have my word doubted.'

Georgie could not have softened my words much, for Petchi flushed deeply. The Partisans, he said, loudly and with great vehemence, had begun their war against the fascist invaders without any help from the Allies, and though he would not deny that help was badly wanted yet, if need be, the Albanian Partisans would continue to the end without it.

The Brigade Commander had put himself into such a passion of rage that I did not find it difficult to remain calm, and I pointed out to him that however the Partisans began their fight, they had not lacked for support since the arrival, some months back, of British missions. Large quantities of material, as well as considerable sums of gold, had been given to the Central Partisan Council, quite apart from the assistance given to individual groups and brigades.

Petchi merely shrugged and said that he didn't care what had been given to others – the Fifth Brigade had gone without help.

Now Besnik interrupted, using a boyish and extremely genuine smile. He apologised for the outburst of the Commander, an emotional man, he said – so much so that he had earned the nickname of 'The Thunderer' – and he hoped I would not be offended by the bluntness of Petchi's speech.

'Of course,' he went on, 'of course we need your help, and badly. We should be grateful to hear your suggestions on that score.'

Now for it! If I could only get them to accept the Dukat proposal and so get the two parties thoroughly interdependent, I might be in a fair way to stopping the civil war in my area, thus leaving both sides free to concentrate on the common enemy.

I explained that for my stores I was dependent on the sea, and that this fact, therefore, limited me in the location of my base. The only possible place for a sea base that I could see was behind Dukat mountain.

'However,' I continued, 'I think there is a solution which I hope will be acceptable to you... I will retain my base in Balli territory, where it is unlikely to be suspect by the Germans, and the material I bring ashore can be secretly transported to you across Dukat valley by night.'

I made Georgie translate so far. A look of amused incredulity came over the faces of the two men.

'And Dukat?' asked Besnik.

'The men of Dukat are agreeable if you, in return, will give them an assurance that you will not attack them.'

At the translation of my last words, the two Partisans smiled broadly at each other.

'Splendid!' said Besnik. 'Dukat evades any dangerous work and asks us not to attack them!'

Another talk between the two, then Petchi spoke.

'Major, we will have no compromise with the men of Dukat. We will enter into compact with them. The right to attack them or to refrain from attacking them, we reserve to ourselves; and if the only way we can get arms is through Dukat then we will do without the arms.'

Full stop. So that was that.

'Why do you not drop arms to us by plane?' asked Besnik.

Now this, I knew well, was what I might have to come to one day, but to agree to it now might be to throw away the one means I had to effect a truce between the parties. It would only confirm the Partisans in their intransigence towards Dukat, and render my own position in that area quite impossible. I could hardly expect the men of Dukat to give protection to my base while I supplied to their bitter enemies the very instruments for their destruction. Yet the maintenance of the sea base was part of my allotted task. Besides, in one sea sortie we could bring into the country more stores than in six air sorties, and I was unwilling at the first sign of difficulty to discard the whole organisation of sea supply which had been so carefully built up and which I was there to employ. I therefore dodged that one.

'I have been told to depend for supplies only on the sea route,' I said. 'We have not enough planes to supply the whole of the Balkans.' And I enlarged on the advantages of sea supply.

'But you can have a sea base in Partisan territory.'

This was new to me, and I was genuinely glad to hear it. I had no idea that the Partisans controlled any suitable part of the coast.

'I can? Where?'

'South of your present base. At Vuno.'

Vuno. That was the village whose lights we had seen from the *Sea Maid* as we were approaching the coast ten days ago – or was it ten years?

'Then by all means let me see the spot,' I said. 'If it is possible I will run the stores in there.'

'Good! Then you can make your base with us and leave the Balli.' Besnik smiled. 'If only for the sake of your own safety you should do that. We would put a company, a battalion even, at your disposal as a guard; but among the Balli you will never be safe. They are fighting with the Germans. Any day they might betray you.'

I knew that in this he might well be right, yet still I was unwilling to commit myself at this early stage. Until I saw their proposed sea base with my own eyes I preferred to be sceptical about it, and not run the risk of losing one sure sea link before I had established another. My reply was that I would certainly establish a base with them, but that I would retain Sea View as well for the time being.

'Major,' said Besnik, 'we feel that you are a little over-concerned about the relationship between ourselves and the Balli.' His voice was silky and his smile disarmingly frank, but he could not hide the subtlety of his face. 'Let me remind you of two statements, both of them made by your own government. The Allies have said that they will help all those who fight the common enemy, regardless of their political opinions. I therefore demand help from you; we are fighting the Nazis. The Allies have said that they will not interfere in the internal affairs of other countries. I demand, therefore, that you leave us to settle our domestic quarrels in our own way.'

And now get out of that one, his expression seemed to say.

'In spite of your argument,' I replied, 'my path is not as clear as I could wish it. To give you arms with which to fight the Germans' – I deliberately avoided the use of the word 'Nazis'; that would be to concede to these Partisans their own political angle on the fight – 'may, in certain circumstances, be equal to interfering very seriously in your country's internal affairs.'

The interpreter had hardly finished before Petchi broke in.

'It is perfectly clear,' he blurted. 'We Partisans are fighting the Nazis. If you want to help us you can; there is nothing to stop you.'

Besnik glanced quickly at his commander. I fancied he would have liked Petchi either to be more tactful or else keep his mouth shut.

'That is an argument into which I do not want to be drawn now,' I answered. 'This is what I will do. In six days from now I shall be at Vuno; I suggest that your representative be there to meet me, and that he is competent to discuss the problems of transport inland as well as the actual reception of the sortie. Six days from now is the earliest that I can be at Vuno, since I must first go back to my own base. Let us for the moment go no farther than that.'

This seemed to content them, and we broke up the conversation to eat lunch. The goat, now carved into lumps and gobbets, was contained in a large dish, and the dish stood on a low stool round which we squatted. Eight or ten other Partisans joined us for the meal, among them a young girl, the first so-to-speak emancipated woman I had seen in Albania. Every other I had seen hitherto had been extremely ugly, dressed in peasant costume, and both segregated from, and subordinated to, the men. But this girl was pretty; she had bobbed hair, and wore a skirt instead of the usual baggy trousers, and she sat eating and talking with the men like an equal. She could hardly have been more than seventeen, but she looked as though she took life very seriously, writing a number of notes and never smiling once. She appeared to be Besnik's secretary, and I wondered if she was also his bed-fellow, but decided that this was unlikely, or she would have looked less solemn.

The head of the goat, as being the greatest delicacy, was courteously placed in my hands by Petchi, but as yet I was too much of a novice to extract from it more than the obvious brains. The meat was very tough, as was to be expected with an animal that had been killed only two hours, but it disappeared in a flash. Fingers were licked. Petchi jumped to his feet and a moment later, with a final brandishing of clenched fist; and a battery of 'Deaths to Fascism!' he and his little staff had gone stamping off.

Besnik remained behind with me to discuss details of the material that was needed by the brigade, and it was only now that I discovered that he spoke good French. This meant that we were able to dispense with the services of Doctor Georgie – which was just as well, for the undercurrent of emotion that had flowed through the meeting, coupled with his dread of offending either side, had reduced the little man to such a state of nerves that he was incapable of further translation.

Besnik's first request was no modest one. 'I want seven hundred rifles.'

'What is the size of your brigade?'

The brigade, apparently, numbered a thousand, all of whom had rifles, though little ammunition. There was also a reserve, a kind of 'Home Guard', of about the same number, but lacking arms of any kind. '

The revelation of such numbers came as a surprise to me. It also struck me that their advantage, since there was little to be gained militarily from a half-armed mass, could only be political.

'Please don't think,' I said, 'that I am trying to teach you your own business, but would it not be better to organise your brigade in small raiding parties, highly mobile and well-equipped, rather than in such unwieldy numbers?'

Besnik smiled. 'You do not understand our type of warfare.'

There was a firmness in his voice which decided me not to pursue that point for the time being.

'What priority do you want given to food and clothes?'

Again the smile, this time with a trace of bitterness.

'You have seen for yourself what we look like. We have no coats, and the snow will soon be here; but arms and ammunition are our greatest need. Do not send food and clothing at the expense of ammunition. If we have arms we can still fight – even if we are a little cold and hungry; but we cannot kill Nazis with blankets and tins of meat.'

As he was leaving, he turned in the doorway. 'You must excuse any hot words that have been spoken. Our need is very great.'

He took a step back into the room towards me.

'There is a reason why I do not think that you will fail us,' he said quietly. 'It is because you, too, are young – and the young do not fail each other.'

FIVE

AT THE FIRST SUMMIT of Dukat mountain Chela and I paused to rest. We lay down among the scrub and the tumbled rocks; Chela lit a cigarette.

'Are you glad to be back among the Balli?' he asked.

'I don't know. I am glad to see you again.'

'You liked the Partisans?'

'Liked them?... I don't know that either. I was impressed by them.'

It was true; the ardour and purpose of the Partisans had made a great impression on me.

In a matter-of-fact voice Chela said: 'I think they will soon attack Dukat again.'

'You don't seem very concerned about it,' I observed.

He pulled his mouth down at the corners. 'It is no concern of mine. I am no longer a man of Balli; I am no longer a man of Dukat; I am only soldier of the Allies.'

'You are an Albanian and have your country to think of. Chela – there is an idea that I want to put to you, and I want you to understand that I am speaking not as a British soldier, but as a man, as a friend.'

He nodded. 'I understand. This is personal: Overton – Chela.'

'You are a man with the capacity of being a leader: you have shown that already here in your own valley. Since I met the Partisans I have been wondering if your right place is not with them.'

He shook his head. 'Impossible.'

'It's a strong movement,' I persisted. 'And whatever its politics may be, it's a patriotic movement. You must be realistic about this, Chela. Some forces are too strong to fight against; the best course then is to try to influence them from within.'

'Major,' said Chela after a pause, 'once I was a very strong Balli, until one day I saw with my own eyes what I could not otherwise have believed. I saw men of my own party, shoulder to shoulder with Germans, fighting against other Albanians – against the Partisans. I took the Balli emblem from my hat and threw it on the ground, and since that day I am no more with the Balli party.'

I glanced at the man's fierce profile as he gazed moodily down upon his valley. He was not talking for effect; this speech was coming from his heart.

'In that time I was in great troubles. I could not be a Partisan – a communist; I could no more stay in my house in Dukat valley, living among Balli. I must be having nothing to do with the politics of my country; I wished only to be private person, only Chela. I decided to leave my house and my family, and go and live in the mountain and look after goats – like a poor one. Then one night there comes to my house Major Keith, and he says – very stiff: 'I am British officer. I am Major Keith.' And I say: 'And I am Chela.' And he says: 'Will you help me to find a base in your area?' So I help Major Keith, and he takes me to live with his mission. And since then I am nothing any more Albanian – not Balli, not communist, nothing, nothing – only against Germans, only soldier of the Allies. Major, believe me,' he pleaded, 'I tell you that for me it is impossible, impossible, to put a red star in my hat and do so...' He raises his fist in the communist salute. '"Death to Fascism!" He giggled at himself then suddenly turning serious he added ironically: "The Freedom of the People!"... Freedom! No, Major.' He scrambled to his feet. 'Let us go on.'

At the next ridge we came on two Albanian guards, sent there by the village, so they told us. Other guards, they said, were posted all along the ridge, watching every approach to Sea View from the road.

Immediately Chela's spirits rose. 'You see, Major, they have kept their promise to you. They are good boys really. And this is only the beginning.'

He pointed to the valley below us and the mountain on which we stood.

'Can you think of a better place to fight the Germans than this?'

It was indeed a miraculous defensive position.

'If you will wait a little, we shall have a fine, fine battle here.'

His voice was filled with excitement. 'You shall have three hundred men of Dukat.'

I raised my eyebrows, and he went on: 'Yes – five hundred. I, Chela, guarantee. And, Major, you will see then how the men of Dukat can fight. We are men, and when we fight – then – we – fight. Not like Partisans always to run away.'

'Chela,' I said, 'don't boast.'

As we came into Sea View I could see that it had filled up during my absence. The camp was full of woebegone Italian soldiers, most of their faces new to me.

In the cave I found Benson sitting alone.

'Why, hallo there! Welcome home!' he called out.

'Where's Trent?' I asked.

'He's gone.'

'Gone! Where?'

'Out. With the nurses. The boat that came for them brought him orders to leave. He went out that same night with the gals.'

'Well, I'm damned! Did he leave a note for me?'

Benson shook his head. 'He left in quite a hurry.'

I found it difficult to adjust myself to Trent's departure. I should certainly miss the only other British officer, yet in a way I was glad he had gone; the triumvirate was dissolved and now it would be a straight contest between Benson and myself. But chiefly I had an odd feeling of dismay. Trent had appeared to me as an important factor in my Albanian life; he had a definite significance. And suddenly, there he was – gone! I felt cheated.

'You must have been relieved to get the girls out safely,' I said.

I was crouching in a corner, taking a bath in a pail of hot water provided by Alpino. I was covered with flea-bites as a result of my trip, but I seemed to have collected no lice.

'I'll say I was. Though there was one little blonde I could have fitted inside my sleeping-bag.' Benson's tone was regretful. 'Unfortunately she didn't seem to have read Hemingway.'

I came and sat down on a box by the fire. The clean clothes felt wonderful, and my hands smelt no longer of stale goat-grease, but of some soap that I had bought in London.

'Tonight,' I said, 'I'd like to be going out to dinner with a very beautiful woman.' I meant Ann.

'May I join your party?' Benson asked. 'I'll bring my own woman. Say,' he went on, 'I'm beginning to feel self-conscious about staying on the Overton-Benson basis. Besides, it looks stupid in front of the women. I take it you have a Christian name?'

'John. And I've heard Trent call you Tank, but I didn't know why.'

Benson smiled. He had very good teeth, white and even.

'That arose from a corrupt signal,' he explained. 'They couldn't decipher my name properly in the signal that announced my impending arrival in this country; it should have read Benson, but they thought it was Sherman, so naturally I was called Tank. Actually,' he added, 'my name is Macavoy.'

'Any particular reason,' I asked, 'why I should believe that either?'

He laughed. 'For Christ's sake, here are we nattering away and I haven't yet asked you how you got on with the bold, bad Partisans. I suppose you did find them all right?' he asked.

'I found them, and I'll tell you the whole story after dinner.'

Just then a small man in American uniform came into the cave.

'Oh! I forgot to tell you. We have a guest for the night,' said Benson. 'Let me introduce you: Ismail Carapizzi – Major Overton.'

We shook hands.

'This is one hell of a swell little guy,' said Benson. 'He's an Albanian and he speaks no English, so he won't get embarrassed if I tell you about him.'

Carapizzi, it seemed, although an Albanian, had spent most of his life in Italy. He had been a member of the Communist party for thirty years, though his last five years had been spent in prison. Sentenced to life imprisonment, through implication in a plot to assassinate Mussolini, he had been set free by the American army, and had volunteered to return to the land of his birth as a secret agent working for the Americans.

'He's as brave as a lion,' Benson finished, 'and he's turned in some wonderful Intelligence work.'

'Do I take it that he goes round the country in this uniform?' I asked, ' – gaiters included?'

'Ah! No.' Benson shook his head. 'This is just what he wears when he comes to call on me in Sea View. He's madly proud of it.

61

He keeps it in Chela's house and changes into it before he crosses the mountain.'

The little man's beady, black eyes were switching from one to the other of us as we spoke. Though he understood no English he could follow the gist of what we said, for he smiled and raised his leg, patting his American infantry gaiters.

'What did I say?' Benson asked. 'You see: they're the pride of his life!'

Carapizzi and Chela ate with us, and when the meal was over Benson said: 'You're being very cagey about your trip. We all want to know what happened. Come on, now – Uncle John's bed-time story.'

I told them all that had happened, though not all of my conclusions; for Chela was listening, and for all his avowal of being only a soldier of the Allies; I was sure that he would not hesitate to pass on my plans to the Old Men of Dukat. I ended by telling them of the big concentration of Partisans which I was sure was taking place in the region of Gjormi and Gumenitza.

'The brigade is short of food; soon the snows will make the situation worse than ever. Before that time comes they are going to make a raid and replenish their larder. The question is, where is the raid going to come?'

'Perhaps Valona,' Benson suggested.

'I think Dukat.' I glanced at Chela, who nodded agreement with me. 'The Partisans dropped a lot of hints about Valona, but Valona is too tough a nut for them to crack at present. I believe their target will be Dukat, on some trumped-up grounds.'

'In spite of that, they seem to have taken you into camp all right,' said Benson evenly.

'Yes, they have. I admit it. Though why,' I added, 'I should use the word "admit" I don't quite know. It sounds grudging, and I don't fell at all grudging towards those Partisans.'

'In fact,' said Benson, 'you've got a lot of use for them because they're at least fighting the Germans, which the Balli are not. Am I right?'

I nodded. 'That's about it.'

There was a silence while Benson lit a cigarette.

'Would you object if I made a speech?' he asked. 'I feel one coming on.'

'Please go ahead.'

'Thanks, I will – even at the cost of boring the pants off these two.' And he nodded at Chela and Carapizzi.

'As a start, I'll admit that my own professional bias is in favour of the Balli, as they're the only people who can give me any information on the Germans; but I'll make an effort to rise above that slightly parochial point of view. O.K.?'

I made a sound of assent, and he went on slowly thinking aloud.

'There was a time when the Allies were in such straits that they took the decision to supply war material to anyone who, in return, would kill Germans. Being only a humble Intelligence officer, I have no way of judging how desperate our position was or is, so I am not criticising that initial decision; I am only stating that, as a result of it, numbers of intrepid young men have descended by parachute all over this part of Europe – and over other parts as well for all I know. These men are now engaged in handing out to guerrilla forces the arms that are dropped to them by other, no less intrepid, young men, who fly their planes by night among these God-awful mountains.'

He saw me draw a breath.

'No, don't interrupt me,' he said. 'I told you this was going to be a speech and so it is, by God! Well, now – the most striking symptom of this whole guerrilla movement, as I see it, is that by far the most competent and best-organised bands are those composed of, or at any rate led by, communists. As a result it is the communists who get the major share of the arms which we – I should say, *you* – are dealing out.

'Is this a coincidence, this communist efficiency and zeal for fighting? Let me quickly say that that question is purely rhetorical, for without giving you a second to reply, I'll furnish the answer myself... No, it is not a coincidence... And I'll tell you for why.

'Once upon a time there was a little chicken whose name was Comintern, and one day that little chicken had its head cut off; but although its head was gone, the chicken's body continued to run round for quite a while. The Joes who were trained in Moscow are now back in their own countries, in Spain, and France, and Greece, and Jugoslavia – and Albania. Comrade Stalin took a lot of trouble with those boys' education, and now it's repaying him.

'Just look at the technique – organise the patriotic resistance movement in a country; see to it that communists have the key positions; rough-house other resistance groups till they're pushed into the Germans' ready embrace; show a few corpses and German pay-books to the unsuspecting British officers, who promptly supply a few more thousand rounds of ammunition. It's a natural!'

'I presume,' I said, 'that a few corpses are considered better than no corpses – or I for one should never have been sent here.'

'Maybe,' returned Benson. 'Maybe. I can only say that we're paying a hell of a political price for carrion.'

'Supposing you're right,' I asked, 'what then? What alternative do you propose?'

'None! I can think of no alternative whatsoever!' He laughed delightedly. 'That's the whole beauty of my position. Here I can sit in this cosy little cave, a thousand miles from responsibility, throwing out my criticisms with all the assurance of the uninformed!'

'Then why the speech?' I queried, ' – which, by the way, I thought was very good.'

Benson's face became serious.

'Perhaps just this,' he said. 'To sound a note of presumptuous warning in case you were carried away too rapidly in your enthusiasm for the clenched-fist boys. And to suggest that you make damn sure that the guns which you'll soon be giving to the Partisans are used to provide German corpses and not Albanian.' He leaned forward, his voice very earnest. 'John, I am delighted that our two countries, together with Russia, are now engaged in overthrowing the Tyranny of the Right. But I feel it would be quite a pity if, in the process, we merely established an even greater tyranny – the Tyranny of the Left.'

Benson changed his tone.

'We'll ask Carapizzi his opinion of the Partisans,' he said brightly. 'As an old communist he should be worth listening to.'

And he switched the conversation into French since Carapizzi had no English, and I spoke no Italian.

The agent's shrewd face broke into a smile when we asked him the question.

'*Partigani?*' he repeated, laughing. Then he made a derogatory gesture with his hand. 'God damn!' he said with emphasis. They were the only two words of English that he knew and they made him laugh afresh.

We told him to be serious, and he made an effort to stop laughing. 'But *they* are not serious,' he protested.

'How do you mean?' I asked.

'Major,' he said, 'for thirty years I have been a communist, hein? For thirty years I have worked, but worked, for the party. I tried to kill Mussolini, hein? Well, I tell you – of these Partisans I am ashamed. What are they?... Boys, irresponsible boys. What do they know of communism?... Nothing. What do they do?... They make piggeries.' He was serious now, almost ridiculously serious. 'I am a communist – yes.' He leaned forward, and with his finger tapped the machine-gun case. 'But I am not a terrorist.'

'And they are?' I questioned.

The gesture he made in reply was eloquent.

For long after the others had turned in I sat smoking by the fire, thinking of Benson's words. His voice, coming from out of the darkness of the cave, startled me.

'John.'

'Yes?'

'You're not angry, are you?'

'No. Why should I be?'

'I thought maybe I'd said something to offend you.'

'Not at all.'

'That's all right then.' There was a rustle as he turned over in his sleeping-bag. 'I didn't like to think of you going to sleep with those tiny fists clenched in anger.'

When Ismail Carapizzi left Sea View in the morning, he took with him thirty gold sovereigns with which to buy himself a car. Albania's public transport, he explained to Benson, was inadequate for the amount of travelling he had to do.

'Did you ever find your mother and sister in Valona?' Benson asked the Albanian as he counted out the sovereigns. 'How's this for self-control?' he went on, turning to me. 'Ismail has a mother and sister in Valona who haven't seen him since before he was imprisoned – six years now, and he refuses to go and make himself known to them.'

The little man smiled, a little sadly.

'I took a room in the house opposite to theirs,' he explained, 'and all one day I sat there and watched them going in and out of their house. But I did not speak to them.'

'Why not? ' I asked.

Carapizzi shook his head.

'They are women,' he said, 'and they love me. When they see me again, after thinking me dead, they will surely become excited, and by their excitement they will betray me.'

He stood up. 'Now I must go, and when I come back in ten days I will bring some very fine informations.'

'If I were you, Ismail,' said Benson, as they shook hands, 'I should speak to your mother and sister. Because they are women, and love you, I think they will know how to keep silent.'

'Perhaps this time I will speak to them.' Ismail spoke slowly. 'It is a temptation very hard to resist.'

He went to the cave entrance and called to the guard who was to escort him across the mountain. 'Misli, I am ready.'

As he left the camp he stood very correctly to attention in his American uniform and gaiters, saluted, and with mock solemnity produced his only two words of English.

'God damn!' he said.

Then he turned and went scrambling up the hill after the young, curly-headed guard.

My own departure for Grama was delayed by the arrival in camp of a wounded Italian, an army doctor, who came riding down the mountain-side on one of Chela's mules, led by one of Chela's men. His left arm was badly shattered, shot through, he explained, by a young Partisan boy who had tried to rob him of his box of instruments and medicine in the hills near Trajas.

The man was suffering from pain and loss of blood; splintered bone was sticking out through the flesh. But beyond sending off a signal urgently requesting a boat to evacuate him, there was little I could do.

'Thank you, oh! thank you,' he said to Benson when he learnt that we should try to evacuate him. 'You see,' he explained, 'I am a doctor: so I know well my own condition. Gangrene will cost me my arm in any case, but perhaps if I could get it amputated within, say, six or eight days, then I might live. If not...' He pulled a wry face.

As I walked to Grama that day, my mind was busy with the whole Italian problem. In every village through which I had passed I had seen these ragged, half-starved men working and living as little better than cattle, and in every village the Albanians had begged me to send them back to their own country. The Albanian hill-men were too near the border-line of starvation themselves to indulge in charity to their late enemies.

Chela had come along to guide me, for the ground between Sea View and Grama was so rough and fissured that even though I made the journey half a dozen times, I still found it quite easy to get lost.

'Why are you yourself so kind to these Italians?' I asked him when we halted once.

Chela assumed an expression of great disdain.

'I help them,' he said, 'because they are no good to fight. They are only poor things, only good to make love and to work.'

I did not press the point, although I knew that contempt alone could not explain the risks which he ran on behalf of the many Italians whom he had harboured in his house, and helped on their way to Sea View. One of the traits that endeared the man to me was this schoolboy reluctance to admit an emotion so unmanly as pity.

Drake had done wonders with the camp at Grama. From a collection of rough bivouacs it had grown into a small village of squat huts with grey, stone walls and canvas roofs, all well hidden under the trees. A track had even been built down to the beach for the mules to follow when we received our first load of stores.

The corporal was bursting with pride. 'You wait till you see the house we've built for you, sir. You haven't seen nothing yet.'

When I was a child, I was certain that one day I would finding the roots of some great oak a small, green door – the door of a miniature house within the tree into which I could creep. The certainty had somewhat diminished in latter years, but the hope had remained. Psycho-analysts would have a name for it no doubt, though personally I attribute it to nothing more sinister than a lifelong devotion to the *Tale of Mrs. Tittlemouse*. Be that as it may, it was this desire that found immediate satisfaction in the house that had been set aside or me. It was a crude enough affair, but it grew out of the ground; the trunk of a oak-tree was a part of one wall; it had a fireplace, with a chimney made out of a biscuit tin; it had a bed – a real bed of ration boxes placed end to end, and it was my house, my home, built for *me*.

'Drake,' I said, 'it's wonderful! But damn you for making the place so comfortable; I shall never want to leave it.'

The whole camp had an atmosphere of optimism; the men looked well and happy, and even Adams seemed less surly. They were eager to know how I had fared, and sitting round the fire in my new house I told them all that had happened and what I was now planning.

'I know these are early days,' I said, 'and there is danger in being too optimistic, but I believe, I truly believe, that we've a chance of doing something quite big here.'

I was speaking chiefly to enthuse the men, but I meant what I said. Besnik had pointed out to me the area controlled by the Partisans, or at any rate sympathetic to them, and the possibilities were enormous.

'How do you mean, sir?' asked Black.

'I believe we could capture Valona.'

They looked astonished, so I went on to show them on a map how I thought it could be done. It wasn't such a bad scheme at that.

'Don't ask me what we'd do with the place after we got it.' I said. 'I only want to show you that if these Partisans will play as we want them to, then such a thing is not impossible.'

'And what if they won't play?' someone asked.

'Then we'll try and stir up trouble in this valley and drag the Balli into the war against the Germans willy-nilly. We could have a wonderful battle up here in this mountain.'

For the first time I saw a glint of genuine enthusiasm in Adams's face.

'I like this idea of runnin' arms to the Partisans,' he said. 'I reckon they're the only boys to do business with. I like the Partisans.'

'Why do you like them?' I asked.

We all looked at him, waiting for his reply. Adams smiled sheepishly at the floor. Then the smile went; he lifted his head defiantly.

'Fellow-feelin', I suppose,' he said, looking at me with a strange mixture of humour and bitterness. 'They're a lot of ragged-arsed buggers, and that's what I am – a ragged-arsed little bugger.'

So that was it! Adams's was no local resentment. Here was no wrong that was in my power to put right: the warp was as deep in his nature. And while I had compassion for him in that moment of revelation of his urchin soul, I also decided that he must go out on the next boot. If he were to stay with the mission he would always be a source of trouble, and might even one day be a danger.

I sat up late that night writing a long report to Headquarters, and in the morning I sent Adams with it to Sea View. I wanted neither of them to miss the boat if it came in my absence. I did not tell Adams my real reason for getting rid of him; I merely said that he had been in Albania for close on six months, and that I thought it time he had a change. He seemed to welcome the news.

When Adams had gone, I set off south with Black and an Albanian guide named Morat, the best of Chela's men.

The trip to Vuno, though successful enough in its object, had the quality of a bad dream. First, I had a fever, which lasted till I got back to Grama four days later. Next, Black, who was not ready to start at the appointed time and so kept us waiting for half an hour, maintained a moody silence during the whole of the first day because he was rebuked. The ground itself was the roughest I had yet encountered, and as a result we could carry only meagre rations.

On the second day we made contact with the young commissar of Vuno and with Dr. Georgie, sent down by Besnik to act as interpreter. I liked the look of the proposed beach, its only drawback being that the coast-road, which was in constant use by German traffic, ran within four hundred yards of it. Still, the cover was good, and with care and secrecy the unloading could be managed.

As a headquarters the commissar proposed an old, ruined monastery, hidden in a fold of the hills high above the road; this, too I approved. Georgie and the young commissar were delighted, and Black was so enthusiastic that he forgot to sulk.

'We'll fix Jerry a treat now,' he said. 'Them Dukats can go stuff 'emselves. If they don't want to fight, then we'll do without their ruddy sea base.'

'This all seems pretty good to me,' I admitted. 'I only hope there's no catch in it.'

Before setting off back to Grama, I wrote a long letter to Besnik which the commissar of Vuno promised to have delivered. I told Besnik that I would immediately signal for a boat-load of stores to be sent to Vuno, but that the size and number of subsequent shipments depended on the Partisans' plan of action. I consequently requested a meeting, as soon as possible, with the Partisan Central Council, so as to co-ordinate our plans. I also told him that I was leaving Black behind in the monastery so that there would be a reliable messenger to carry his reply into Balli territory.

Black rather liked the prospect of being left on his own. 'But I only hope I get hold of an interpreter quick,' he said. 'I can't understand none of this lingo.'

'I'd like to stay with you,' suggested Doctor Georgie hopefully, 'only...' He hesitated.

'Only what?' I asked.

The little man looked acutely miserable. Well, Major, Besnik kind of wants me to go back to your Dukat base with you. I thought it wasn't such a good idea, but...' He gave a feeble laugh. ' – But I couldn't say so.'

Georgie, I could see, was in a difficult position. Besnik had almost certainly ordered him to go with me to Sea View and there spy on my activities with the Balli, and the doctor had probably good reason to fear for his life if he failed in these orders. At the same time, he was afraid of what would befall him at my hands if I caught him carrying them out – and he was terrified of being shot by Dukat for even venturing into their territory.

'I don't know what you mean,' I answered. 'I think it's a splendid idea. Black stays here and you come with me. Exchange of diplomats. Besides, we've got a badly wounded man that you can take care of.'

There was a nervous smile on Georgie's face. 'But, Major, you don't understand. Maybe they'll bump me off.'

'Who will bump you off?'

'The Balli. They'd do that to me.'

'What nonsense,' I answered. 'Of course they wouldn't; not unless you go and do something silly.'

I was damned if I would afford Georgie this loophole by refusing to take him with me. His fear was so abject that it made me cross, and besides, I thought the least he could do as a doctor was to help the unfortunate Italian who had been wounded by one of his own precious Partisans.

'Georgie,' I said, as I saw him about to protest again, 'forget it. You're coming back to Sea View with me.'

Black had no pack, so when I said good-bye to him, I lent him mine; left on his own he might be needing one. We were hungry and tired after two days' hard walking with little food, and we decided to risk entering one of the villages which lay on our way back in order to get a good meal and a night's sleep under cover. The headman of the village received us well, assuring us that the coast was clear, and we were just sitting down to eat some cheese and raw onions when the alarm was given.

Some German trucks were just entering the village.

Within five minutes of the alarm every man in the place, young and old, had taken to the hills, dragging us with them. They were none of them Partisans, but they were taking no chances.

On the hill-side we stood in a knot, looking down on the village. Lights were moving round the narrow streets, flashing on the houses.

'They're probably looking for billets for the night,' I said.

Not at all, I was told, it was a search.

'How do you know?' I asked.

They didn't know.

'Do you even know how many Germans there are down there?'

They had no idea.

'Then why not send someone down to find out? We may be standing here in the cold for no reason at all.'

No, that would be too dangerous.

'In that case, I will go,' I said.

– And what did I think would happen to their village if the Germans were to catch a British officer in it?... In case I tried to act upon my suggestion, they turned and took us farther into the mountain.

They were panic-stricken, and aimless in their panic. One man said he knew of a cave where we could shelter for the night, so in single file we started to follow him. After half an hour it was found that our leader had got lost in the darkness.

I was nearly crying with tiredness and rage – rage at being so ignominiously driven by the Germans from my well-earned supper and sleep – and I was very rude to the Albanians around me. But it did no good; nothing would induce them to return to their village that night.

We spent a bitter night on the open hill-side, and when the dawn came, Georgie, Morat and I started for Grama.

It was a tiring walk back, and since we skirted the villages, we were unable to get food. Georgie, between his fright and his physical exhaustion, was in a lamentable state when we reached Grama in the evening, and I was little better. Morat, on the other hand, showed no distress at all; he sat down under the trees, produced a safety-razor from his pocket and proceeded quietly to shave.

'Do you think Sea View have had a sortie?' I asked Drake.

'Not that I know of,' he replied; 'and I think we'd have had word if the boat had come.'

There was nothing for it but to plod on the next morning to Sea View; if the boat came that night I wanted to send out written instructions for sending stores to Vuno. But when we reached the top of the gorge and looked down into the camp, my heart sank; the place was fuller than ever. There had been no sortie.

Benson was talking to a strange Albanian as I entered the cave with Georgie close on my heels. He looked up.

'Oh! hello,' he said in his calm way. 'You're back. Did you have a good time in the south?'

'Not very,' I replied.

'That's too bad,' he said, 'because you've come back to plenty of trouble here.'

He drew a cigarette out of a packet and tapped it on the table. 'Twenty more Italians have arrived; Dukat have withdrawn their guards; and Carapizzi has been murdered.'

SIX

HODO WAS THE NAME of the stranger. He was one of Tank's Intelligence contacts, a young man with a scarred face who looked like a Slav and spoke perfect English.

'Begin your story again,' Benson told him. 'He's only just arrived,' he explained to me, 'and I know nothing yet beyond the bare news.'

For all his outward calmness, I could see that Tank was very upset.

Hodo began. Four evenings ago (the day on which Carapizzi had left Sea View), the young, curly-headed guard, Misli, had arrived alone in Dukat valley with a confused story that Carapizzi had been shot by two unknown assailants. When asked what he, the guard, was doing while the shooting was taking place, he answered that he had become frightened and had run away.

'This reply,' said Hodo, 'was enough. Misli was arrested at once.'

'Why?' I asked.

'I will explain. Albania, as you know, is a very wild country. Under King Zog there were gendarmes to see that the people kept the laws, but that was only for a short time and in the towns; in the hills, the only laws have always been our own special code of honour. If you disobey the old laws of the mountains, then the penalty is death.' He smiled. 'So, you see, the laws are kept. Now,' he went on, 'one of the strongest points is that the guard of a man who is attacked must die with the man he is guarding. If he survives and the other is killed, then he has lost his honour, and it is the duty of the dead man's family to kill him.'

Hodo explained the point with the precision of the Peckham town clerk outlining one of the borough's bye-laws.

'So,' he pursued, 'the story of Misli was unbelievable and at once the village arrested him.'

'And Carapizzi?' asked Benson. 'Was the body found?'

'Yes. We went into the mountain to look for him and on the second day we found him. Three shots had been fired into his back and one into the palm of his hand, all from very close range. He had been stabbed also, many times.'

'The palm of his hand,' Tank repeated. 'Poor little devil, he must have caught hold of the muzzle trying to push the gun away. Did you find his papers?' he asked.

Hodo shook his head. 'We found Carapizzi; nothing else. He was naked.'

Tank made a noise through his teeth. 'Whoever stripped that body got hold of some mighty interesting documents. I'm sorry to have lost those. The gold doesn't matter.'

'Gold?' Hodo had caught the last words. 'Was Carapizzi carrying gold?'

'Thirty pieces.'

'Ah! Then that is why he is now dead.'

'But would Misli have killed him for a few pieces of gold?' Tank's voice was incredulous.

'For thirty pieces of gold,' replied Hodo, 'a poor man like Misli would murder his own grandmother. He knew that Ismail Carapizzi had no family to avenge him; he would have killed Ismail for five – for three pieces of gold.'

'No family to avenge him!' Benson spoke quietly. 'It was as well he never spoke to that mother of his in Valona.'

Of the murder Hodo could tell us no more; he had left immediately to carry the news to Sea View, leaving Chela, who was also in Dukat, to stay and witness Misli's trial. He could confirm, however, the other alarming piece of news. The village, without giving us any explanation, had ordered the guards down off the mountain.

That many more Italians had arrived to swell the numbers of the camp I could see with my own eyes.

'Now tell me that the Italian doctor has died,' I said, 'and the happy story is complete.'

'He's alive,' Benson answered, ' – just.'

The next day brought Chela with a pale face and the story, emotionally told, of Misli's trial and the subsequent happenings.

Two hundred men of the valley had assembled, had judged Misli, and had unanimously found him guilty. The boy – he was no more than twenty – had been handed over to the commander of the village guard to be executed at dawn.

Why the men of Dukat, dispensing their own rough justice, had clung to the quaint custom of carrying out an execution at dawn rather than performing the ceremony then and there, was not clear to me. At any rate the respite had saved young Misli's life.

In the middle of the night the guard-commander had been woken up by a deputation of the male members of Misli's family; there were some thirty all told, what with brothers, cousins, nephews and uncles. They had come quickly to the point. If one hair of their darling's head was touched, they declared, they would go straight off and reveal to the Germans in Valona the full story of Dukat's complicity with the Allied mission.

Nor was there the slightest doubt, apparently, that the family would have failed to put their threat into execution.

Dukat was faced with nothing less than a civil war all of its own. In order to execute Misli with impunity they would have to put to death every male member of his family – and even if this operation were successful there would be nothing to stop a revengeful female from telling the whole story to the Germans.

I began to see by what strange counter-forces the social structure of Dukat was held together, and on what a delicately adjusted balance we ourselves were poised.

'Then where is Misli now?' I enquired.

'He is at home. He is free.' Chela's cheeks were more sunken than ever. 'I am ashamed,' he said, between clenched teeth.

'Ashamed?' I asked. 'Why?'

'Because it is my duty to kill him. Here you are in my territory. I am responsible for you, and Carapizzi was your man. If I do not kill Misli, I am dishonoured. But I cannot kill Misli!' he burst out. 'Oh! Major, I do not know what to do.'

There was nothing that Chela could do, though it took us some time to convince him.

Hodo handled Chela well, speaking always in a low, calm voice. The man had a certain authority about him and his confidential manner implied: 'In a world of knaves, I alone am to be trusted.'

'Well, what *are* we going to do?' Benson demanded. 'This is an act against the Allies. If Misli did it, he must not be allowed to go free.'

Hodo said: 'There is only one thing to do. We must send for Mucho.'

'And who, pray, is Mucho?' I asked.

Benson explained that he was the leader of all the Balli in the south of Albania.

'And the only man who has any influence in Dukat,' put in Hodo.

'I think maybe Hodo's right,' said Benson. 'I've had two talks with Mucho and he's a guy that makes sense. Quite apart from this Carapizzi affair you ought to hear his version of the civil war story before you go all out for the Partisans.'

'Mucho is now in Valona,' said Hodo. 'I will leave at once and tell him that he must come immediately to Dukat.'

I asked what good it was thought this Mucho could do if he did come.

'Major,' said Hodo, 'the only way for Misli to be executed, without his family going to the Germans, is for the family to execute him themselves. Mucho must persuade them that they should shoot him.'

It struck me that this would take persuasiveness of a quite unusual order, but since anything seemed possible in this peculiar country I did not demur.

'And tell those damned Old Men of Dukat to send a deputation over here as quick as they know how,' I told Hodo when he left. 'We want an explanation for this guard withdrawal.'

My own immediate problem was the composition of a signal to Cleaver. I had promised the commissar at Vuno, and I had confirmed it in my letter to Besnik, that I would run a cargo to them during the first week in February – only a fortnight off. If I was to keep my promise, I would have to tell Cleaver at once what stores I wanted.

Benson and I were alone in the cave when I asked his opinion.

'If I bring them food and clothing,' I said, 'it's exactly what they need the least, and they'll be convinced that I'm double-crossing them. If I send them machine-guns, I have an uncomfortable presentiment that they will use them against Dukat.'

Benson combed his beard with his fingers. 'You have cordial talks with the Partisans, Dukat withdraw their guards, and poor

77

little Carapizzi gets murdered. Do you see,' he asked ruminatively, 'any connection between those three events?... In other words, do you think that the Old Men of Dukat, those masters of insinuation, are spelling out to us: "You Have Been Warned?"'

'But how should they know my talks have been cordial? How should they know that I've promised to send anything to the Partisans at all?'

'Oh, come, come!' Tank replied. 'Friend Chela is no fool, and however weak his party allegiance may be he's a true son of Dukat.'

'And therefore,' I cut in, 'warns his fellows that they are shortly to be mown down by the weapons supplied by us.'

'Supplied by you,' said Benson.

I accepted the correction.

'You may be right. And you might say,' I went on, 'that we ought to move right out of Balli territory and make our base with the Partisans...'

'I'd say nothing of the sort,' Benson interposed. 'I'd trust those babes just as far as I could throw them. And anyway,' he insisted, 'it's no use asking my opinion. I've told you before that my interest in this country is very different to yours. You're a professional throat-cutter and bridge-blower; I'm a peaceful fellow with an enquiring turn of mind; and the Balli are the only people who can tell me what the Germans are up to. They should know, too,' he concluded wryly. 'They have dinner with them every night.'

In the end I compromised: I sent a signal to Cleaver telling him to make up a cargo mostly of food and clothing, with a few rifles and some ammunition, but to send the boat as quickly as he could. If the Partisans complained, I could blame it on the fools who had loaded the boat wrongly in Italy. It was a compromise that could only serve me once, but for the moment the only course seemed to be to play for time till the situation became clearer.

Cleaver signalled that he was trying to send a sortie to evacuate the doctor, but that he was not hopeful as there were 'difficulties'. I knew what that meant: probably our destroyers were submarine-hunting in the Adriatic, and the *Sea Maid* could not make the night crossing for fear of attack by our own ships.

I kept away from the wounded man. Daily he sent messages asking if a boat was coming to take him out, and daily I found that I could not face him with a negative reply. Dr. Georgie found a bottle of sulfaguanadine in the cave, and the Italian took large doses of it to counter the septicaemia that was spreading up his arm. Then the sulfaguanadine affected his bladder, and he had to stop taking it. The worst of it was that the patient himself was the best judge of his own condition, and knew only too well how slender were his chances of living unless a boat came at once.

Georgie himself seemed to have got over his fears and forebodings. He had been fitted out with new underclothes and boots on his way through Grama, and with reasonable food he began to gain weight. I think, too, that it made him happy to hear English spoken again.

America was for Georgie the land of his dreams, and his four years there seemed to him now like a fairy tale that he was always re-living. Tank's prestige with Georgie was immense, for he alone could understand the snatches of campus slang which the little man so proudly produced.

Why Georgie had returned to Albania at the outbreak of the war I could not understand. Patriotic reasons were the ones he gave, yet I found them hard to believe. And why had he joined the Partisans? He had been a man of some little property. I could not even make out his function: he did not fight as a soldier; he had never been in an action; he did not even act as a doctor with the front-line troops, but wandered round the country writing prescriptions for sick women and malarial babies. It seemed as though a genuine idealism led him into courses of action in which his courage was not sufficient to sustain him – was not even sufficient to let him withdraw.

I found him both touching and infuriating.

On the third morning after Hodo's departure, the Old Men of Dukat arrived. About a dozen appeared as we were eating breakfast; they had been climbing and walking all night. What with the delay in the sortie and the unexpected number of Italians in the camp our food stock was very low, and I could offer them little to eat but some chocolate I had brought from Italy, and some tea without milk.

They gave a long apology for the withdrawal of the guards – a measure, they explained, due to the increased danger of the village from attack. The Partisans, they assured me, were massing in great force round Gumenitza and Gjormi, and attack was expected daily. Every man was needed for the defence of Dukat.

They talked a lot, too, about their failure to execute Misli... 'But what were they to do? They were helpless.'

Round and round the talk went all day long; the deputation had climbed a long way for this meeting, and they were not going to allow any quick decisions to cut short their pleasure in debate.

I began to see that there was a sharp division in the village between those who were generally in favour of supporting the Allies, and those who were very much opposed to it. Perhaps Tank had been near the truth when he had suggested that the withdrawal of the guards and the murder of Ismail Carapizzi had been intended to warn me against getting too friendly with the Partisans. If this were so, I made no attempt to conceal my intended help to the Fifth Brigade.

'The Partisans,' I said, 'refused your offer to permit the passage of arms across Dukat valley. I am sorry for that; it would have been an ideal solution. As it is, I must get arms to them some other way. I want you to know that; I wish to make no secret of it; and the same material help will be available to you on the day you join in the fight against the Germans.'

Another point that emerged was that the village was furiously jealous of Chela, who they believed was receiving thousands of gold sovereigns from the Allies. The guards who had been removed had been nominated by Chela, and, as each man of them was to draw two gold sovereigns a month, this had only increased the belief of the villagers that Chela and his friends were pocketing all the golden eggs, while they could scarcely obtain a glimpse of the goose.

The venality of their outlook was so revolting that I kept my temper only with difficulty. But in the end it was settled that the guards should be restored; only this time they were to be nominated by the village, and were to work in rotation. In this way every family would have a share of the spoils.

When at last compliments had been paid all round, protestations of friendship had been made and listened to, and the deputation had departed, I found that all my chocolate had been eaten.

I turned to Tank.

'In the words of the late Ismail Carapizzi,' I said, '"God damn!"'.

Doctor Georgie was thrown into a panic of fear by the advent of the deputation.

'Please, Major,' he pleaded. 'Oh! please let me go away. They will kill me, I know.'

'But what about the doctor?' I demanded.

'He can look after himself,' replied Georgie, white-faced. 'Gee!' He gave his nervous smile. 'I'm only a bacteriologist. This guy knows much more than I do.'

'Maybe he does, but a man who is only half-conscious and is having a haemorrhage every day cannot look after himself. And you know that damn well!'

George moved his head impatiently, but I pursued my point.

'For months this man has been doctoring one of your own Partisan bands. Now that he's been shot by a Partisan, the least you can do is to try and save his life.'

Georgie gave an indifferent shrug. 'He will die in any case,' he stated.

'Then you,' I said, 'will stay here till he does.'

If Georgie had been less callous about the Italian I would have let him go, but his indifference to the man's suffering and his fearfulness for his own skin only hardened my resolve to make him see the job out till the doctor was saved – or had died.

At last came a signal from Cleaver that we were to stand by for a boat. It would come on one of the next five nights, between the hours of eight and eleven. We were to flash the letter L.

The sea was calm, the weather perfect. During the afternoon the Italians carried the wounded man down to the beach. The descent took them two hours, and though every movement caused the jagged bone to cut into the vein and bring on a haemorrhage, yet he somehow survived it.

That night, just in case the *Sea Maid* had mistimed her landfall, we started to flash an hour early and continued till midnight; but no boat came. The doctor could not be carried up to the caves again, so a bed of leaves was made for him in a tiny grotto near the beach.

The next night it was the same. Each man carried a glowing brand to light his way down the steep track to the beach. From the cave I watched the procession of glow-worms winding down the hill, and at midnight saw their dim light twisting and bobbing as they climbed back again.

On the third day the weather broke. For two days the wind blew strong from the south, the sky piled up, and to hope for a sortie was madness. All the same we signalled every night, just on the off-chance.

When the sea calmed there came a signal to say that the sortie had been postponed for a week.

Then Drake sent a message that Grama was running short of food. It was a problem to know how to supply them, as our mules were too weak and too few for the task. Many were sick, and several had been killed by wolves at night; those that remained were just strong enough to carry the daily wood and water for Sea View.

I decided to try and supply the other base by sea, using our small canvas boats and paddling down the coast when dark had fallen. It was an idea which I had suggested once before to Trent, but he had ridiculed it.

'My dear fellow, it's quite impossible. Take my word for it. I've been messing about in small boats all my life.'

We proved him wrong by doing the journey in fifty minutes. By the upper route the mules would have taken six hours, and three hours was the best time a local shepherd could make on the lower track. From then on we repeated the journey every night that the sea was calm enough, each time shipping larger loads. We would have done it by day as well, only there were too many German reconnaissance planes patrolling the coast.

Through each day of inactivity, while the doctor lay in his grotto and fought for his life, I would long for night to fall when we could begin our nocturnal voyage. During the long, silent paddle, the mind regained peace and proportion – so tiny was our craft, so immense the sea, so serene the moonlit mountain whose base we skirted.

At last one morning came a signal telling us to stand by again for a sortie, and that very night the *Sea Maid* came. It gave me a quick stab of excitement to see her answering flash – excitement, and also that queer emotion of being linked secretly with one's kindred which I had felt the night I landed.

Rawlinson came ashore himself in the dinghy.

'You haven't changed a bit,' I said, as I wrung his hand.

'Why should I?' he asked. 'Dammit, it's only a month since I landed you.'

A month! It seemed a year.

The doctor had been under morphia for the last few days, but though he was breathing heavily he was quite conscious, and when I came to say that we were ready to move him, he smiled, and a look of utter happiness came into his face.

Gently, gently, we carried him down the beach and placed him in the boat, and as we pushed off I thanked God that after this long ordeal his life was going to be saved.

But God decided otherwise. The doctor died as we lifted him aboard the *Sea Maid*.

Apart from the doctor's death, it was a successful night. Rawlinson sailed down the coast and unloaded the bulk of the stores at Grama, so that in one stroke the place was established as our main base. Benson had agreed to join me there in two days' time, leaving Sea View as a kind of evacuation centre for Italians. Adams went happily out, and Nigel Samson, a young Irish captain, bringing a wireless operator and a pile of heavy equipment, came ashore. His orders, he said, were to make his way down the coast and open a sea base for the supply of the Partisans in the south. He was full of eagerness and seemed very disappointed that I would not allow him to go plunging off then and there into the night.

When the boxes and bundles had been stacked out of reach of the waves we climbed up to the camp, and as Samson was preparing his bedding, I said:

'I suppose you've no mail for me, by any chance?'

I said it casually and tried to make myself feel casual in case the answer should be 'No'.

'My goodness!' he exclaimed. 'I'm most frightfully sorry. Yes, indeed, I have got something for you.'

In the long minute of suspense while Samson rummaged in his pack, a few heavy drops of rain hit the roof of the hut.

'I've got them!' he cried. 'Here you are.' And he held out to me a couple of letters.

'Not very much, I'm afraid,' he apologised, as though his was the fault.

'It'll do,' I replied. The writing on one of the envelopes was Ann's. 'It'll do very well.'

I sat down on a box by the fire and opened the other, a typewritten envelope. It was a printed notice asking for the renewal of my subscription to the Times Book Club. I threw it in the flames.

I turned Ann's letter over in my fingers; it was a bulky envelope, containing something heavy and stiff. I longed, yet feared, to open it.

Samson made a remark, but the rain was now making such a noise on the roof that I missed it. I turned round and saw him struggling into his sleeping-bag.

'What d'you say?' I queried.

'I just asked,' he replied, raising his voice, 'if it often rains like this?'

He peered anxiously at the roof through which some drops of rain were already leaking.

'This is the first rain we've had in a month,' I said. 'There'll be snow on the mountain tomorrow.'

Samson snuggled down into his bag. 'Well, I'll leave you to your mail. Good night.'

'Good night.'

There was a feeling of constriction up the back of my neck and a hollowness in my stomach as I ripped open the envelope and drew out a thin leather case; it contained a photograph of Ann.

For a time I could only sit still, looking at this confirmation of the image I had carried so long in my mind – the soft line of the hair where it sprang from the forehead, the wide-set, amused eyes, the sad mouth. It was so vivid that I could almost feel Ann's physical presence.

God! how the rain was coming down. A sudden stream fell on my knee; I shifted my box a foot or two.

But was there no letter? I looked again in the envelope to see if I had missed it... No. Perhaps she had written a letter and forgotten to enclose it? Not likely, I admitted to myself, but it might have happened. Perhaps there was a message on the photo itself? I drew it out from behind the mica, and there on the back she had written:

'John darling, with my love and special wishes for the new job – Ann.'

The fire had sunk very low; water was trickling down the biscuit-tin chimney, sizzling as it fell into the hot ashes; through the rotten, canvas roof, a hundred miniature spouts were pouring into the hut. The driest place to be was in the sleeping-bag. On the wooden case by the head of my bed I placed a tin on its side, and inside the tin I stood the picture, so as to protect it from the rain. When I had done that, I lit a candle stump and put it in front of the photograph; then I lay on my side looking at it, till the half-inch of candle should burn itself out.

Why had Ann sent it to me? It was the only one she had ever given me. And what was the meaning behind the restrained, half-cold, half-affectionate message? I couldn't persuade myself that it was very loving, and yet – perhaps it was something. So I lay gazing at the inarticulate image, while my mind pushed out its antenna, touching the words that she had written, quickly recoiling from them, then cautiously feeling out again.

A fierce gust of wind flapped the canvas violently; a gush of water from a fresh rent in the canvas fell on my neck, and the candle went out. I wormed deeper into the sleeping-bag and pulled my raincoat over my head: but it was a long time before I could sleep.

That was the night of February the third.

SEVEN

'MAJOR OVERTON! Wake up! Wake up!'

I pulled the raincoat from off my head, spilling onto the floor the pools of water that had formed in its folds. Chela was standing by my bed.

'What's the matter?'

'I have some news for you. Bad news.' The man's face was strained and startled.

'What is it?'

'Messengers have arrived; they crossed the mountain during the night. The Germans have begun a big drive against the Partisans. They have moved into Vuno.'

'Are you sure?'

He nodded.

'Blast!' I swore quietly to myself. Fools, idiots! Just when I was about to run them a cargo they *would* have to concentrate their forces and call down a German drive. I extricated myself from my damp bedding.

'Well there's no need for you to look so gloomy, Chela. You ought to be glad. The Partisans are your enemies.'

'That is not all, Major. The Germans have also occupied Dukat.'

There was a pause. Then I asked: 'Are you certain of that?'

'Yes. I am quite sure. My own men have brought the news – Zechir and Old Ali.'

'Thank you, Chela' I said. 'Now will you go and talk to them, and find out all the details you can.'

The young captain was sitting up on the floor, rubbing his head after sleep.

'Bad news?' he asked, his face crinkled with good humour. 'Bad news?' he repeated eagerly.

'It might be,' I replied. 'Let's have some breakfast. I'll think better when I've eaten.'

The news, though not so tragic as Chela had made it, was

certainly disconcerting. 'And you, my dear Captain,' I told Samson, 'are the one most immediately affected.'

'How's that?' he asked. 'My God!' he added inconsequently, 'this is a good breakfast. I'd no idea you lived so well here.'

'Eat well,' I advised him. 'The great thing in this country is to fill your belly while you can – because it's quite possible that tomorrow you can't. However, to return to your journey...' And I explained to him that to get south with his radio, batteries and charging engine – and to go without them was useless – his way would have to lie inland through Dukat, since the direct route down the coast, through Vuno, was impassable for mules.

'Now,' I said, 'if the Germans have occupied Dukat, and are frisking about in the mountains of Trajas and Gumenitza, it looks as though that route also is barred for the time being.' Men alone might slip through, but not leading two or three heavily-laden animals. 'Look,' I continued as he started to protest, 'we can settle this beyond doubt in a minute.' And I led him outside the hut. It was as I thought; in the night snow had fallen right down to the lower slopes of the mountain, and a heavy snow-cloud still hung about the summit.

'No mule will get across that,' I said. 'I'm sorry, but I'm afraid you'll just have to put up with inactivity for a bit.'

Samson's face had fallen, but suddenly he cheered up. 'Never mind!' he said. 'Perhaps the Germans will come here looking for us!'

'That is a possibility,' I replied, 'which has not escaped me.'

But Nigel could not stay inactive for long. He spent the day sorting his kit, and the following morning he set off down the coast with Doctor Georgie to do a reconnaissance. The bacteriologist was as glad to go as I was now to be rid of him. Since his charge was dead, there was no medical reason for keeping him, and I had to admit to myself that the chances of his being assassinated had all along been considerable.

'Don't come back with the captain,' I told him. 'Try and get through to the monastery and join Black; he'll be needing an interpreter now more than ever... And try and send us some reports on the German movements.'

It was quite a relief to see the little figure shambling away southwards and not to have his blood on my hands.

The knowledge that Germans – a company of them, it appeared – were established in Dukat made a change in the atmosphere of Grama. The camp that had felt so secure felt so, indeed was so, no longer. The Albanians sat about in groups, discussing the news with long faces: Old Ali, alone among them, preserved his detached and philosophic air. No doubt long years of knavishness had inured him to life's vagaries.

In due course, Tank arrived from Sea View. He brought with him Sergeant Butcher, his Marine wireless operator, and the ever-faithful, if bedraggled, Alpino. He also brought news which did nothing to dispel the feeling of uneasiness that pervaded the camp.

On the very morning following the sortie no less than thirty Italian soldiers had crossed the mountain and dropped down into Sea View. The Dukat guards, in spite of my orders to the contrary, had apparently allowed them to pass. No doubt they felt that Dukat, with the Germans installed in it, was well rid of their dangerous presence. Nor was this all: another large party was believed to be on its way and expected momentarily. It seemed that the movement I had always feared had started, and that all the Italian soldiers, scattered in the mountains for miles around, were slowly on the move towards the pin-point on the coast whence they hoped would come their salvation.

I sent Old Ali to Dukat with instructions that the flow must somehow be stopped. For one thing there was no way of finding out if there was a spy among them, and anyhow I had no desire to have a few score unarmed and moribund Italians on my hands should the Germans come to smoke us out.

I sent an urgent signal to Cleaver; he was to cancel the Vuno sortie but send a boat at once to take away the Italians. I also begged him to send me a British second-in-command, and a good Italian officer to handle the whole business of Italian evacuation.

To go to Dukat and have a talk with the Old Men was out of the question. Though they were probably in need of a little fortification and encouragement it would have entailed a three-days' trip, and I dared not leave the camp so long for fear of missing Mucho, who was now daily expected.

Nigel returned – alone. He had been unable to enter Vuno; there were too many Germans about for a man in British uniform. But Georgie had gone on, saying that he would make his way to the monastery and join Black; he had promised to get word to us of how the drive went.

And every day by the coast it poured with rain and sleet, and every day the snow on the mountain deepened till messengers from Dukat found it difficult to pass the summit, so deep were the drifts. If this limited our supply of news from the valley it also gave us one less approach to watch, since an armed German was as likely to get stuck in the snow as an Albanian shepherd – and it did not appear that the men in Dukat were ski-troops.

It was important to decide our plan of action should the enemy appear. When I was clear in my own mind what we should do I called the British and Americans together; I wanted every man to feel that he had a share in the decision so that he could act with conviction. As there were only six of us, one man in disagreement meant a high proportion of doubt.

'What we have to decide,' I said, 'is whether we sit and fight, or whether we clear out if we get news that the Germans are coming. One of our main troubles here is lack of reliable information. There aren't enough of us to maintain a guard on all the approaches to this camp: for that you'd need twenty Allied soldiers. I've moved a party of Albanian guards down to the south, but I haven't much confidence in them.'

'Nor I.' The Marine sergeant spoke with great emphasis. 'These Albs won't fight. Leastways,' he corrected himself, 'not unless they're properly cornered.'

'I agree,' I said. 'Further, if the Germans do come, I don't even trust the Albanians to give us reliable information.'

Nigel cut in. 'Excuse me,' he said quietly, 'but I don't understand this discussion. It seems perfectly clear to me. Haven't we been sent here to kill Germans? Then why should we complain if they save us the trouble of looking for them?'

He gave a smile, so as to take the asperity out of his words.

'Certainly we're here to kill Germans,' I replied. 'But surely at a time and place of our own choosing. The one thing we want to avoid is to get pinned down in a futile scuffle at this stage, before our work is really started. If we can avoid a fight now, we should; we can do more damage later on.'

So it was decided. Every man, had orders to prepare, and keep at hand, a pack of his essential belongings and some 'K' rations, so that we could abandon camp at a moment's notice if necessary. Wireless operators were to carry with them their crystals, cipher pads and radio plans. We spent an afternoon stowing away the heavy radio equipment; charging motors, batteries, and cased petrol were hidden in holes in the cliff face, then covered over with brush-wood, so that the Germans, if they came, could not find them.

'I suppose you're pleased now, you damned old reactionary,' I said to Benson. 'Now the Partisans can get nothing from me – neither bombs nor biscuits. Come to think of it, I wouldn't be surprised to hear that you had engineered the whole thing.'

Tank shook his head, smiling. 'I'm much too afraid for my own skin to do that,' he said. 'Although I might, even at that,' he went on after a moment's reflection. 'Do you know Italy well?'

The sudden question was surprising.

'Not particularly,' I replied. 'Why?'

'Because,' said Tank – and his dark eyes took on a fixed, hot look as they always did when he spoke of women – 'because I have two passions in life, and the other one is Italy.'

'What's that got to do with supplying the Partisans through Vuno?' I asked.

'Because whatever happens this side of the Adriatic is going to affect Italy, and I love Italy as though she were a woman. I love her for her experience and her beauty, for the way she thinks and talks, for her very smell...' He broke off and looked at me. 'You and your God-damn communists will kill Italy.' There was real bitterness in his words. 'She has thrown off the domination of one lover – Fascism, and now you blind soldiers are busy injecting virility into another husky brute – Communism.' He gave a short laugh. 'I guess

I've a right to protest against the rape of a woman I love.'

On the tenth of February the wind was blowing strong from the south, but a signal came saying that every attempt would be made to send a boat that night to take off the Italians. I sent an Albanian runner up to Sea View to collect them, and by six in the evening they started coming into Grama.

'I thought you said there were thirty,' I said to Benson. 'I've counted over sixty.'

They were in a very emotional state at the prospect of returning to Italy. We had no huts for them, but they made little fires under the shelter of the cliff and huddled round them quite happily. As darkness fell they began to sing; there was a Neapolitan among them with a good voice, and Drake too, who had a fine baritone, could not resist giving a spirited rendering of the 'Song of Songs'. He was loudly applauded.

Looking at the grey, tumbled seas, I thought it only humane to go round and warn them against over-optimism, but nothing could depress them that night. They were convinced that dawn would find them back in their beloved Italy.

Eagerly they took it in turns to signal, starting an hour earlier than the boat was even expected and taking turn and turn about for the coveted position of look-out. Discretion was forgotten; a continuous flow of Morse shot out over the waters, but it was of no avail. The hours went by; spirits slowly sank; the singing round the fires died down; but not till two in the morning would the poor fellows reconcile themselves to the obvious fact that the sortie had failed, and stop their flashing.

The Italians, in the morning, were woe-begone and disconsolate. The sea still ran high and offered little hope for a sortie, so we took the last part of the day in rigging some rough shelters to protect them from the continuous rain.

It was about four o'clock in the afternoon when I heard running feet outside my hut, then Chela's voice, an octave higher than usual, crying:

'Major! Quick, quick! The Germans are coming!'

The alarm and urgency in his voice brought me squirming out

through the doorway. He must have given a general alarm already, for the Italians had caught fright and were running helter-skelter out of the camp towards the track that led down to the beach. Chela was jigging about with nerves.

'Major,' he pleaded. 'Please... Please... We cannot stay... run quick.' He wrung his hands.

'Shut up, Chela,' I said. 'Calm down and tell me what has happened?'

The whole of Chela's face was contorted with fear. He started to gabble.

'They are coming. They are coming. From the south.'

'How do you know this?'

'A shepherd has come running. They have just shot his dog.'

The last sentence had a ring of truth: it decided me.

'Major.' There were tears in his eyes. 'I am responsible for you... *Quickly.*'

By now there was a knot of Americans and British round us, most of them ready carrying their packs and weapons.

'All right. Leave camp. Quick as you can. Operators – don't forget – hang on tight to your crystals and signal plans.'

I dived back into the hut. I had few signals to burn; all was ready. I grabbed my pack and gun, and in a moment we were all running down the only track that led out of camp northwards – down the hill to the beach.

'How much of a start have we?' I called to Chela.

'Perhaps ten minutes, perhaps half an hour,' he called back. 'I don't know.'

The steep track was sodden with rain, and the running feet of seventy men had turned it into a slippery morass. Drake's feet shot from under him and he landed on his back in the mud.

'___ this for a lark,' he declared as he was pulled to his feet.

As I ran I found that I was half frightened and half enjoying myself, as though I were taking part in a very exciting game of hare and hounds.

Now we had reached the beach, and now the only way of escape was up three hundred feet of absolutely bare hill-side. Already my back was aching under the heavy pack, and my heart sank as I surveyed the precipitous slope.

'This is where we'll get it,' said Nigel. He was fetching his breath in gulps, but at the same time laughing. 'They'll pick us off like rabbits as we go up this.'

'The only alternative is to be trapped here on the beach,' I said. 'Come on. Up we go.'

We began the climb, digging our fingers into the ground, the loose shale slipping away beneath our boots. All about men were swarming up the scree. Grunting and panting we toiled upwards till we were on a level with the abandoned camp. The American sergeant, coming behind me, stopped for a moment to look back. Suddenly he gave a great cry.

'There they are! I seen 'em! I seen 'em!'

'Where are they, Butch?' I called over my shoulder.

'Coming into camp,' he panted. 'I seen 'em duck behind some rocks.'

As I climbed on I thought: 'This is the end then. I have often wondered how it would come. Now I know. Any moment a bullet will smack into me, and a khaki bundle that was Overton will go tumbling down the hill on to the beach.'

I didn't think it *might* happen. I *knew* I was going to be killed – knew it so well that I asked myself why I bothered to claw my way up to the distant ridge. Why exert myself so painfully when death would overtake me in any case? Yet I had the feeling of taking part in a ritual; of being impelled to play the scene out to the end. So on I climbed as fast as my aching legs and arms would take me.

And all the while I felt no fear at all – only a great, great sadness, an intolerable regret that now Ann would never know what it was that I had been trying to say to her; she would never know how I had loved her; she would not even know how that khaki bundle had rolled down the hill.

But the ridge came nearer and still there was no shot. I heard myself calling: 'Come on. We're nearly there.' And in another minute we were on top of the ridge and crouching for cover behind the rocks.

I grabbed an Italian officer as he came past.

'Collect all your men in the next valley to the north. We are staying here.'

He wanted to stay too.

'But you're all unarmed,' I replied. 'Do as I say. We'll get in touch with you in the morning.'

Another minute or two and all of our party were present. The light was fading fast; the distant camp under the trees was indistinct, and looking down on it from our ridge there was no way of telling if it was occupied by the enemy or not. I could have sent a patrol back to find out, but there was not a man whose loss would have been justified by the gain of such knowledge. We should know all right when the light came.

It was a cold, wet, and comfortless night on the hill-side.

When the morning came, I could see no sign of movement in the camp below us, so we began a cautious return. Of Germans there was not a trace. We began to feel foolish, and walked on more boldly. The silent huts, as we entered the grove of oak trees, seemed to reproach us for their abandonment. I put my head into my own hut; it was ransacked. Shouts of dismay from the other houses showed that they had been pillaged too.

'Chela!' I called. He came running up.

'If the Germans have not been here, the only people who can be responsible for this robbery are the shepherds. Look! Everything's gone – clothes, blankets, boots. You must get them back.'

Chela tried to look serious, but he could not keep the smiles from his face. He was now in an ecstasy of relief that the danger was past, and he could take nothing very seriously.

Albanians began to drift back into the camp, sheepishly bringing the goods they had stolen. All swore that they had only taken them to prevent them falling into the hands of the Germans.

I set about tracing the origin of the false alarm, and after a lot of questioning the story became clear. The 'Germans', whom the shepherd had seen approaching, were merely a score of unhappy Italians wending their way up the coast in search of Grama. These were the men that Butch had seen when he gave his now famous cry of: 'I seen 'em! I seen 'em!' He was stating the truth when he said that they had dodged behind the rocks; so they had – terrified at the mystery of the deserted camp and the sight of the figures swarming up the opposite hill-side. They had thought a German attack was impending, and had crept back again to the south, where they had spent a wretched night cowering in a fold of the hills.

The part about shooting the shepherd's dog was quite untrue. No dog had been shot. The man had invented that to lend credence to his tale.

The whole story was farcical, and discreditable to all concerned, yet it contained a disquieting moral. If twenty harmless Italians, in broad daylight, could approach within a rifle-shot of the camp before they were spotted, what was to prevent the Germans from doing exactly the same?

The day was spent in putting the camp in order, in feeding the newly-arrived Italians, and in sending food to those who were sheltering in their valley to the north. I thought it best to leave these where they were for the time being; I wanted no recurrence of the stampede.

Drake had radio contact with Italy twice a day, morning and evening. Schedules these were called, with the American pronunciation, and the word was abbreviated to 'sked'. Owing to the general confusion, Drake missed his morning 'sked' that day, but he went on the air at seven in the evening. He had no signals to transmit, but, sitting in my hut, I could hear a lot of traffic coming in. Then the sound of Morse ceased and I heard the corporal's voice outside my door.

'Got three messages, sir. One of them's urgent.'

'Come on in, Drake. We'll decipher it together.'

'It's good to be on the air again,' he said as we settled round the fire with paper and pencil. 'This time last night I didn't reckon I'd be hearing the old da-di-da for quite a while!'

The urgent signal was a short one and we soon had it finished. Nigel read out:

'Bad weather has prevented sortie but will try again tonight February twelve Stop Stand by period twenty hundred hours to twenty-three hundred hours.'

I looked at my watch. 'Well, it's five-past eight now,' I said to Drake. 'You'd better go straight off and organise a flashing party. There's not a hope of a sortie tonight in this sea, but we'd better he on the safe side.'

Drake crawled out of the hut and Nigel and I settled down to the next priority signal, but we had hardly begun it when there was a shout from the corporal outside.

'Major Overton, sir. They're here!'

'What!'

'The boat's here now. Down in the bay. Flashing like blazes.'

'All right, Drake,' I shouted back. 'Signal them to come ashore. Then get down on to the beach with all the men you can collect.'

Nigel was already pulling on his boots, while from outside came the sound of shouting and men running towards the cliff path.

'Damn it!' exclaimed Tank. 'I *must* finish a report I'm sending out. I think I could get it done in half an hour. Can you cope with the reception?'

'Of course we can,' I said. 'And take it easy. We'll be at least two hours unloading and getting the Italians on board. Stay here quietly and finish your work.'

My own written report was all but finished. In five minutes I had it sealed up in an envelope with my personal mail, then Nigel and I were plunging and slipping down the track.

As we reached the beach and rounded the shoulder of the cliff the bay became visible, and there – a mere dark shape on the tossing waters – was the little ship. But there was no time to stand and look; shaded torches were shining in the middle of the beach, and it looked as though a boat had already come ashore. We lunged on over the shifting pebbles.

A heavy wooden dinghy was drawn up on the beach with a small knot of men standing round it. Drake was there with Nigel's operator, Cooper, and I could make out Alpino in the dark. Slightly apart from the rest was a tall man, standing by himself. When he saw me he moved towards me.

'Are you Overton?' ...American voice.

'That's right. Who are you?'

'My name's Meredith. I've brought the *Yankee* across tonight. Say, what the hell's going on here? I've been standing around on this beach for ten minutes.'

The man's offensive tone made me wonder if there was trouble ahead. It was the right kind of night for trouble.

'I'm sorry,' I said. 'You caught us by surprise. You were here before we'd finished deciphering the signal.'

'I see.'

I couldn't understand what had happened to Rawlinson.

'Did the *Sea Maid* not come then?' I asked.

'I've just told you,' the other replied. 'I've brought over the *Yankee* – and I'd be grateful if you'd start to organise something. We've a lot of stores to get off, and I can't stay here all night.'

The man was being unnecessarily truculent, but this was certainly neither the time nor place to start a quarrel. For the first time I noticed that the waves were coming in with a crest on them and breaking viciously on the steep beach.

'What's the boat situation?' I asked.

'We've brought just the one dinghy,' the tall American replied. 'We were told you had boats here.'

'We have two canvas assault boats but in the sea that's running tonight they'll not be easy to handle.'

Meredith grunted. 'You'll have to use my dinghy then; but whatever you decide, for Christ's sake let's get started.'

I could see him now in the torch-light – a handsome, blond giant in heavy sea-clothes; about six feet four. The anger was bubbling inside me, but I managed to control it.

'Drake,' I said, 'will you take the dinghy out? ...And you'd better take Alpino along to help you,' I added.

'I'll go back to the ship with them,' said Meredith 'I can supervise the unloading.'

Thank God for that! We were headed for a fight if he stayed on the beach much longer.

'I believe you've got an American officer here by the name of Benson?' Meredith produced an envelope from an inner pocket. 'This is for him: it's urgent. Where is he?'

Butch answered. 'He's up in the camp, finishing a report. I'll give it to him.' He took the envelope and disappeared in the direction of the camp.

'Look, Meredith,' I said. 'Before you go out there and we lose touch, you must get an idea of our situation ashore here. These half-dozen men you see are all we have in camp at present. As I've told you, we weren't expecting you. Now, hidden in a valley three-quarters of an hour to the north are sixty or seventy Italians whom we've got to evacuate tonight. I'll send a runner for them at once, but they certainly can't get here for an hour and a half. Can you wait that long?'

'We'll have to,' Meredith replied shortly. 'Anyhow,' he added, 'the unloading is going to take quite a while. We've got ten tons on board.'

Ten tons! – and, till the main party arrived, only a handful of men to off-load and stack them.

'All right, Drake,' I said. 'Get going!'

The boat was pushed down into the thrusting breakers and vanished into the dark, carrying Meredith with it.

I called to an Italian soldier who was standing near: '*Senti!*'

'*Commandi.*'

'*Andare subito alli alteri.*' O God! my stumbling Italian. '*Digli venire qui presto presto. Capisce?*'

'*Sì.*'

'*Sicuro?*'

'*Sicuro.*'

The man went climbing up the ascent northwards. I hoped he would find his friends on this pitch-dark night, but if he didn't there was nothing I could do about it.

By the time Drake returned the two canvas assault-boats had been carried down to the water's edge and, with some difficulty, launched. The corporal ran the bows of the dinghy ashore, but we had to grab the boat quickly to prevent the waves from slewing round the stern and capsizing it. He had brought two passengers ashore with him. One of them, immensely tall in the darkness – it seemed to be a night of giants – splashed ashore and came up to me.

'Are you Major Overton?'

'Yes, I am,' I replied.

The stranger came to attention and, with great correctness, saluted.

'I am Captain Marson,' he announced, 'reporting to you as your second-in-command.'

'You're very welcome,' I said.

I liked the man's appearance and the way he spoke, and on that bedlamite beach I liked the deliberation with which he saluted.

Marson turned to the second figure who had come ashore. 'And this is Lieutenant Manzitti. He has come to help run the Italian evacuation.'

'You couldn't have come at a better time,' I said as we shook hands. 'We have sixty of your men to get out to-night, and by the look of the sea, it's not going to be too easy.'

There was something familiar about the Italian's face, about his thick-lensed spectacles.

'What did you say your name was?' I asked.

'Manzitti.' He spoke in a quiet, almost shy way.

'Manzitti.' I said. 'Welcome back! We seem to meet always on beaches.'

He smiled. 'Yes: it was on New Year's Eve.' His English was good but slow. 'As you landed I went out. I had malaria, and Commander Trent sent me to hospital in Italy. Now I am better, so I have come back.'

When I had explained the position to them both and told Manzitti to look out for the arrival of the big party from the north, I got into the dinghy and pushed out towards the *Yankee*; I took Alpino again as crew.

To come alongside the *Yankee* was no easy feat. She was rolling badly, and all the while manoeuvring to save herself from being driven on to the reefs. Alpino and I yelled to attract attention, and after a time a rope was flung to us. We pulled ourselves as near as we dared while, from above, the stores were hurled down into our boat. Communication with those aboard was difficult, for the crew appeared to be Jugoslav and spoke no language but their own. When the dinghy could hold no more we shouted '*Basta!*'; cast off our rope and made for the shore, passing, as we did so, an assault-boat on its way out.

We had been away from the beach perhaps thirty minutes in all, but even in that short time the sea had grown rougher. As our bows grounded, a wave got under our stern and swung us broadside to the next breaker; this in turn lifted us, and neatly tapped into the sea ourselves, the oars and all the cargo. By the time we had retrieved both of the oars, and the bundles of stores and pulled the boat firmly on to the beach, I was in a filthy temper. There was a long evening ahead of us, and I had not wanted to start it soaked to the skin.

'For God's sake,' I told the men who were humping the stores on the beach, 'when you see a boat getting near the shore, stand by. Then go into the water to steady it in the breakers. If you don't, we'll have all our stores ruined.'

As I spoke there was a shout from out of the darkness, and next moment we could make out the shape of a canvas boat approaching the beach. We judged where it would hit the land and four of us waded into the sea to meet it. The light craft slipped into the trough of one breaker, then, before the crew, paddling desperately, could control it, the next wave crashed down, swamping it completely. Once again we went through the salvage operations.

We got the dinghy launched again, and this time Alpino and I made a more successful voyage. It was on the third trip, while we were fending ourselves off from the threatening sides of the *Yankee*, that the dinghy suddenly shipped a great lump of water.

'Hey!' I shouted up to the deck above, 'throw me down something to bail with.'

Apparently someone understood English, for soon a coal shovel was dropped down into the boat. But I had hardly begun to scoop the water out before there was a thump and a splash as a bundle of stores landed in the boat in front of me. I yelled at them to hold hard, but it was no good; the Jugoslav element aboard was hell-bent on unloading and the English speaker, whoever he was, had vanished. Bang! a second bundle hit me square in the back as I bent over the first. Just then a cheerful American voice from aboard – Meredith's, unmistakably – called out: 'Is that Overton?'

'Yes,' I shouted back.

'Come aboard and have a drink. Do you good.'

I wanted to answer that it would do me more good if he would come and give me a hand, but the offer of a drink was no doubt a conciliatory gesture, so I merely called out that I was too busy – 'but thanks all the same'. The business of offloading, when conditions were difficult, required great understanding – intuition almost – between those afloat and those ashore, and as I pulled the heavily-laden and half water-logged dinghy towards the beach I cursed Meredith for his lack of understanding.

Once again the landing cost us and the stores a ducking; the only difference was that this time the breakers capsized us while we were still out of our depth, and we had several yards to swim.

Now the Italians started to arrive; twenty or thirty had already reached the beach and more were trickling in. They were wildly excited and wanted to begin embarking at once. But before I could allow them to go out to the ship I needed to use their labour. Until their arrival there had not been enough men to do more than pile the stores out of reach of the waves, so that a stack of material had collected by the water's edge. On a calm night it would have been sufficient to move it thirty paces up the beach and hide it under the shelter of the cliff; there it would have been safe from air-reconnaissance in the morning, and we could have collected it at our leisure with the mules. Tonight, however, it looked as though the sea might increase in strength, and if so it would be washing the foot of the cliff. There was nothing for it but to carry the stores to the southern end of the beach and store them far up a gulley where the sea could not reach them.

Manzitti listened quietly while I explained to him what was needed.

'I hate having to ask this of them,' I said, 'but there's nothing else I can do unless I risk losing all these stores.'

'It is a small thing to ask,' he replied. 'Are you not sending them back to Italy?'

Already in poor condition, the Italians had finished two days of exposure in the drenching and continuous rain by walking for an hour in the darkness; but they set to with a will. Half of them stood by to receive and unload the boats as they plied to and fro; the other half shouldered the heavy, sodden bundles and sludged with them four hundred yards across the pebbles.

The unloading itself was going badly. The dinghy, though small, was very heavy, and took such a toll of our energy each time it came ashore that we decided to use it no more. We pulled it up onto the beach and there it lay with a quantity of water in the bottom; its floor boards were washed away, and so was the coal-shovel bailer. Marson, Nigel and Drake were manning the canvas boats, and as these came hurtling in on the breakers I tried to get the Italians to wade deep into the sea and man-handle them. But they couldn't do it. They would see the boats approaching, go into the sea no more than knee-deep to meet them, then jabber loud recriminations at each other after the inevitable capsizing had taken place. I became furious and yelled at them; all our precious stores would be ruined in the salt water.

'Manzitti,' I cried, 'explain to the men that they've got to go into the water. Right in. Like this.'

To encourage them I waded into the sea till it was high up my chest. Even as I did so it struck me that, as I was already drenched, it was not a very difficult gesture to make.

'Now organise them, Manzitti: three men to either side of a boat. They must rush into the water and keep the boat steady through the breakers.'

They tried, but it was beyond them. Poor devils! I think none of them could swim, most had a mortal dread of the sea, and all had reached the end of their endurance.

Yet still the boats came in and overturned, and still the Italians were hopelessly ineffectual.

'Damn and blast these men!' I shouted. 'Manzitti! Manzitti!'

'Yes?'

Behind his smeared glasses I could see the distress in Manzitti's eyes, and even in my exasperation I could admire the way in which he was controlling himself. Here was a good man.

'Listen,' I spoke deliberately. 'First of all stop these men arguing among themselves. I want silence.'

At last he silenced them.

'Now explain to them that if they don't handle these boats properly, and unload the stores without getting them ruined, I won't send a single one of them back to Italy. Not one. Tell them that.'

Manzitti told them. It was a filthy threat, and I didn't mean it but it seemed the only way to get results.

'John.' Tank's voice at my side made me turn. He was hatted and coated and looked oddly tidy.

'I'm going out on this sortie,' he said. 'I've had orders.'

'Oh!' I said. There was a pause. 'Well, that will save you writing a report anyway.'

'I feel like a heel running out on you like this.'

'Don't be a fool. If you have orders, that's that. But I'm very sorry.'

'So long John. Look after Butch for me.'

'I will. So long. By the way,' I added, 'you'll find an infuriated compatriot of your's out there on the boat. Tell him we're doing our best this end.'

Tank decided to go out in the dinghy, taking three or four of the Italians with him. It required a big effort to get the boat launched, and I began to feel that I had not much strength left; all the time I shivered, and I couldn't stop my jaw from rattling up and down. Twice the waves swept the boat back on to the beach, but we managed to hold it and prevent it from overturning. The third time, heaving and shouting, we rushed it into the waves, wading in till our feet no longer felt the ground beneath them. Tank had the oars poised and he timed it perfectly; for a moment the boat hung balanced, then, as he drove the oars hard into the water, it slid forward, topped a breaker, and moved out into the bay. We gave them a cheer as they disappeared.

The crew of the next canvas boat to come ashore announced that theirs was the last load of stores to come off; there were no more. I looked at my watch: to my surprise it was still going. Though 'Waterproof' was written on its face I had never expected it to prove so. It was twelve-thirty. In four and a half hours we had cleared ten tons. But I was finished; I felt very sick and was shaking all over.

'Manzitti!' He came up. 'Well done! all of you.'

Except for a small pile that was now being lifted, the beach was completely clear of stores.

'You can go right ahead now with the evacuation,' I said.

For a while longer, after the first boat-load of Italians had been pushed off towards the ship, I stayed on the beach hesitating between my craving for warmth and my feeling of duty that I should stay to the end and see them all off. But what good, I asked myself, could I do now by staying? It would be a long business, another hour at least; and, after all, this was now an Italian affair. Beside Manzitti there were several other Italian officers. I told them that I thought of going back to the camp and asked them if they could handle the evacuation themselves.

'Yes, yes,' they said. 'Go on back.'

But in my heart I knew I should be staying.

I said good-bye to all the men I knew, and turned towards the camp. Marson and Nigel were the only two of our party at hand, and since I could not expect them to stay when I was leaving I took them with me. As we moved off I said to them:

'They'll manage all right. Their own officers will look after them.'

And now we were walking away, and with every step we took the fault became more certain in my mind and the effort to right it more difficult to make.

The little house on the cliff-top was warm and cosy after the wildness of the beach. We put fresh wood on the fire, and when it blazed up we made some tea. We stripped off our sodden clothes and threw them into a corner; we rubbed our bodies hard with a towel, then put on dry clothes and sat sipping the hot, sweet tea. Conscience still told me I should have been on the beach, but as the fire blazed and the tea warmed my body it spoke in a smaller and smaller voice. I slipped into a feeling of drowsiness and well-being.

Suddenly there was a noise of feet outside, then Drake breathing heavily, burst into the hut.

'There's been an accident, sir.' The words came between pants. 'Six Ities drowned.'

'O Christ! Who? . . . Not Alpino, Manzitti?'

'No. They're both safe. Boat overturned in the bay and they were all drowned.'

'Where's the *Yankee*?'

'Gone, sir.'

'Gone!'

'Yessir. After the accident none of the Ities dared go out to her and she signalled she couldn't wait no longer.'

'How many have got away then?'

'I reckon we got off fifteen before the accident. Then the others couldn't face it. They just couldn't face it. We must be left with fifty.'

Fifty still on our hands... six drowned... and if I had been there perhaps all would have got safely off. I hated the fire. I hated my dry clothes; I hated the mug of tea in my hand; I hated myself.

Nigel said: 'Don't take it too hard. You couldn't have done anything.'

And I answered: 'No, perhaps not.'

But in my mind I was saying: 'You fool; you cursed, weak fool. You should have stayed; you know well you should have stayed – and much comfort may you find now in railing at yourself.'

EIGHT

FROM THE DAY that broke, all violence had been washed away. The wind had dropped, and the sea, streaky and grey, had calmed with surprising speed. Down in the bay the waves were playing with the broken remains of our canvas boats smashed on the previous night, but of the bodies of the drowned men there was no sign. The rain fell in a steady drizzle.

Tank's departure wrought in me the same emotions as had Trent's. Normally we do not accord to all men the same attention since all men do not play a role of equal importance in our lives, but in this strange existence every man encountered had a special significance, for on the correct assessment of his character might at any moment depend life itself. So the days were spent in a continual and heightened sense of awareness, and while I now partly missed Tank and partly was glad he had gone – since I was now indisputably in command – yet chiefly I felt cheated of the energy and thought I had expended in gauging him, in winning him, in finding a formula for living and working with him.

His unexpected disappearance, the enforced inaction, the thwarting of my plans, and finally my self-reproach for the death of the Italians, were driving me into such a state of frustration that I would have almost welcomed the arrival of the Germans in Grama – anything so long as it provided action. It was a mood against which I knew I must guard.

Nigel must have been suffering from the same prickings, for he suddenly announced his intention to try at all costs to get through to the south.

'I'll leave all my heavy gear with you,' he said. 'There's another fellow in the neighbourhood down there – Harvey; I'll try and make contact with him and organise my first sortie with his wireless set. The first boat to come can bring me a fresh receiver and transmitter. Oh! I know it's a bit hare-brained,' he went on in answer to my silence, 'but at least there's a chance in it. Here I'm absolutely useless.'

I was not sanguine of his chances of getting through, but as his mind was made up, and as he was not in any case under my command, I thought it best to keep my mouth shut.

I came into the hut to talk to him while he packed, and found him standing looking at Ann's photograph. He turned quickly when he heard me and blushed very red.

'Hope you don't mind my admiring it,' he said.

'On the contrary.'

'It's such a lovely face,' he pursued – awkwardly, but reassured. 'Fact is... well...' Nigel was not very articulate. 'It really does something to this hut,' he got out at last. 'It's almost as though this – ' he hesitated slightly, seeking for the tactful word, ' – this friend of yours were actually in the hut with us.'

'I thought I'd be the only one to feel that,' I answered.

'Oh! no,' he affirmed. 'I do too – very strongly.' He gave a self-conscious laugh. 'It's damn silly, but do you know I look at that picture every time I come into the place.'

He turned away and went on with the business of sorting the kit he was to take with him.

'Nigel,' I said. 'Forgive me asking, but how old are you?'

'Oh, pretty young!' He sounded almost apologetic. 'I'm twenty-two.'

I was surprised and told him so. 'I'd taken you for nearly thirty,' I said. 'Then you must have been at school when war broke out?'

He nodded. 'I was eighteen when I joined the army. I suppose I've grown up a lot since then. Only – ' he gave a look at the photograph, ' – only I seem to have left out some of the stages. Still,' he finished cheerfully, 'let's hope there'll be time for that yet.'

Nigel and Cooper, his wireless operator, set off at midday, aiming to reach Vuno as night fell and to pass through the German patrols in the dark.

One relief in an otherwise depressing situation was the arrival of a second-in-command. David Marson – he was the Honourable David Marson, I discovered – looked as English as a hayfield. His fair, straight hair might fall in a few years to come and the blue eyes become watery, but he would still remain, what he was now, a very handsome fellow.

'I can't say how glad I am to have you here,' I told him. 'Though I'm afraid this is not a very gay opening to your Albanian adventures.'

Marson grimaced. 'Probably improve soon,' he replied, and continued to busy himself with the sorting of the stores which the Italians, in utter dejection, were carrying up from the dump on the beach.

Marson was being assisted in his task by the wireless operator he had brought in with him, a wiry man with a spiky forelock. I said good morning to him and asked him his name.

'Trotter, sir.'

'What part of England do you come from?'

'Wolver'ampton!'

'Wolverhampton?' I repeated. 'How are the Wanderers doing?'

A look of fervour came into Trotter's face. He gave me a quick look to see if I could be mocking him, and having decided that I was serious he answered: 'Passing through a bad patch what with the war an' all. But get this little lot over – ' he gave a suck at his teeth and a confident smile, ' – and we'll ' ave the finest football team in all England.'

By a merciful stroke the rain stopped for a while, and the sun came out sufficiently for us to spread the bundles of gear and dry them; fortunately, they had been so well packed that their immersion in the sea had done them no great harm. It was ironic to see every packet stencilled 'Sea Elephant' – the code name of the proposed Partisan base at Vuno. Clearly the stores I had requested for the Partisans had been ready loaded on the *Yankee*, and sooner than unload them the supply people had sent the boat-load to Grama. As a result, I now had hundreds of suits of battle-dress which would have been very useful to the Partisans, but which were no good at all to Balli, who would not dare be seen in them.

Morat, however, proved an exception to this. An inveterate dandy, he immediately donned British boots and battle-dress and spent the rest of the day preening and posturing round the camp. He enlivened the drabness of the uniform by lacing his boots with bright red string.

It was soon after Nigel's departure when we saw two strange figures coming down the mountain towards the camp. They were unknown to me, but Alpino borrowed my glasses and stared through them.

'It is Skender Mucho!' he stated.

'Are you sure?'

Yes, he was quite sure: he had seen Mucho once before and he was right. Fifteen minutes later, followed by a single bodyguard, the Balli leader walked into the camp. He wore a motor-cyclist's black leather jerkin, and black leather cap with ear-flaps.

Even on a first impression the man was likeable. He was slight and frail-looking, with a worn face and a smile of considerable charm. His age I judged to be around thirty-five; I learned afterwards that he was forty-two. He introduced himself, speaking excellent French, then I took him into my hut, sat him down and gave him a stiff drink of rum – the only liquor we had.

The talks which we started after lunch lasted two days, and except to eat and sleep we never stopped talking. We did not talk only of Albanian affairs: Mucho was a cultivated man and was at pains to show it. From Albania, where he had practised law and had become a leading barrister, he had travelled all over Europe for his holidays. He spoke endlessly of Paris, enthusiastic to find someone else who knew the city. He had he said a great admiration for the works of Clemenceau.

'I believe in one thing.' He was speaking tight-lipped, gazing hard at me. 'I believe in the freedom and dignity of the individual, and I will fight against any form of compulsion, be it of the Right or of the Left.'

I said nothing, so he went on:

'I was an anti-Zogist, since Zog was a tyrant. I was condemned to death by King Zog, but my sentence was commuted to life-imprisonment.'

'How many years of it did you serve?' I asked.

'Seven.' He smiled. 'They were very useful years. Save for the separation from my wife I would not regret them at all. During my imprisonment I read all the books for which I had never had time. When the Italians invaded my country I was set free.'

'And then?'

'Then I went into the mountains and fought against the invaders.'

'You are not fighting the Germans now?'

'No. I am fighting with them.'

His frankness took me somewhat aback.

'You are surprised to hear me say that?' He leaned forward. 'I will tell you the reason. Our war is not your war. For us Albanians that is a great pity, but it is true.'

I asked him to explain what he meant.

'One day,' he said, 'the Allies will defeat the Germans. That is certain. One day the Germans will either be driven from the Balkans or they will leave of their own accord. Then will begin our troubles – the real troubles for Albania, and Jugoslavia, and Greece.'

'Why?' I asked, not out of ingenuousness, but because I wanted to hear him give the answer.

'Because we shall then be left with the communist in our midst, with the terrorist and the anarchist, and for us those are worse enemies than the Germans. Albania is a very small country, and a very long way from England and America. Are you going to take a part in our affairs once the war against Germany is over?'

I shrugged my shoulders.

'You know quite well you are not. We shall be left to settle our own disputes.'

'Then,' I said, 'why not settle them when the war does end, and not do so now in the middle of it?'

Mucho gave a patient smile. 'Because,' he said, 'the communist movement – under the guise of a patriotic movement – will then be too strong. Then every man will have a pistol pushed into his ribs and be ordered to salute with the clenched fist. Sooner than that I will use the Germans, who are now in Albania, as a weapon with which to destroy the communists.'

Certainly Mucho was laying every card he had on the table. Probably he had decided that concealment was impossible, and that extreme frankness was the best policy.

'You are playing a very dangerous game,' I said. 'You say that you are confident that the Germans will be defeated. You imply that post-war assistance, or interference, from Russia would be distasteful to you. There remain England and America as potential helpers – and yet you do your best to antagonise them by collaborating now with the Germans.'

Mucho made a gesture of assent. 'I agree: it is a risk. But I am used to taking risks. I take a considerable risk in coming here to talk to you now. If the Germans were to know of it I should be...' He snapped his finger and thumb.

'Look,' I said. 'If I advise you to change your policy, you will suspect my words, seeing that they come from a British officer. All the same I am going to do so, and I can only ask you to believe that I speak as a man who likes you, and who wishes the good of your country as well as his own.'

'I believe that,' Mucho replied.

'Whether or not I share your fears of a communist domination of Albania is beside the point. I tell you, as an impartial foreigner, that you have made a fatal error in allowing yourself to be manoeuvred by the Partisans into collaborating with the Germans. An ignorant young peasant has no political discernment. If he sees a band of men fighting against the invaders of his country, then his instinct is to join them; if the leaders of that band tell him that the opposite of a fascist, or of a nazi, is a communist, then he is ready to believe them and become a communist himself. By your alliance with the Germans you Balli must have forfeited the goodwill of every ignorant young patriot in Albania. Further, the Partisan movement is now too strong for you ever to stamp it out: particularly since it is being fostered by the Allies. If you pursue your present course certain failure awaits you. Your only hope is to begin to fight *against* the Germans... and if you cannot bring your party with you, then you would be well advised to come yourself, with as large a band of followers as you can muster.'

It was very dark in the hut. There were no windows, and the canvas room shut out most of the light: even at noon two lamps were kept burning. The resultant gloom gave our talks a conspiratorial feeling, focusing attention on the words spoken rather than on the faces of the speakers. Now, during the long pause before Mucho replied, I could hear from outside the sounds of the camp – a man chopping wood, the Italians calling to each other, the peep-peeping of Drake's radio as he received a message that was coming in at strength.

At last Mucho said: 'I cannot change. My party is committed to a course and there is no turning. Do not forget, either, that history decides whether a man is right or wrong. Success is its own justification. If I succeed, then I shall be judged to have done right; if I fail, then certainly my enemies – who will be my historians – will condemn me.'

'But, Mucho,' I said, 'even if you succeed in defeating the Partisans, what then? How do you hope to ingratiate yourself with the Allies, having virtually fought against them?'

'As soon as the Partisans are destroyed we shall turn on the Germans and fight them.'

'And you think you will destroy the Partisans?'

'As I think you well know, Major, there is now a very big drive against the Partisans – not only against the Fifth Brigade, but over the whole of southern Albania. The drive is going well – very well. You, if I may say so, are in the position of a man who must make a bet. Whom are you going to back – the Partisans or the Balli? It would be useless for me to try to influence you at this stage, and I would not expect you to believe my prophecies, but in three or four weeks' time I hope you will recall what I now say: *the Partisan movement is on the eve of destruction.*'

David put his head into the hut. He had begun by sitting in on the talks with Mucho, but as he spoke neither French nor Italian it had availed him little and he had soon given up.

'Excuse me butting in,' he said, 'but Drake's just received a long signal which you might like to decipher right away. It's Top Priority.'

I left Mucho in my hut and joined David outside.

'I thought it might have some bearing on your talks now,' he explained. 'And we'll get it deciphered much quicker with three working on it than two.'

We walked a few paces through the drizzle, which had begun again, and crawled into David's shelter; Drake was already there at work, squatting on the muddy floor.

It's an exciting game deciphering an important signal. Till the last moment the jumbled letters make no sense whatsoever and as you begin the last stage, you hold your breath and pray that there has been no mistake in any of the processes through which the message has passed. If there has been a fault in any of the phases of enciphering by the sender, of deciphering by yourself, or if there has been an intervening slip in transmission or reception, then your work is wasted, the letters are as unintelligible as when you first saw them, and there is nothing to be done but gnaw your thumbs in impatience while you wait for a repeat of the signal to be sent. And for that you will probably wait two vital days.

We had been working on this signal for half an hour when there was a scuffling at the hut door and Nigel Samson appeared. He looked wet, tired and dispirited.

'It's no good,' he announced. 'I can't get through. Vuno is alive with Jerries, and those blasted Albs are scared out of their wits.' He eased off his pack and flopped down on the floor by the smoking fire. 'Those rocks too!' he went on. 'They've about done for my feet.'

David handed him a mug of rum. 'Drink this,' he said 'then tell us how and what.'

Nigel stopped tugging at his boots. 'They've caught Black and Georgie,' he said.

Drake looked incredulous. 'They've – *what?*' he demanded.

And I thought: 'That's right; they've caught them; that's the kind of thing that does happen; caught.' And I also thought: 'Damn! I shan't see my pack again: that's a nuisance.'

'That's right,' said Nigel. 'They've caught 'em both. That's definite.'

He gave another pull and his boot came off with a sucking sound. Tenderly he rubbed his feet, then glanced around.

'It's nice to be home again;' he grinned. 'I spent last night in the Vuno mosque under arrest – waiting to be handed over to the Boche.' He lifted his mug. 'Astonishing success!' he said, and drank down the rum.

Nigel's story was a depressing one. Arrived on the outskirts of Vuno, he and Cooper had sheltered for the night with a goatherd. They had not wished to make themselves known to any of the locals, but they had found the area too full of Germans and the ground too difficult for them to hope to get through without a guide. Nigel had seen six armoured cars in the village, as well as what he judged to be a company of infantry. The goatherd promised that while they slept he would go into the village and find a man willing to guide them through to the south. It was a task, he made clear, which he would have been honoured to perform himself, but regretted that he did not feel sufficiently sure of the way. He went off and left them.

An hour later he was back with twelve armed men from the village. Politely, but firmly, Nigel and Cooper were led off through the dark and placed under guard in the village mosque. The head-man of the village was sent for, and it was while waiting for his arrival that Nigel learnt of the capture of Black and Georgie. They had actually been seen by the villagers, passing through in a truck, guarded by Germans, and travelling in the direction of Valona. From their description there was no chance of mistaken identity.

The arrival of the head-man, a trilby on his head and a rifle over his shoulder, was the signal for a tremendous dispute. At first Nigel could not follow it at all, but it gradually became clear to him that half the men were in favour of handing the two Britishers over to the Germans, while the other half thought that they should merely be told to go back whence they came. As to anyone helping him get through to the south that was quite out of the question, and when he asked what had become of the Partisan element in the village he was told derisively that they were *tutti scapati*. Luckily for Nigel and Cooper the more moderate element won the day, and after being told by the head-man that the presence of British threatened the safety of the whole village, and that if they returned they would run the danger of being shot by the village guard, they were led through the darkness and put on the track that led back to Grama. It was then three o'clock in the morning.

'Did you gather at all how the drive against the Partisans was going?' I asked.

'I can't understand Italian very well,' Nigel replied, 'and I think the men left behind in Vuno were somewhat biased, but if they're at all to be believed, the Partisans are being smeared all over the mountains. It must be bloody cold up there too,' he added.

We returned to our work on the signal. It came out flawlessly and in a few more minutes I was able to read out: 'German troops in the

Southern Balkans are expected soon to withdraw northwards. An operation, to be known as Operation Victoria, is planned with the destruction of the divisions withdrawing from Greece as its object. The inland roads are to be rendered impassable by guerrilla action and the columns forced to move by the coast-road where they can be kept under continuous – attack from the Air Forces based in Italy. All other activity will be subordinated to the successful operation of Victoria. No action will be taken against the Germans that might jeopardise the operation. Liaison officers will indent for the arms they need for their part in the scheme. They will formulate their plans and signal them as early as possible to Headquarters. They are to keep in touch with and encourage all parties and bands now offering, or likely to offer, resistance to the enemy.'

David pulled at his moustache. 'What d'you make of that?' he asked.

'Make of it?' I repeated. 'It's wonderful! The first clear instructions we've had yet; and coming at this moment it's a godsend. Ever since Mucho arrived I've been wondering how far to play ball with him, but now this makes it clear. "They are to keep in touch with and encourage," I read out again, "all parties and bands now offering, or likely to offer, resistance to the enemy". Well, we can't keep in touch with the Partisans for the time being, or encourage them. That only leaves us the Balli – "likely to offer resistance".'

'We could try to find the Partisans and arrange some air sorties for them,' David suggested.

'How are you going to set about finding Besnik now?' I asked. 'From all I've heard the Partisans split up into small units when they're attacked, and get right up the mountains. I doubt if many of the Brigade even know where their commissar and commander are to be found. And how are you going to arrange air sorties without a wireless set?'

'You'd pass a loaded mule through those Boche patrols,' said Nigel, 'as easily as an elephant with a howdah.'

'Besides,' I continued, 'from what Mucho tells me, this is a real, all-out attempt to finish the Partisans. Unless he'd been pretty sure of the outcome he wouldn't have dared tell me so. Of course, he may be wrong: the Partisans may survive. But what if they don't? What if they're broken up in spite of the little help that we might be able to bring them by air? How are we to carry out our part in this operation Victoria then? Only with the Balli... Come on, David, let's go back to Mucho and get down to facts and figures.'

As I crawled out of the doorway, Drake said: 'What'll happen to Black, sir? They wouldn't put 'im through the 'oop, would they?'

'I don't know,' I replied. 'I don't think so.'

He was quiet for a moment; then, 'I wouldn't like to think that,' he said. 'Black was a mate of mine.'

Whatever was Black's fate, Mucho had no doubt as to the treatment that was in store for Doctor Georgie.

'It would have been better for him to have been shot on the spot,' he said. 'In Valona he will have an unpleasant time – I may say a very unpleasant time. Is he a brave man? Will he be able to keep silent?' I shook my head. 'Then for your sake as well as the doctor's I hope he may have been shot quickly. You realise, Major, that your base here is now compromised? I advise you to find an alternative hiding-place!' He smiled. 'You may be having visitors.'

I told Mucho that I would represent his views to Headquarters, and that I now wanted to discuss what joint action we might take on the day the Germans started to withdraw.

'But I warn you,' I said, 'that it is not enough to declare your intentions; you must give proof of them.'

'What proof?' he asked.

'Hitherto all my dealings have been with the village of Dukat, but I do not wish to continue on that level. You have come here representing the whole Balli party, so now, as a start, let the party see to it that justice is done on Misli – the boy who murdered Carapizzi.'

Mucho assured me that he would try.

'Next, let the party send twenty of its soldiers as guards for this base. The men of Dukat have too many domestic ties.'

'I agree,' he said.

'And let us receive regular and full information on German strength and movements.'

'Agreed.'

Till late in the night David, Mucho and I sat working out the number of mortars and machine-guns we should need to take effective action.

Before he left in the morning, Mucho gave me a list of points which he asked me to communicate to Headquarters, and so to the Allied Governments. They were chiefly demands for various forms of indemnity against the Italians, a plea for the retention of the Kossov Ar oil-fields by Albania, and a strong request for some sort of representation in London and Washington.

'I can assure you that you haven't a hope of getting that,' I told him. 'The Partisans are not represented outside Albania, and they'd be more likely to receive recognition than you.'

'I know,' said Mucho. 'But you who belong to a great nation cannot realise what it is like to be a small nation of only one million people and to receive no guidance except what we hear on the wireless. Left isolated, of course we make mistakes.'

'I can give you all the guidance you need at this moment, I replied. 'Fight the Germans. Until you take that step you cannot hope for recognition by the Allies.'

He inclined his head. '*Au revoir*. Thank you for your hospitality. These two days have been my happiest for a long time.'

I watched Mucho and his bodyguard begin their climb, two slowly-diminishing shapes on the vastness of the mountain-side. Very small figures they looked, on a very large canvas.

With Mucho departed the semblance of activity that had reigned for two days, and the camp relapsed into realisation of its own precariousness. Every Albanian for miles around knew of our whereabouts; it only needed a careless or malicious word to bring the Germans down on us from three directions at once and to this danger was now added the information that might have been wrung out of Georgie or Black.

To my urgent signals for a boat in order to evacuate the Italians there was no reply at all, and even if a boat could have been sent the weather would have prevented it from making a landfall. Day after day the south wind blew and grey seas piled up and broke against the ragged cliffs. Day after day more Italians dribbled in from the mountains. Twenty arrived from the area of Vuno. They had been fighting with the Partisans for the last five months, and had some first-hand intelligence to give.

In my hut, hollow-cheeked and serious-eyed, a young lieutenant told of the present plight of the Fifth Brigade. They were up above the snow-line, he said; they had little food, no blankets, and their ammunition was almost exhausted.

'Will they survive this attack?' I asked.

'Individually, yes,' was the reply. 'But as an organised body, perhaps no. Many followers will fall away: the hardships are too great. Frost-bite and pneumonia are worse enemies than the Germans.'

I asked how he himself had gained permission to leave the Brigade, and he explained that he had been in command of a mortar platoon which for several days had been without ammunition. He and another Italian officer had each a revolver, but only six bullets between them; their men were quite unarmed. In this plight they were more of a liability than an asset to the Partisans, as they still consumed a precious daily handful of maize. When they had asked if they might go and search for the Allied base which, they believed, existed near the sea, and which offered the possibility of return to their own country, the Partisans had readily given them permission as much in order to be rid of useless mouths as a reward for their past services... The responsibility for them now devolved upon me.

I asked the lieutenant what he knew of the politics of the Partisans.

'Most are ignorant and have no opinions,' he replied. 'But the leaders are communist. I have often spoken of politics with my battalion commander. His attitude is very hostile to the democracies. He wishes to use their material aid in this war against the Nazi-fascists, and then prepare for the final war of liberation in Europe in which the United Soviet Republics will overthrow the capitalist democracies.'

I was amazed to see how proud these Italian soldiers and officers were of their achievements with the Partisans. They, who so recently had been the soldiers of Fascism, now quarrelled over the rival merits of the Fifth or Fourth Partisan Brigade, according to which they had belonged.

The days passed in increasing anxiety and frustration. Physically immobilised, we were also mentally thwarted. There was no positive action for us to take till the situation changed one way or another. Our duty was to sit warily, endeavouring to assess the true situation, ready to throw in our weight wherever Allied interests could best be served.

We took steps to improve our defence system. Inland, the deep snow on the mountain would protect us from surprise attack; to the north we could rely on the goodwill and sharp wits of the goatherds; from Vuno, however, a force could set out and reach Grama between dusk and dawn. I strengthened the screen of Dukat guards to the south and armed them with Breda machine-guns. I did not expect them to provide any protection, for I was sure they would run away, but they might give a reliable alarm.

I signalled yet another urgent request for a sortie, and then set off on a two-day trip north with Chela and David Marson: I wanted to find a secure hide-out should we be driven from Grama. We could find no place where the local goatherds would not immediately know of our presence, and it was Chela's opinion that under German pressure they would certainly betray us. Nor was there any place suitable, and at the time sufficiently accessible, to which stores could now be moved by way of preparation.

And all day long, day after day, it rained.

'Have you got a reply to that signal?' I called to Drake as we came back into Grama, picking our way over the wet rocks.

Drake had been on look-out, and in a dripping gas-cape was watching our arrival.

'I've got a signal, sir, but I'm afraid it's not the one you want.' He squelched off to the men's hut to get his signal-pad.

The message he brought to me read: 'Sorry. Realise your difficulties but impossible repeat impossible send *Yankee* before March 3.'

'And to-day's date?'

'February 21st,' David said.

'Dear God!' I exclaimed. 'Have they gone raving mad at H.Q.? How do they expect us to go on living under the Germans' noses with sixty-odd Italians on our hands?'

I went round that night telling the Italians that there was difficulty over the boat and that they would have to spend a few more days in Albania: I did not tell them how many. In their makeshift bivouacs they were worse housed than goats, but like goats they huddled together and kept warm. They were very good; they knew well the danger they were in, but they took my news with complete stoicism.

Nor had they been idle in my absence. All the clothes, food and ammunition that had been landed in that disastrous sortie were now safely cached and covered with ground-sheets in a well-hidden cave belonging to the nearest goatherd. To act as guardian of the storehouse the old ruffian had driven a hard bargain; three gold sovereigns a month was his price. Neither was there any alternative but to pay what he demanded.

In my hut the conversation went round and round, never reaching a decision, while the rain dripped drearily through the roof. Even our rum was finished.

David made an attempt to start brightly the morning of the twenty-second. 'Nigel,' he ordered with mock solemnity, 'listen to me. Being virtually the staff Captain of this outfit I will give you your orders for the day. We two will present to the Major our own fresh and independent points of view, and to that end we will today sit down and work out what is known in the military text-books as an "Appreciation of the Situation". Get that?'

Nigel was lying on his bedding whistling the 'Londonderry Air', out of tune. He stopped the dismal noise and sat up.

'By all means, dear Captain Marson,' he said. 'Though as far as I can see the situation is past appreciation. It is fit only to be deplored.'

Their talk I knew would be fruitless, but it would help them to pass the time and perhaps clear their minds a little; I left the hut and wandered through the camp as far as the cliff-top. Here I found Manzitti standing, looking out to sea.

I had seen little of the Italian since the night of the sortie; he had been avoiding me – not, I felt sure, out of dislike or reproach, but through reluctance to intrude where he might not be wanted. I had respected this withdrawal, and, though I liked him, had not sought to know him better. During the last few days I had been glad of his quiet presence about the camp; he alone seemed contented and resigned.

'Munzi,' I said – his name had soon become abbreviated – 'what are you thinking about?'

'I am thinking,' he replied, 'that when the boat comes I should go with it.'

'Why do you say that?'

'Because I came to work and there is no work for me. With the situation as it is now you can evacuate no more Italians. I am only useless.'

I pondered his words a minute before answering.

'Munzi,' I said at last, 'if you want to go you must go, and I will not stop you; I can only tell you that I should be dismayed to lose you.'

He gave me a quick look through his spectacles.

'Then I shall be glad to stay,' he said quietly, and, turning, he walked back towards the camp.

I stayed a while longer looking out over the grey Adriatic where in the distance, the island of Corfu was dimly visible between the rain squalls. It was an afternoon on which to recall the hissing of logs in the hearth of an English home and the sound of the muffin-man's bell in the street outside.

The sound of a fast-approaching plane made me sit motionless among the rocks; and a moment later there appeared from the north the evening reconnaissance plane. It flew low over the waves, its German markings clearly visible, and disappeared down the coast.

As the sound of its engine died away I was turning to go when my eye was caught by an object lodged in the rocks a few feet below me. I climbed down and picked it up. It was a boot – an old, worn boot; the upper had come away from the sole and its alpine nails stuck out sideways like a ragged moustache.

It was the discarded boot of Doctor Georgie.

NINE

IT WAS ABOUT ten o'clock in the evening of February the twenty-third. Hodo had appeared that morning; I fancy he had crossed the mountain in order to see Benson, not knowing that the American had gone. Now, after dinner, he, David and myself were sitting by the fire in my hut.

'Look at that!' I held up my boot from which the rocks had ripped a piece of the toe that morning. 'There's a good pair of mountain boots gone in under two months.'

'I'd change into your spare pair if I were you,' said David. 'You never know when you'll be needing to move in a hurry, and I shouldn't like to trust my life to those boots!'

I was starting to take his advice when he asked: 'Would you like some really good laces?'

'I would indeed.'

David left the hut and returned in a minute with a pair of well-oiled leather thongs. 'They are good,' he agreed as I admired them. 'An old man on my father's estate makes them. I bought a whole lot from him for the squadron at the beginning of the war, and I've still got a few pairs left.'

I thanked him and began to thread them into my spare boots. Their strength and suppleness were satisfying to the touch.

Hodo was sitting cross-legged on the floor, scowling thoughtfully at the fire. When I had met him at Sea View a month ago, I had taken to the man, but now there was something furtive and scheming about his manner that I did not like. His every proposal seemed to be solely for the advancement of Hodo. Now he stirred a little and drew in a noisy breath through his nose. 'Major,' he said, 'believe what I say: the Partisans are finished. This last drive has destroyed them. Besnik is wandering in the hills behind Trajas; he has only three followers; no one but his uncle will give him food. If he is allowed to continue, he may build up his force again, but if he were to be sent out of the country' – Hodo's voice dropped insinuatingly – 'then I could easily take over all that remains of the Fifth Brigade. You know me, Major; I have a great sympathy among them. Be sure of this.'

'And how,' I asked, 'do you propose that Besnik should be sent out of the country?'

'Major, he is in danger. He has killed many men. Now he is weak their families can take their revenge. I think if he was given the chance he would be glad to leave the country.'

'From what I know of Besnik, I do not agree with you.'

'No, Major?' Hodo was looking distastefully cunning. 'Perhaps not if you asked him directly. But a little trick?... You invite him to a conference in Italy – and then it becomes impossible to return him to Albania... and beside, Major, that when I take over his old brigade, they will not be Partisans: they will be patriots, soldiers of the Allies.'

'Hodo,' I said, 'I have no intention of playing that kind of game. The end is not certain. If I were sure that the salvation of Albania and the winning of the war lay in removing Besnik I might do it, but that is very far from clear.'

The flap over the entrance was pushed up and Chela crawled in, followed by Morat and another Albanian. Before he opened his mouth I knew by his face what Chela was going to say.

'They are coming.'

I knew perfectly well that he meant the Germans, but I asked: 'You mean the Germans?'

'Yes.'

'How many, and where from?'

'Five or six – a patrol. They come from the north. This man,' Chela indicated the stranger, 'is one of my own shepherds. North of Sea View, three hours ago, the German patrol stopped him and asked for the British base. He showed them a track – the wrong one – then ran ahead of them to warn us.'

'David, go and get Nigel, will you?' I said, and as he left the hut, 'You'd better not tell Manzitti yet,' I warned. 'We don't want the Italians catching fright.'

Till the two returned I sat by the fire struggling against the wave of inertia that had suddenly come over me. I didn't want to cope with this situation; I didn't want to have to take decisions; I only wanted to go to sleep. Was this fear, I wondered?

'Let's think this out aloud,' I said when David and Nigel were in the hut; indeed, it was the only way in which I could think for the moment. Without the stimulus of speech my brain was quite inactive. 'Three hours ago' – I looked at my watch – 'that is at seven-fifteen, this patrol was north of Sea View. My guess is that they'd never try to cover this rough ground in the darkness. They'll probably sleep near Sea View – perhaps in our caves if they come across them – and move on towards Grama with the first light. That gives us plenty of time to decide what to do.'

'Chela,' said David, 'ask your man if the Germans were carrying a wireless.'

The man did not know what a wireless was, but he could describe a box which one German carried on his back; it had a stick, he said, that 'grew longer'. It was a wireless all right; probably the equivalent of our '18' set.

'Sounds to me like a company patrol,' said Nigel, 'with the rest of the company maybe a mile behind.'

Chela had been speaking in Albanian to his shepherd. 'He says,' he now broke in excitedly, 'that there is with the Germans an Albanian. He is dressed like a German, but he spoke perfect Albanian to my shepherd. Major, I believe it is Doctor Georgie leading the patrol.'

David whistled. 'It might be, mightn't it? – Leading the Germans to our base in return for having his life spared.'

'Major, we must leave Grama at once.' Hodo's voice was low and urgent. 'If Georgie is leading them, then be sure they will find us here. And they will not only be coming from the north: they can come from many places at the same time.'

'Any news from the south?' I asked.

There was none, but unfortunately that meant nothing: previous experience had taught me to expect little accurate news from that quarter. The feeling of sleepiness was wearing off now, and my mind was working better. What the devil did this patrol mean? I asked myself. Of course they might be an isolated and quite innocent coastal reconnaissance party – but that seemed unlikely. The

Germans would hardly send half a dozen men, unsupported, into a potentially hostile mountain. And besides, why the questions about the British base? And why the wireless set?

'Well now,' I said. 'We've got to reach a decision. We have definite and conclusive information that a small patrol, almost certainly with a wireless, is coming down the coast from the north. That's all we know for certain. There may be no troops behind them; on the other hand, there may be lots. From Dukat and from the south we have no news. That similarly means nothing.' I looked round the ring of faces. 'I hate to be turned out of our homes at this hour of night, but I think that to stay here is a risk we simply cannot take. There may be a company behind this patrol; there may be a battalion. In case there is, it's our job to be clear of the place by daylight. David, Nigel, do you agree?'

They agreed, reluctantly; Chela and Hodo with alacrity.

'Right. Everyone is to collect his essential kit. Operators will carry their wireless sets. They're useless without batteries, but they're much too precious to leave behind. We'll leave camp in half an hour.'

'You changed your boots just in time,' said David as he left the hut.

While David and Nigel organised the Allied party, I sent for Manzitti and spoke to him.

'Munzi,' I said. 'We're pulling out. What are we to do with your Italians? There are sixty of them, and I'm afraid I just cannot take them with me. It might mean the loss of everyone.'

I felt very mean as I said it, but there was nothing else to be done.

Manzitti just said quietly: 'I will go and talk with the Italian officers. It will be all right. Do you wish me to come with you?'

'Indeed I do. Of course.'

'I am glad,' was all he said.

'And we'll take Alpino,' I added. I couldn't have left him behind.

Alone in the hut, I stood wondering what to carry with me. The drowsiness and inertia were quite gone now; the decision was taken; a new chapter was beginning; I was almost enjoying myself. I had a feeling that within a few days we would be reduced to no possessions, so I might as well start reducing myself now. There was little that could not be eliminated: my precious photograph went into my trouser pocket; round my waist I fastened a money-belt containing three hundred gold sovereigns; into a sack I thrust the rest of our gold – five hundred pieces of it, a blanket, my sponge-bag – minus the soap which I could find nowhere, some 'K' rations and a Shakespeare. I hesitated a moment over the Shakespeare, then, with a feeling of guilt, I pulled the book out of the pack and put in its place some more 'K' rations; I could carry enough poetry in my head to last me for a few weeks. I put on all the warm clothes that I could pile on top of each other and found, when I was dressed up like Father Christmas, that I had left off my uniform jacket: I couldn't undress again and put it on, I couldn't be bothered to carry it, so I left it.

I was in the middle of burning my papers – signals, notes on the Mucho talks, sketch maps – when Hodo put his head through the entrance.

'Major, I have no gun. You have your revolver. May I borrow this?'

He reached out and touched my Tommy-gun leaning against the wall.

'Thank you. Thank you, Major.'

Before I had time to say anything he had disappeared with it.

A last look round the disordered hut... Good-bye, house! Good-bye the hopes that had been built there!... and I crawled out into the open. The others were collecting. Radios and batteries had been hidden in the rocks.

'All signals burnt?'

'Yessir.'

'Got food?'

'Yessir.'

'All set to go?'

A murmured 'Yes.'

'Right. Lead on, Chela.'

It was a foul night for walking, without even starlight, and we were all heavily weighed down. Every half-hour we stopped for a short rest, less out of fatigue than to prevent ourselves from becoming soaked with sweat, for we were wearing every stitch we could carry. We started in silence, since for all we knew there might be enemy patrols about, but our nailed boots made a terrific clatter on the rocks, and after a couple of hours it became impossible to stop men swearing. David was a particular offender; he was some yards behind me, and after a deal of stumbling I heard him fall full length with a great crash. Thereafter his profanity flowed unchecked.

Hodo and Chela were scared, and as they led us on hour after hour signs of rebellion became apparent from the rear of the party. By three o'clock Nigel and David were in revolt. It was absurd, they said, to walk so far from a danger that might not even exist. We had gone far enough and would soon be completely out of touch with Grama, unable to keep a watch on what happened there. Chela and Hodo, on the other hand, continually urged us to do just half an hour more and 'we would be in a perfect place'; but at the end of each half-hour we were invariably told it was 'only half an hour more'. The Albanians were being irritating, but I myself sided with them; I knew how slowly we were moving and that dawn would find us far nearer to the camp than the others believed. I knew too that David and Nigel were suffering chiefly from wounded pride, from the indignity of being chased out of camp by half a dozen Germans. The line I decided to take was to cajole them as long as I possibly could, and then, when I judged that they really had reached breaking-point and were about to mutiny in earnest, to forestall them by telling Chela we would not go a step farther and meaning it.

At one of the halts I was sitting beside Hodo when he whispered to me: 'Major, one thing. If we are surrounded, what will you do?'

'What do you mean?' I asked, though my mind guessed at what he would say.

'If we are surrounded Chela and I will surely fight. Will you fight too?'

I restrained the desire to strike him then and there, and instead asked: 'What would you expect us to do?'

'You might surrender. Perhaps they will only take you prisoner, but Chela and me they will surely kill.'

'We will fight,' I said.

'Thank you,' he whispered. 'Because we will surely fight.'

'Yes,' I said, 'you've told me so already and I never expected you would do anything else. Now will you stop talking? We're making too much noise.'

Breaking-point came at five in the morning: Nigel and David refused to go an inch farther.

By God's good grace we had just reached a dried river-bed, overhung with cliffs and hidden by trees, and it satisfied even the Albanians as a resting-place. We all got under the lee of the cliff and lay down. Those who were carrying blankets wrapped themselves up and fell asleep. The rest of us sat waiting for the sun to rise, or collected wood against the time when it would be safe to light a fire.

Even when the sun rose Hodo was against lighting a fire on account of the tell-tale smoke, but I felt the danger was not so pressing as all that, and that the men's spirits would sink extremely low with nothing warm inside them. Accordingly, a small fire was lit, water was found and heated, and soon we were eating a welcome breakfast of 'K' rations.

During the night we had collected an old shepherd who belonged to that part of the valley. In the dark I did not see him join us; he seemed to materialise with the light – conveniently in time for some hot coffee. Him we sent back towards Grama to find out what news he could of the Germans. Morat was precluded from a similar task by his battle-dress.

Till the shepherd returned with some definite information we ourselves decided to stay where we were. David took his boots off and went sound asleep. Chela sat very silent, smoking cigarette after cigarette. Hodo unfolded his plan; he must have been thinking it over all night, for he had it pat.

'Major, this is now a very dangerous time for you. I have decided to go into Valona, and into Tirana if necessary, and find Mucho. Now is the time for him to help you.'

'That is how it strikes me too,' I replied.

'One thing, Major.' He glanced to make sure Chela was out of earshot. 'You must keep Chela with you. He has an influence with these shepherds; while he is with you they will not betray you. If he goes away they might do anything. His presence with you is your best protection.'

He had been lacing his boots as he talked and now he stood up.

'Good-bye, Major. I shall be back in a day or two with Mucho. Now he must show he is a serious man and that his words are not empty.' He turned, and went climbing up the valley out of sight.

He had been gone an hour before I realised that he had taken my gun.

It was ten o'clock when the shepherd returned. When the man had told his story, Chela turned to me. 'He says that the patrol has been seen to the north of Grama, coming over the hill. They are going straight towards the camp and they should be there in an hour.'

David rose to his feet. 'We'd better go and kill them,' he said abruptly.

Nigel got up too. 'Well?' he asked. The two stood looking down at me, waiting for my decision.

I knew what was in their minds. They were smarting under the indignity of being chased out of camp, and after the weeks of frustration inactivity had become intolerable. As if their feelings were not written in their faces, Nigel uttered them:

'For God's sake, we're not going to let them move into Grama and do nothing about it, are we?'

Into my mind came Cleaver's words: 'Your job is to kill Germans!' I could remember the way he had looked as he said it, clenching his teeth and writhing his lips back until the gums showed. He was right too; our job was to kill Germans, and here to hand were six good specimens... and yet... and yet...

'Just a minute,' I said, 'I don't think it's quite as easy as that. Let's try and reason it out loud. There are two courses of action: to kill them, which we can easily do, or to let them go free. First of all let's consider what will happen if we let them go free. They'll find that there was a big camp and stores at Grama, and they'll either go back to report or they'll sit in Grama and whistle up more troops by their wireless. In any case, we can assume that troops, sooner or later, will arrive. But we also know that those troops can't live at Grama indefinitely; the supply problem would be too difficult. After a ten-days' stay they'll have to leave. So what would it all amount to? We'd lose the base temporarily; we'd lose the stores perhaps permanently; but when the road was clear we could still come back and open another base. And if Dukat was charged with complicity they could deny all knowledge of us and blame our presence on the wicked Partisans.

'Now let's see what happens if we kill them. The moment these boys go off the air their headquarters will realise that they've run into trouble and come in search of them; no doubt they'll have a pretty accurate idea where to look, too. So by killing them we shan't avoid the presence of troops in this mountain, or the discovery of our base. On the credit side we should have the destruction of six Germans and the recovery of our self-esteem – both pretty good gains. On the debit side will be the reprisals which will certainly be taken against Dukat. If these men are killed in Dukat mountain the village will get ripped in half.'

David asked if that mattered much.

'Yes, it does,' I answered, 'and that quite apart from humanitarian reasons. We're agreed that our part in "Victoria" may possibly depend on the Balli. It's not a very good beginning to antagonise violently the one part of the country which at all costs we want to keep friendly.'

I looked at the two faces before me; they were not convinced, or if mentally convinced then not emotionally. Their manhoods were insulted by the presence and continued existence of these six Germans, and no reasoning could repair that insult. I could feel that I was stretching their discipline dangerously in running so counter to their deep instinct and that I might be in danger of losing my authority in their eyes, but there was nothing else that I could do.

'I'm sure I'm right in this,' I insisted. 'Their headquarters, or whatever formation these Germans belong to, is bound to know their approximate position – and Dukat will surely pay the price for their deaths.'

They were silent, and in that silence we rounded our perilous corner.

'All right,' said David. 'You know best. What do we do then?'

'We send a patrol to keep contact with them and see what they get up to. You two had better get off straight away. Take Sergeant Butch with you – and take Manzitti in case you need an interpreter with any of the shepherds. I'll stick right here with Chela – I expect we'll be getting some word from Dukat during the morning.'

The word from Dukat arrived even sooner than I had expected, for the four had hardly moved off towards the coast when Chela, through my binoculars, picked up two figures coming down the mountain-side at a great pace.

'It is Old Ali and Zechir,' he declared, handing me the glasses. The two men were fairly running down the hill, jumping from the rocks; and half an hour later they had arrived at our resting-place. They had met Hodo on the mountain and he had told them where to find us.

Old Ali saluted with his usual elaborate courtesy, sat down on the rocks, rolled a cigarette and lit it, and only then produced from the recesses of his clothing a tightly-folded pellet of paper which, he handed to Chela. I could see the fear coming into Chela's face as he read it.

'What does it say?' I asked.

'It is from the chiefs of the village; they order me to come back at once.' He was already on his feet collecting his belongings, slinging his automatic over his shoulder.

'What reason do they give?' I asked.

'They say there is danger and that they must make plans. Major, I must go at once.'

'All right, all right, but don't be in such a hurry. We must make some arrangements for keeping in touch. If the Germans come, shall we cross to the other side or stay hidden here? We cannot stay here many days or all our food will be gone.'

'Major, I cannot talk now.' The man was in a great state of agitation. If I do not go at once I cannot cross the mountain before dark. You have Morat with you; Ali and Zechir will stay also. I will keep in touch.'

There was no use trying to get any sense out of him. He was as panic-stricken as on the day of the false alarm. I let him go and he went racing away up the mountain.

Hodo's desertion I could have expected, but Chela's was surprising and at the same time dismaying. Drake at my side murmured: 'The ship must be sinking pretty fast.'

At three in the afternoon Nigel and Butch returned. 'We've been in touch with the sods the whole time,' Nigel told us. 'They've been right into the camp, poking around and photographing everything.'

'Sons of bitches,' Butch muttered. 'Jesus Christ! What a target they made!' He lay back on the ground. 'And to think I gave that little swine Georgie a pair of my socks,' he added.

'I don't think the Albs had left them much to photograph,' Nigel continued. 'The camp is ransacked; hardly one stone on top of another.'

'Could you make out if one of them was Georgie?' I asked.

Nigel shook his head. 'They're wearing parka hoods. You can't make out their faces. But there was one much smaller than the rest; it could have been Georgie.'

'Well, I can't blame him,' I said. 'God knows I might have done the same myself. What was happening when you left?'

'They were pulling out – moving in the direction of Dukat. They can't be far behind me.'

'Any sign of the Italians?' I asked.

Nigel shook his head. 'They've left the area of the camp. Probably trying to escape in the direction of Vuno.'

'And David and Munzi?'

'They've stayed behind for a last scout round. They'll be back soon.' He shook his head and laughed. 'I'd like to meet that German patrol when the war's over and tell them how near they were to death today. I'll bet it would scare the guts out of them even ten years afterwards.'

David was half running when we saw him, clattering up the river-course as fast as he could go with Manzitti behind him. When he reached us he tried to speak, but he was too spent to get a word out. The two of them lay on the ground regaining their breath while we sat waiting for whatever it was David had to tell us. At last he got out between gasps: 'There are two hundred Germans to the north of us now – moving this way.'

'Who told you this?' I asked. 'Have you seen them?'

David shook his head. 'I was told by a shepherd who had seen them. It seems they're quite near. There's talk too of another big party working up from Vuno. The shepherd swore to it.'

'It may still be untrue,' I said.

'The fellow believed it all right,' David replied. 'He was already on the move with all his goats.'

'I'm afraid we must assume it's true too,' I said. 'Which means that once again we move.'

'Where to?'

'We must get across the mountain tonight and be in Dukat valley by morning. If we stay here the cover is not bad and there's a chance they might not find us, but on the other hand the shepherds know just where we are. In any case we have no food: we can get food on the other side. D'you all agree?'

No one demurred; indeed our course was obvious. We decided to split into two parties, dividing between us the radio sets that we were carrying, and to cross the mountain independently; in this way concealment would be easier and also, if one party came to grief, there was a good chance that the other would get through. Nigel took Cooper, Butch and Trotter, with Zechir as guide; my own party consisted of David, Drake, Manzitti and Alpino, with Morat as guide and Old Ali as a messenger.

Each party was to find its own way over the mountain and get in touch again on the other side – probably through Chela.

'So long, Jim,' I heard Trotter saying to Drake as he shouldered his pack. 'This is the life, eh?... Just like Wolver'ampton.'

'Munzi,' I said. 'Will you ask Morat what on earth is the matter with him?' The Albanian was sitting some paces from us, apparently sunk in misery.

'*Non possibile passare la notte,*' he replied to Munzi's question. '*Troppa neve. Niente luce. Impossibile.*'

'*Impossibile*' or not we had to do it, and we told him so. He only pulled his mouth down at the corners and shrugged. There was nothing to be gained from further discussion; we divided up what little food we had left and in a few minutes Nigel's party had gone tramping off. Soon we too were climbing up through the trees towards the snow line.

The money-belt with the three hundred sovereigns I wore all the time, though it was an uncomfortable weight. The bag containing the five hundred sovereigns David and I took it in turns to carry, as it was extremely heavy. We had tried to effect each transfer secretly, since I was anxious that the Albanians should not know how much we had or who was carrying it; in our present predicament they might have been tempted to invest in a little speculatory murder. This time it was David's turn to carry the heavy bag, for which I was not sorry; it was a steep ascent.

We reached the topmost fringes of the wood and above us extended a snow-covered expanse of open hill-side, utterly devoid of cover. As I looked I saw a line of figures in the distance climbing upwards across it. It was Nigel's party. Damn fools! I thought. We had decided that each party must take all the cover possible even at the expense of time lost, and there they were, visible for miles around, crossing open ground in broad daylight.

David and I consulted together and decided to wait where we were until it was at least dusk; in the half-dark we would traverse the bad patch of open ground and get across the top somehow during the night. Morat pulled a grimace when we told him our decision and his sulks deepened. But I was quite decided not to cross that open patch in daylight, so we squatted down in a little gulley where there was some protection from the wind, with the idea of getting as much rest as we could before night fall.

Ever since Chela had left in the morning Old Ali had been flitting about us like a goblin: he would go off towards the south to see if there was any sign of German movement there, then back he would come to see how we were getting on. Now as we sat huddled in the gulley, disconsolately munching biscuits, I felt glad to have him around. He was a picturesque ruffian; he had been useful to us during the day, and I fancied he would be staunch in a fight. Ali caught me looking at him; he gave a resigned shrug of the shoulders and his moustache twitched in a smile.

Suddenly we heard a voice shouting. '*Italiani!*' it cried. '*Italiani!*' And again, coming nearer: '*Italiani!*'

Before I could give him the order. Old Ali had gone to investigate. Who on earth could be wandering high up here calling out for Italians? In a moment we knew, for Ali appeared over the ridge leading a man in Italian uniform, and I recognised him as one of the officers who had been in Grama – a solid-looking fellow. We crowded around him in welcome, offering him cigarettes and broken biscuits from our pockets. I think he was very glad to have found us, and we felt happy about it too: in saving him our sense of guilt at leaving the others was lessened.

We bombarded him with questions. What was the news from Grama? What had happened to the Italians? What was he doing up in the mountain alone?

Most of the Italians, he told us, had moved southwards, but a few, of whom he was one, had remained near the camp where there was food to be had, hoping that they would escape discovery. Unfortunately, he himself had walked straight into the German patrol that morning; they had shouted and fired at him but he had managed to get away and had gone climbing up the mountain, becoming more and more lost, and at last in desperation calling out to his friends.

To our enquiries as to the numbers of Germans alleged to be approaching from north and south he replied that he had seen only those Germans who were in the patrol, and that though the report might be true he was inclined to disbelieve it.

This statement quite decided Morat: he announced firmly that it was madness to try to cross the mountain by night, that he refused to lead us, and that we had much better lie hidden somewhere on the seaward side till we knew positively what was the situation. The news of Lieutenant Tallei, as the Italian was called, had also heartened us, and we now took little persuading to postpone our assault on the mountain which, as darkness fell, grew every minute less and less inviting. We humped our bundles and trudged downhill again to our old resting-place.

We were preparing ourselves for a night under the lee of the cliff when Butch, prowling round, discovered a small cave which offered some protection against the storm that appeared to be brewing. It was two hundred yards farther up the river-course and had clearly been in long use as a goat-pen. But though the floor was deep in droppings it would at least be soft to lie on; we would be dry if it rained, and, if we screened the entrance, we would be able to light a small fire without it shining all over the hill-side. Some of us started to carry our gear along and stow it for the night, while others set about making a fire and fixing a blanket screen across the mouth of the little cave.

David had made several trips to and fro carrying kit when he asked: 'Anybody brought my pack along?'

We looked around. It was nowhere to be seen.

'I saw it last trip I made,' I said. 'It was there under the cliff with Old Ali sitting by it.'

'That's what I thought,' replied David. 'But it's gone now and so has Ali.'

'He's probably gone off into the bushes for a minute. They're very reticent, these Albanians.'

'But I've been shouting for him,' said David, 'and he doesn't answer. Damn it, it's only two minutes since I saw him last. He can't be out of earshot so soon.'

'Never mind,' I said. 'Don't worry about that now. He'll turn up and so will your pack.'

'Yes,' said David doubtfully. 'I hope so, because all the gold was in it.'

I checked.

'Did I hear you alright?' I asked.

'I'm afraid so,' David replied.

'In that case,' I said, 'I think you may save your breath and stop calling, for I don't think we shall be having the pleasure of Ali's company again for quite a time.'

I noticed that Morat was looking at us queerly; he must have seen from our faces that something was very amiss. The best course was to try and keep concealed the magnitude of our loss. If the Albanians still around us realised that our gold was stolen, I surmised that we might see a marked falling off in their loyalty. I told the others to act as though nothing had happened.

Thank God I still had three hundred sovereigns in my money-belt; our position was not desperate. Temporarily worse than the loss of the gold was the loss of our reserve 'K' rations which David had carried in his pack.

But we still had a few packets of powdered soup in our pockets, and some biscuits: enough for a meal. The screen was rigged up, the fire lit, and when we had eaten we stretched out on the dung and gazed at the flames, almost bemused with so much warmth.

That night I was wakened by the din of a thunderstorm that broke over the mountain, and by the sound of the rain falling in torrents. I raised myself on my elbow; by the light of the still glowing sticks I could make out the forms of the others unmoved, deep in sleep. A good job we didn't try to cross the mountain, I thought; up there, there must be a blizzard. Much better in our snug, dungy little cave. As I pulled my blanket around my ears and settled down to sleep again I thought: 'How cold and wet those Germans must be – I hope.'

Normal means of communication might not exist in Albania, but bad news travelled with the same rapidity as in any part of the world. So I was not altogether surprised when, with the sodden dawn, there arrived half a dozen guards and shepherds all demanding payment. Their demands, I had to admit were rightful; their monthly payment was in fact due. Nor, although I guessed as much, did their insistence betray whether or not they were aware of our loss. Morat at all events had become aware of it and, though he knew that I still retained a quantity of gold, firmly counselled me to make no payments. Once paid, he said; the guards would disappear and be of no further use to us.

But the guards were of no use to us in any case, and their payment I now regarded merely as a bribe, without which – and particularly if they thought we had no gold left – they would not hesitate to betray us to the Germans. I decided to pay them.

By now, however, I had become cautious. I did not want the Albanians to see how much money we had left or where and how it was carried, but as I had half to undress to get at the stuff this secrecy was difficult of achievement. There was no privacy, since the blanket screen had been taken down; my efforts to coax them away by guile were unsuccessful; there was nothing for it but to undress and take the gold out of the bag before their eyes.

They went away well contented – to their look-out positions in the hills, so they said, but more probably, I felt, to their respective homes. They had brought no factual confirmation of the Germans' approach, only an atmosphere of fear and foreboding, but what they bore away was concrete enough. Besides the two pieces of gold which we had wittingly paid to each man we discovered, when they were gone, that in that short interval we had unwittingly become separated from two pairs of binoculars, a revolver and a raincoat. So adroit was the technique that at any other time it might have been worthy of a certain admiration, but now it only served to increase in me a growing detestation of these Albanians.

Morat now urged us to move again. Our lair, he said, was too well known, and he claimed to know of a better hiding-place on this same side of the mountain. Whereas he had previously refused to cross the mountain by night he now refused to cross it by day, owing to the danger of being spotted. I decided to follow his advice. We were very dependent on him and, anyhow, argument was useless; Morat arrived at his decisions through instinct, not reason. By seven-thirty we were again on the move.

Shepherd's Valley was our destination – the high, inland end of it, and an unpleasant three-hours' walk it was over country devoid of cover. We hadn't a rifle between us, no weapon with a longer range than a Tommy-gun's. The only pair of field-glasses left to us were my own, and through them we continually scanned the desolate slopes around us; there was no sign of movement. The heaviest burden was Alpino's, who had become the self-appointed bearer of Drake's wireless set; this, though only the size and shape of a suitcase, was extremely heavy. We had wrapped it in ground-sheets to protect it from the rain, and Alpino carried it over his shoulder with the haft of an axe pushed through the handle.

By ten-thirty we were high up the mountain-side, near the head of Shepherd's Valley. Somewhere in this vicinity was the hiding-place, but Morat was not sure of its exact position; we had to wait while he descended into the valley to find a shepherd friend who knew it. The wind was cold and it had started to rain, so we sheltered as best we could at the foot of a rock face and watched Morat's figure grow smaller as he ran down into the valley.

'Munzi,' I asked, 'is there anything wrong with your hands?'

I had noticed that he was handling his bundle very gingerly.

'I cut them yesterday on a tin,' he said. 'They are a little sore.'

'Let me see them. Go on,' I insisted, 'take off those gloves and let me have a look.'

With difficulty he drew off his woollen gloves and held out his hands. They were blue and swollen, with a gathering of pus round the cuts; he could not move his fingers. To carry his bundle must have caused him a lot of pain, but he had made no complaint.

'I think we shall have to let that poison out,' I said.

He nodded. 'Yes – if they are not better by tomorrow.'

I noticed then that he was shivering. 'Have you a fever?' I asked. 'A little malaria,' he replied.

As my mind leapt ahead to possible implications, I suddenly realised how important Manzitti had become to me personally, and how, through his very quietness and self-sufficiency, he had become a stabilising factor in our party. Both Nigel and David I had to nurse along; even Drake could be temperamental; but on Manzitti I could count for immediate and unquestioning acceptance of my decisions: I could rest on him. I prayed now that he was not going to become seriously ill, for we had no medicines at all.

We huddled against the rock, speaking little, fighting off the cold that attacked our bodies and, far worse, the depression that assailed our minds. This hill-side on which we were now fugitive had belonged to us; we had felt that it was our territory: as though this were a game in which each side was inviolable when in his own base. Naturally, we had expected trouble with the Germans on the other side of the mountain, on their side. But now they had most unfairly broken the rules; they had brought the fight on to our side: the basis of our plan was destroyed.

At length Morat returned with the same old shepherd who had given us hospitality that day when I had first come south in search of Grama Bay. He gave us an expressionless salute, then led the way still upward for half an hour along a narrow, rocky track from which we could look down on Shepherd's Valley lying peacefully below us;

the huts looked no bigger than flies, and the goats mere grey dots.

The rock by the side of the track was curiously weathered and fissured so that holes had formed in it as in a cheese. Some were quite small, some large enough to accommodate a man. Suddenly, with a cry, David stopped and put his hand into one of these larger holes.

'Look!' he called triumphantly, pulling his hand out and holding up a small tin. 'Band-Aid! My tin of Band-Aid! It was in my pack. I saw it shining as I walked past.'

'Are you sure it's yours?' said Drake.

'Don't be a damn fool!' replied David. 'Of course it's mine. It doesn't rain tins of Band-Aid in Albania. I'll bet that old devil Ali slept in this hole last night.'

Morat, who was small enough, had crawled into the hole to see what else he could discover, and now emerged holding some bits of David's clothing and a bedraggled prayer-book. David made a little noise when he saw the prayer-book and, taking it quickly, started to straighten out its muddied pages.

'*Niente aro?*' Drake demanded of Morat. The Albanian shook his head ruefully. 'That bloody old Ali!' the corporal burst out. 'I'll kill him if I catch him.'

Manzitti's face broke into a broad smile. 'I think it is a nice picture,' he said. 'I like to think of Old Ali last night, r-r-running between the rocks in the thunderstorm.'

I saw what he meant. It must have been like a scene from a Fritz Lang film – the little scuttling guilty figure bent under the weight of the stolen gold, his coat blowing out wild while the thunder crashed around him and the lightning flashes lit the rocks. There was something so dramatically satisfying in the scene that I found it took away my anger against Ali and somehow compensated for the loss of the gold. I was grateful to Munzi for appreciating it.

After another twenty minutes the shepherd stopped and pointed to a blank wall of rock. We stared at it, bewildered. What hiding-place was there here? The guide smiled, climbed up on to a ledge of rock some eight feet high – and disappeared behind it; then his head reappeared beckoning us to follow. We did so, and found that although the ledge appeared to be part of the cliff face, there was actually a narrow cleft behind it. Down this cleft we lowered ourselves one by one, crawled on hands and knees for a yard or two, then stood up erect in a cave that lay just behind the rock face. It was indeed the most wonderfully hidden cave I had ever seen. A man could walk past that ledge of rock and look hard at it, yet never suspect the cleft that existed between it and the rock face, or the cavern that lay behind.

A drop of water splashed on to my shoulder; then one fell on my hand; I looked upwards, and one hit me full in the face.

'Keep quiet a moment!' I said.

We stood in the murk listening, and to our ears came the manifold and complicated rhythm of innumerable drippings... drip, drip, drip, plop... drip, drip, drip, plop... I shifted my ground and the rhythm changed... plop, drip, plop, plop, plop, drip, plop, plop...

'What's the matter with this bloody cave?' said David. 'It's raining!'

Drake shone a torch; its battery was flat and its feeble beam was engulfed in the ponderous darkness, but it was sufficient to reveal an enormous cavern, large enough to hold a hundred men. He turned the light upwards, and there was an exclamation from us all; from the roof, in single, giant daggers and in intricate and elaborate screens, hung a forest of stalactites, every one of them dripping. He shone the light on the ground, and from the rocky floor the stalagmites aspired upwards in moist sympathy.

'I don't see "Welcome" on the door-mat,' Drake objected.

It was not a very funny remark, but it made us laugh uproariously. We couldn't stop laughing, and the more the drops fell down our necks the more we laughed.

At last we pulled ourselves together.

'We could stay hidden here,' I said, 'for the rest of our natural lives, but unless we get some food quickly that's likely to be a short span.'

Slightly protesting, Morat was sent off to our cache at Grama to collect some biscuits, sugar, and tea. He also had instructions to change back into his Albanian costume if he could lay hands on it; his usefulness to us was curtailed by his battle-dress.

When Morat had departed we set about making the cave more habitable. Our first need was a fire, in order both to dry our clothes and give some light; we decided to risk one. Some dead trees stood outside the entrance to the cave, but we dared not cut them for fear of the new axe-marks that we should make, so we collected the few sticks and broken boughs that lay beneath them and took them inside the cave to be chopped.

'You'll never get those to burn,' we warned Alpino as he hacked at them in the semi-darkness. 'They're much too damp.'

But Alpino felt that his reputation as a champion fire-lighter was at stake. With meticulous care he arranged his sticks near the exit, where he hoped there might be a draught, and put a match to them.

By the end of half an hour's blowing, re-laying, more blowing, re-lighting, more blowing still, plus the expenditure of a great deal of nervous energy, Alpino had coaxed into life a few half-hearted flames. He had also filled the cave so full of smoke that it was impossible to see and scarcely to breathe. We looked longingly at the unpromising pyramid; certainly those few flames were comforting and would in time provide the means for a hot drink: with equal certainty they would provide the means of asphyxiation. Reluctantly, as we would have put to death a favourite but ailing dog, we extinguished the fire. Strenuous fanning of the smoke towards the exit tunnel seemed to clear the air a little.

His fire having proved a fiasco, Alpino set about rigging a screen of ground-sheets to protect us, as we slept, from the ceaseless drips. Hands willing to help him were not lacking, but Alpino was now on his mettle and had worked himself into a state where he resented assistance. For a time I watched him wrestling with ground-sheets, and pieces of cord for which he could find no hold-fast, and bits of stick that were too short and could not be driven into the rocky floor, but it became painful to watch his efforts. I turned away to see if there were indeed no place where we could light a fire and brew some tea.

During the first attempt at fire-lighting, some of us had crawled out into the open to get the smoke out of our lungs and smarting eyes, and we had noticed that smoke was oozing from a small fissure some yards away from the main exit. The fissure itself was concealed under tufts of grass, so that it looked as if the smoke was issuing from the very hill-side. Now we began to search for this fissure from the inside, and at last found it. It was at one extreme end of the cave, at the bottom of a funnel down which we had to squirm on our stomachs. Sure enough there was the suspicion of a draught. We laid a small fire and with no great optimism, lit it. To our joy it drew – filling the cave again with smoke, but not unbearably.

Snow lay in patches on the hill outside, so some was collected in a canvas bucket and melted in a mess-tin over the fire. The water was boiling by the time Morat returned, a tin of biscuits strapped to his back and his pockets filled with tea, tinned milk and sugar. He received a great welcome, and our mouths began to water at the prospect of the feast before us.

Without artificial assistance there was not enough draught to keep the fire alight, so we took it in turns to crawl down the little funnel and, lying full length, blow till we could blow no longer. Then we crawled out again backwards and made way for the next human bellows. An added difficulty was the fact that we had only one mess-tin in which to melt the snow, boil the water and brew the tea. But we drank in relays, and at last everyone had had a good drink of strong, sweet, hot, wonderful tea. The effect was extraordinary: our spirits went up with a bound; we no longer minded the drips that fell down our necks with such devastating accuracy; we started to talk and laugh – all except Alpino.

Poor Alpino! For two hours in the smoke and semi-darkness he had been struggling to erect his shelter. Half a dozen times he had nearly succeeded, only to see as often his edifice of string, sodden ground-sheets and bits of stick collapse on the ground. He was nearly weeping and all the time talking to himself... 'Oh! God, why was I born a man to endure this misery? Why was I not born an ass? Why was I born at all?...' As the silly structure collapsed yet again I saw the tears in his eyes and ordered him to stop. Only then would he accept his portion of tea.

'Where's Munzi?' David asked suddenly. 'Munzi!' he called. There was no reply.

'My God!' I said. 'What's happened to him?'

No one had noticed his disappearance, but he was so unobtrusive that this was not altogether strange.

'He came into the cave all right,' said Drake. 'I followed him in when we arrived.'

'Perhaps he wandered out again,' I suggested. 'He had a bad attack of malaria on him.'

'Munzi!' David called again.

The pile of gear on which I was sitting stirred a little, and a muffled voice said: 'Yes?'

I jumped up and began to delve into the stack of guns and packs and blankets. At the very bottom lay Munzi. As Drake shone his torch he looked up smiling, his spectacles hanging by one ear. We pulled him to his feet and gave him some tea.

The malaria had made him feel ill, he explained, so he had lain down on the slimy rocks and fallen asleep. In the darkness we had covered him up.

'But didn't it hurt when I sat on you?' I asked.

'No,' he replied. 'I only woke up when I heard my name called.'

It was now about six o'clock and dusk had fallen outside, putting an end to the little light that had come through the exit-hole. The best thing we could do was to lie down and sleep. We reconnoitred for sleeping places and shared out the groundsheets and blankets. Morat chose to sit on some rocks which were jagged but dry, and Alpino joined him. Drake found a place on his own to lie down; Munzi and Tallei bedded close together, and so did David and I. The ground we chose was a patch of wet shale, but we elected to put up with the damp in order to be able to stretch out flat. We had a ground-sheet under us and my rain-coat over us, and when we pulled it over our heads we could hear the water-drops come plopping down on it. With masculine reticence we avoided physical contact to begin with, but before dawn the cold and wet had driven us to lie as close as two puppies.

David and I stood on the ledge outside the cave, each wrapped in an army blanket, watching through my glasses the hill opposite and ready to bolt back into our hole if we saw a sign of the enemy. The wind flapped the corners of our blankets and occasionally there was a scurry of rain, but wind and rain were preferable to the plipping and plopping that continued ceaselessly inside the cave. We had stood on the ledge for two hours, sometimes talking, but for the most part silent.

'When will Morat be back?' asked David.

For some reason or other Morat had failed to change his clothes the previous day, and soon after dawn had been despatched again to do so. 'Tell him,' I had said to Munzi, 'that we are not going to spend a second night in this cave. Unless a message comes from Dukat to the contrary we're going to cross that mountain tonight, come what may.' Morat had shrugged and departed.

'He could be back by noon,' I answered, 'but he'll probably take much longer than he need.'

There was a long silence. Suddenly, and with a deal of irony in his voice, David blurted out: 'Balkan Campaign, nineteen forty-three!'

I wished David had not said that. God knows we all felt depressed, but the best service we could do each other was to keep our depression to ourselves. Certainly I had no energy to spare on coping with David's disillusionment. I could have answered that it was no use his resenting a world that turned out contrary to his expectations, but that would only have sounded unctuous and done no good. So I asked: 'What made you take on this kind of work?'

'Because I thought it would give me action.' David snorted. 'Seems I was wrong.' I made no comment, so he went on: 'Soldiering in England was deadly dull last summer. The German invasion was obviously 'off', and the signs were that my regiment was not going to be used when we came to invade the Continent. It looked as though we were going to be shipped off to Palestine or some such place to do frontier patrol. I didn't go much on the idea of patrolling some damned frontier when there was a war on in Europe; after all, soldiering is my profession. Then one day we got a letter, all very secret, asking for volunteers – 'for hazardous work in Occupied Europe', I think it said something like that. It sounded to me like my chance to get a crack at the Hun and...' He made a grimace, 'here I am.'

'Then you hadn't expected "Balkan Campaign, forty-three" to be anything like this?'

'Good Lord no! Back in Cairo they told us a lot of tales that we'd be welcomed with open arms by the inhabitants, that they'd give us all we needed and not allow us to pay for a thing, and that from the moment we hit the ground we'd be in the midst of the fighting.'

'Perhaps there are parts of the Balkans where it's like that,' I said.

David merely grunted, pulling his blanket closer round him and gazing at the hill-side opposite with a hostile blue eye.

Though I did not resent our altered condition as David did, I had to admit that it called for considerable re-adjustment. Until now I had pictured us sallying forth from Grama to do desperate deeds against the enemy, returning triumphant to our snug base. Well, the snug base was snug no longer – was not even a base; we had little or no food; we were out of wireless contact with our Headquarters and God alone knew when we would regain it. Now we had more immediate adversaries than the Germans: cold, fatigue, sickness, the tortuousness of our Albanian allies, our own depression. All right, I thought; so be it. Now it is going to be a test of endurance. In my battle-dress pocket my hand touched the leather photograph-case. It would be another facet of my gift to Ann.

Possibly our minds had been following similar channels, for David said irrelevantly: 'Anyway, I'm glad I've got my prayer book back. My wife gave it to me.'

Something made me ask: 'Are you a Catholic?'

'Yes,' he answered. 'I became one quite recently.'

'Why did you do that?'

'All sorts of reasons. It seems to me the only way to obtain any happiness.'

'Do you believe that there is such a thing?

'Don't you?' he countered.

'I doubt it. Content – through achievement, yes. Ecstasy – very rarely. That's all.'

'I had a more particular reason,' David continued, 'I'm a great believer in marriage – particularly my own. Marriage nowadays is treated so damn lightly, and I'm determined that mine's going to last.' He fell silent, his big, handsome face looking doleful and abstracted.

Of what a strange mixture, I thought, was the man compounded.

Behind that outward reserve and those abrupt phrases of understatement was a dreamer, an emotional romantic. In a previous century he would have been a crusader. The last two weeks must have indeed been galling to him, not least in that he found himself, a professional soldier, under me, an amateur. And yet I knew that there was in David, instilled into him by birth and training, a sense of duty that would be quite unshakable and which, for all his moodiness, made him a very solid and welcome companion at this time. I made some attempt to tell him so.

At last it became too cold to stand outside any longer and we made our way back into the cave. Here an operation was in progress. Finding that his hands were, if possible, worse, Munzi had submitted to Drake's surgery. The corporal's only instrument was a razor-blade, but he wielded it with great firmness and Munzi made not a sound. The relief was almost instantaneous; within an hour he could move his fingers again.

It was about midday when we heard the sound of voices outside. Silently each of us put out a hand for his weapon, while, slowly and cautiously, Drake crept up the tunnel and peered out. Certainly the voices were Albanian, but that did not necessarily mean that they were friendly. For a moment Drake's body blocked the hole, then he moved on and the watery light streamed in again, while from outside we could hear the corporal's voice and laughter added to that of the Albanians. The moment of tension was over. We relaxed, and one after another scrambled out into the open to see who had arrived.

Of our famous guards, three who had not previously put in an appearance stood there grinning at the alarm they had given us. The misfortunes of others were the only jokes at which Albanians laughed, the height of comedy being when another man was killed; as we now emerged from our cave the three guards fell about with laughter.

'Munzi,' I said, 'will you tell these apes to stop laughing and quickly.'

They sobered up when Munzi spoke to them, and one produced a folded piece of paper from his pocket. It was from the head of the village guard and was written in Italian.

'Dear Mister Major' (it ran), 'the Germans say they know you are in the area of Dukat. They say that they will come to look for you with many soldiers and that we must guide them. So it is very important that you keep well hidden, so that we shall not be able to find you.'

'Does that mean,' asked Drake, with a look of dismay, 'that we've to go on staying here in this – cave?'

'It certainly does not,' I answered. 'We're going to cross the mountain tonight. So long as we keep well hidden it doesn't matter which side of it we're on.'

I asked the bearers of the note when this search was expected to take place, but they would give no proper answer; either they were ignorant of what was going on in the village or else being deliberately evasive. They would not even give a firm reply when I asked them if the snow was too deep to make a night crossing of the mountain. On the other hand they made a very positive demand for payment which, once again, I thought it wise to satisfy.

'And now,' I said to Munzi when each had received his two pieces of gold, 'tell them to get the hell out of here. They're an offence.'

I was beginning to understand why Tom Keith had kept Albanians away from Sea View.

When the three had gone we turned back into the cave and began to prepare for our climb. Blankets were rolled and wrapped in ground-sheets; our gear was stowed away in packs so that we should be in readiness to start as soon as Morat got back. But of his return there was no sign.

The hours went by and it started to rain, first a drizzle, then a steady downpour. We sat in groups inside the cave, silently enduring the slow passage of time. But we were no longer depressed, for movement was imminent, and soon we would have quitted this cave which our spirits abhorred, so much had it become a symbol of our discomfiture.

David, Munzi and I held a council at one end of the cave. David was very unhappy about the situation. 'How on earth are we to get started again?' he asked. 'How are we to operate if we've lost our base?'

'David,' I said, 'I've no idea, and I don't think we can look as far ahead as that. The problem now is survival: just that.'

'What's the good of mere survival,' he demanded, 'unless it's to a definite end?'

'Look,' I replied, 'speculation is only going to confuse us and distract us from our immediate task – to keep our whole party in being. While we're alive we're the devil of a potential nuisance to the enemy. True we've lost our permanent base, and no doubt our stores too by now – for what the Germans don't find the Albanians will surely take – and I doubt if we'll ever again be able to maintain a permanent base on this stretch of coast: the Germans are sure to patrol it. But heavens! That doesn't mean the end. The Boche can't occupy the coast: his transport difficulties would be too great. In a little while we should be able to start running cargoes again – under the Germans' noses if necessary. The one thing to do now is to maintain ourselves and avoid compromising Dukat. If we can do that there's no reason why we shouldn't resume our work where we left off, as soon as the commotion dies down.'

David gave a little snorting laugh. 'I'm glad you're so optimistic.'

It was time to lighten the conversation.

'If I am optimistic,' I said, 'the fault is yours.'

'Mine?'

'Yes. No one could be put down with these laces in his boots. I can't tell you how grateful I am for them.'

'I don't see why they should make you optimistic,' said David.

'Because they're the only piece of equipment I have left that gives me real satisfaction. That old man on your father's estate did a good job. Every time I lace my boots I handle a piece of English leather that I know will endure through everything.'

I stopped, and touched Munzi's arm. 'Look there,' I said.

Half-way down the cave Drake was sitting on a rock, the light from the entrance falling on him. He was sitting absolutely motionless, and I wondered what thoughts were passing in his mind to hold him so rapt. The shaft of light fell dramatically across him, giving a parchment colour to his stained duffle-coat while behind him the cave stretched in deepening shades of grey till the far end was lost in obscurity.

'It is a picture by Caravaggio,' Manzitti breathed softly.

'And its title is "Balkan Campaign, nineteen forty-three",' I said.

The moment gave a sense of intimacy and the chance to ask Manzitti a question which I had been wanting to put to him.

'Tell me, Munzi,' I said, 'why did you volunteer to come back to Albania?'

'Because my malaria was cured and I wanted to be useful.'

'Your malaria obviously was not cured,' I said, 'and you could have been very useful in Italy.'

Manzitti faced me. He spoke quietly but, for the first time since I had known him, with emotion.

'I am an Italian,' he said. 'I am pr-roud to be Italian. We have been defeated; now we must show how a defeated nation can behave.' He produced the next words with physical effort. 'Now we must r-r-run, and jump... and do all that we can do.'

Gradually the gloom within the cave deepened as the night fell and still Morat did not return. Twelve hours almost he had been gone on an errand which should have taken no more than five. Added to the sound of the beating rain outside came the rumble of thunder, and a strong wind began to hoot across the entrance hole. Talk languished and died. We could not smoke, for our tobacco was exhausted. We sat in silence, waiting.

It was nine o'clock when we heard the sound of voices outside, then a slithering and scrabbling as bodies crawled into the cave. We shone a light, and there at last was Morat, together with the old man from Shepherd's Valley. Morat had no reason or excuse to give for his long absence and was in no whit abashed for it, but at least he had now changed back into his shepherd's costume.

'Tell him,' I said to Munzi, 'that we've decided to leave this cave and cross the mountain tonight.'

Morat grinned broadly, the rain-water still trickling down his face. '*Impossibile!*' he said with great decision. '*Impossibile!*' he repeated.

'That word is beginning to annoy me,' David muttered.

'Munzi,' I said, 'get it into this man's head that I am not prepared to argue. We are going to cross the mountain tonight, and – he – is – going – to – guide – us.'

There was some conversation between the two Albanians at the end of which Morat made a short speech to Manzitti.

'What does he say?' I asked.

'He goes on saying,' replied Munzi, 'that we cannot cross tonight. They have brought some food. They want us to eat now, then sleep, and at five in the morning we will start to cross. He also says that if we wish to go tonight we can go alone. They both refuse to guide us.'

As if to lend point to his words there came a terrific crash of thunder, then the sound of the rain falling in torrents. Morat caught my eye, his face in the torch-light full of expression.

'*Impossibile*,' he said again, quite quietly.

Then he sat down on a rock and untied a piece of sacking that he carried, revealing some lumps of cold goat. He gestured to us to help ourselves.

'I'm sorry, everyone,' I said, 'I'm afraid these two have got us by the short hairs. We can't find our way alone, and they clearly aren't going to budge. It seems we're to spend another night here after all.'

A silence followed my words. It was broken by Drake. 'I've got here,' he said brightly, 'something as I've been keeping for a time of real gloom. I reckon this is it!' From his pocket he produced a stub of candle and lit it. 'There we are. Just the job! Come on now Munzi, let's get stuck into this goat.'

The meat was good, but as we had no more wood left with which to make a fire we had to go without tea.

As we prepared to settle down for the night I saw the corporal making for his previous resting-place.

'Weren't you cold there last night all on your own?' I asked.

'I was a bit.'

I had a feeling that he had chosen this solitary couch because he neither wanted to bed down with the Italians nor yet intrude on his officers.

'Do you particularly like that spot you've chosen?'

'Not specially, sir.'

'Then why don't you come and sleep with Captain Marson and me? There's plenty of room under the blanket, and we'll all keep each other warm.'

He accepted with such alacrity that I knew my guess had been right.

A lot of water had collected on the cave floor during the day, and to spread our ground-sheet over the patch of shale was a mere gesture of formality; it was at once submerged.

'Come on, Drake,' said David. 'You're smallest. Get in the middle.'

But though sharing our bed Drake was still observing the proprieties, and I could feel that he was embarrassed by such proximity.

'Don't be so stand-offish,' I told him. 'The idea of this is to get as close as we can, not as far away.'

Drake chuckled. 'All right, sir, I'll get close. You'd better watch out though, because my wife says I nearly shove her out of bed in the night.' He pushed up close and in a minute was asleep.

Before morning both David and I had full sympathy with Drake's wife.

A dense, cold mist hung over the mountain as we climbed upwards, blanketing sound, reducing visibility to a dozen yards. We climbed steadily, if a little wearily, the old shepherd leading. Not even Morat could have found his way unaided.

The mist was doubly welcome, for besides cloaking our movement it put us on equal terms with any German patrol into which we might blunder. We were all half hoping for such an encounter as a relief for our pent-up feelings.

Near the summit we stopped to rest, and as we leant back against our packs there came from above us the sound of a man singing. It was a good, clear voice, faint at first but growing louder as the invisible singer came straight towards us. There was no way of telling the singer's nationality, for the song had no words – only a tune. He might be a German; he might be the Albanian guide of a German patrol. We flattened ourselves on the ground and there was a faint clicking sound as bolts went forward. Still the voice came nearer. Suddenly the old shepherd shouted out in his own language. The singing stopped abruptly; there was a moment's silence. Then came a shouted reply from out of the mist; another pause – then the song began again; but now the singer was walking away from us. For a minute longer we lay still, then, with a feeling of relief mixed with disappointment we rose and continued on our way.

The snow was not deep; it seldom came higher than our knees. Doubtless much of it had been melted by the heavy rain, but I felt sure that Morat had been wrong to raise such objections on the first night that we had wanted to cross.

At last we were on the topmost ridge and the old shepherd prepared to turn back. As he went round shaking hands David said with astonishment: 'Good God! Doesn't he want payment?'

'Don't worry,' I replied, 'I paid him before we started – and for the goat we ate last night as well.'

'Too bad!' said David. 'I thought we'd found the one Albanian altruist.'

The mist was not hanging on the inland side of the mountain, and we had to hurry down the two or three hundred feet of exposed hill-side that separated us from the cover of the trees.

As we lumbered through the snow my mind was busy with thoughts of the Albanians who had been round us during the last four days. Hodo had run like a rabbit at the first opportunity. Chela, though possibly for better reasons, had been quick to follow him. Ali's theft of what might well have been the whole of our gold had been followed by the clamour for payment by our so-called guards. Even Morat had misled us, and remained with us, I suspected, more out of hope for personal gain than through any feelings of loyalty.

My foot slipped on a hidden rock and I pitched sideways into a snow-drift.

'David,' I said as he helped to pull me out, 'I think I have never hated – really hated – a country so deeply as I hate Albania at this moment.'

Morat guided us down-hill for an hour until, at the head of a ravine that fell precipitously into Dukat valley, we came upon a large platform, or ledge. In the centre of the ledge, surrounded by tumbled rocks, was a deserted hut. It was a small bothy, just a framework of wooden stakes covered over with branches and leaves, but after our recent habitations it appeared a most civilised and splendid house.

Here Morat left us, saying that he would go down into the valley and tell Chela that we had arrived.

When he was gone we lit a fire in the shelter. It smoked a lot, as the wood was damp, but we felt it to be no great risk: the ledge was well enclosed by the walls of the ravine, and no track, such as a patrol would be inclined to follow, ran nearby. Alpino found a spring gushing from the rocks and made his discovery known to Drake.

'Acqua?' repeated the corporal. '*Malta bono*! *Malta bono*! Now we'll have a brew-up in no time.' He started busying around, invigorated as always by the prospect of tea. 'Now then, Alpino me lad, *prende queste*.' He held out the canvas bucket. 'And *prende acqua – subito subito. Capeesh*?'

Then the sun came out, the sun that we had not seen for days, and with the sunlight the whole atmosphere changed. Everyone began to smile and talk. Alpino sat on a rock, whistling to himself and cleaning boots with a salvaged tin of David's saddle-soap. From inside the hut came a shout from Drake. 'Tea up! Tea up! Come along now! Come and get it!'

It was not only the sun that caused the reaction; it was the escape from our dripping dungeon. Now we could see what was going on: the danger, if there were one, was not veiled and hidden from us. Down there was the valley; there was the road, and there were the trucks driving up and down it – Germans, to be sure, but at least visible. No longer were we dodging through mists and hiding in desolate caves from an intangible and possibly non-existent enemy.

I was lying by the fire in the shelter, the steam rising from my sodden clothes, when there was a cry of delight from Alpino.

'Signor Chela! *Come stai? Bene?*'

Then Drake's voice: 'Chela! Man, but it's good to see you!'

Before I could rise, Chela had come crawling into the shelter. 'Chela!' I cried.

'Major!' was all he said, but I could see that he was moved. And in that moment of encounter my anger against the man evaporated. There was something childish about him that was quite disarming.

Then the hut was bursting with men as they gathered round

him... 'What have you done with your battle-dress?'... 'My! that's a smart blue shirt!'... 'First time I've seen you shaved, Chela. You look ten years younger...'

'How long is it since we last saw you?' David asked.

'Three days,' replied Chela.

'Longest bloody three days I've ever lived,' observed Drake. 'Christ! That cave has put years onto me.'

When the greetings and enquiries had died down and the shelter was a little emptied of men, Chela's face became very serious.

'Major,' he said, 'I am ashamed.'

'Ashamed? What of?'

'Major – the gold: Morat has told me.'

'Yes, it's serious,' I admitted, 'but we'll find a way to deal with it. There are other more important problems.'

'But, Major, I am responsible. Ali is my man. For this he must die.' He was thoroughly enjoying his own drama.

'Chela,' I said 'the thing is done now. If we can recover the gold: good – very good. If not, well, it won't cost us the war. In any case I am much too full of other questions to talk for the moment about Ali and the gold.'

'But first,' said Chela, 'you must eat.'

And from two saddle-bags made of red carpeting he produced vermouth, hard-boiled eggs, brown bread, and – best of all – a tin of honey. He had remembered everything, even some packets of Albanian cigarettes. While we ate he told us his news.

The German patrol that had walked into Grama had descended into the village on the twenty-fifth: They had reported to the officer commanding the company billeted in Dukat, then departed quickly by car for Valona.

The German commandant had then summoned the heads of the village and told them that a British base had been discovered at Grama. He had said that a big search would soon be organised, in which the men of Dukat must act as guides for the German patrols. He had also asked them what they know of this British base.

'But of course,' said Chela with a sly grin, 'what do poor village boys know of such things? The heads of the village were very surprised to hear of this base; they said that it must be something to do with the Partisans.'

'And the Germans believed that?'

Chela shrugged. 'They controlled a few houses.' By 'controlled' he meant ransacked. 'They were looking for Allied material,' he explained.

'Did they find any?' I asked.

Chela smiled. 'We Albanians are very good at hiding things. We have much experience.'

'Was that all the Germans did?' I asked.

'They regulated some men.'

To be 'regulated', as Chela used the word, was to be set upon, beaten, smashed, and left half-dead.

'But the Germans were stupid,' he went on with a contemptuous expression. 'They regulated only ignorant men who knew nothing in any case. Now, if they had regulated me they might have discovered something, but no! With me they come and have dinner!'

'Have dinner with you?' I repeated, astonished.

'Yes, Major.' Chela giggled. 'Last night in my house I give a very good dinner for the German commandant. I kill a very fat turkey. We drink plenty of raki, and the German commandant make a long speech. But tonight will be better. Tonight I kill my best turkey for you.'

'What's the general feeling in the village?' I asked:

Chela giggled and looked uncomfortable.

'They are very nervous,' he replied.

'Of course they're nervous, but are they still friendly to us?'

'Major, you have friends in the village – be sure of that. But there are also many dirty fellows!' He made the words sound like offal in his mouth.

'Do they want to give us up to the Germans?' I asked.

Chela pulled a face of extreme distaste. 'Major, they are dirty fellows.'

He would say no more, but I was sure there were some who wished to betray us. No doubt they would receive a good price too. Chela's story rang true when he said that, since his return, he had been moving continuously between the village and his house in the valley, holding secret meetings, canvassing his friends for our support.

'Have you a plan now?' I asked.

He had. It was to descend into the valley at dusk and eat at his house; then after dinner to walk on across the road, across the river, and sleep at the house of Morat – where we would find Nigel's party already arrived.

'There's just one thing I'd like to know, Chela,' I said. 'Since you left us, has any German patrol, other than the one we saw, gone up into the mountain to search for us?'

'I hear that a force went up from Vuno as far as Grama. It is said that they have taken prisoner all the Italians.'

'Never mind what went up from Vuno. Has there been any search in this part of the mountain?'

'I think not: but now they will surely come.'

'In other words,' I said, 'we need never have passed two nights in that God-forsaken cave. We need not have spent an hour in it.'

'That is so.'

There was no adequate comment I could make.

Suddenly there came the sound of a rifle shot; it was followed by a second, then a third. There was a short pause, and then we heard the sound of two explosions, one after another. The noise echoed from hill to hill, reverberating back and forth across the valley. Chela became taut.

'Those sounded like hand grenades,' I said.

'It is our signal in the village that there is an attack,' he replied. 'Three shots followed by two bombs.'

'A Partisan attack?'

'Perhaps. We shall see.' He looked anxious. 'If you are ready, Major, we will go down now.'

On the lowest ridge above the valley we stopped to rest and to allow the last light to fade before the final descent to Chela's house. From below on the still air rose the familiar tonkle of goat-bells, the cries of the herdsmen driving the animals to their pens, and the barking of their dogs. Suddenly there came to our ears a new sound, piercing sharply through the domestic babel – a weird, half-musical cry; it was so distinctive that we looked at one another questioningly. Farther along the valley another voice took up the cry, high and shrill; then another and another, till all the air was filled with the wild ululation. It was a sound that I had heard once before from an Arab village.

Chela's face was set. 'It is the women crying,' he said. 'Men have been killed. Let us go on.'

Another half-hour and we had reached the meadows at the mountain's foot; silently and in single file we crossed the short-cropped grass. Chela walked towards his house, but instead of entering it he skirted the main building and made for a shepherd's hut four hundred yards distant. At a call from Chela the door was opened; we entered the single, large room, lit only by the fire that crackled at one end.

'You are all welcome,' said Chela. 'In this time I do not take you to my own house. That has to be reserved for the honoured Germans!'

He bustled around, helping men off with their packs, finding them a place to sit on the earthen floor where we made a great circle round the fire.

From the shadows emerged two women with blank, impersonal, peasant faces. They helped to serve out the huge meal of congealed turkey, entrails and spinach which had been prepared. The men sighed and stretched out before the blaze. For my part I wanted to eat, but had a fever which took away my appetite – a conflict that made me childishly cross.

Chela questioned the women about the alarm we had heard, and the wailing.

The village truck, it seemed, on its way into Valona, had been ambushed by the Partisans. The attack had taken place several miles from the village and before the men of Dukat could get to the scene the fight was over; the Partisans had vanished into the mountains, leaving many dead on the road and taking others with them as prisoners. The story was told by the sole survivor.

'Do I know any of the casualties?' I asked Chela.

'Gani is prisoner,' he said. 'That is a bad loss for the village.'

I thought back to my first meeting with the Old Men of Dukat and recalled a small man in a cloth cap who had appeared to me like a French mechanic, very smiling and affable.

'Who else?'

Chela questioned the women again, then turned to me with an expression of delight.

'Misli!' he said. 'They have taken Misli! Now the Partisans will shoot him, Carapizzi will be avenged, and we shall be saved the trouble. Oh! that is very good.'

'If the Partisans,' I said, 'are in a position to lay successful ambushes for the men of Dukat, it does not look as if they have been liquidated.'

'They have not been liquidated,' Chela answered bitterly, 'and the drive is finishing. The Partisans still exist – and Dukat has done some bad foolishness.'

He beat his forehead with his fist.

'What have they done?'

'They sent fifty men to fight against the Partisans. Always till now I have kept them from going outside the village to fight, but Mucho persuaded them to do this. Now where will it end?'

Where indeed, I wondered? Quite gone now were my hopes of reconciliation.

Chela gave us little time to digest our meal, for we had farther to go that night. Morat's house, for which we were bound, lay a mile down the valley to the south, and on the farther side of both road and river. For fear of German trucks we did not walk on the road but stumbled along beside it through the fields. A German staff car flashed past us coming from the direction of Vuno, and went humming on its way towards Valona. There was no other traffic.

After walking south for an hour we turned sharply to the left and crossed the road, then waded through the river that ran beside it. The water was not deep, not as high as our waists, but it flowed swiftly. On the farther bank we turned southwards again, treading warily in the pitch dark, never stopping for an instant for fear of losing touch with the man ahead.

Now we have halted and Morat has gone on alone. Though it is too dark to see, I can feel that there is a building ahead of us... Morat knocking at a door and calling softly; an answering voice from within, an alarmed voice. More talk, then a low call from Morat to come on. We file on, past out-houses, past a door behind which a large dog is whining and scratching with excitement, and in through the door of the house. Till we are all inside, and the door is closed behind us, no one strikes a light; then a lamp is lit, and we see we are in a small one-roomed house. We are all in each other's way, suddenly clumsy and huge in the confined space; there is a suppressed jostling and edging and easing off of packs; I cannot see them clearly but there seem to be some men lying round the dying fire at the far end of the room. Their heads emerge from under the bright-coloured blankets, and as the lamp burns bright I can make them out – Nigel, rubicund and cheerful, already grinning at us; Trotter, his spiky hair tumbling over his forehead; Cooper, still half asleep; and, like a lean patriarch, Butch suddenly comes to life and shouts: 'God damn! God damn!' then roars with laughter.

For a moment, before the talk breaks out, we stand in a ring grinning down at them – we still coated, booted, the river water sodden round our legs, our faces cold with the night air; they warm and sleepy round the fire, only heads and stockinged feet protruding from the furry red-and-white blankets, like figures from a fairy-story – like the Seven Dwarfs awakened on the stroke of midnight.

TEN

MORNING REVEALED that we were no more than three hundred yards from the main road, on which an unusual amount of German traffic seemed to be passing.

Chela left us early, saying that his presence was still needed in the village to prevent opinion from setting against us, but promising that he would return in the morning, bringing food.

To guard against being surprised, we took it in turns to observe the road, and I was crouching by the small, shuttered window when I saw a bunch of men, more or less in formation, coming up the road from the south. Though I was looking through my field-glasses I could not at first make out who they were: they were not in uniform, yet they were not in the usual Albanian dress. Then as they came closer I distinguished them clearly. Two German soldiers, wearing greatcoats, walked at the head of the column, two walked on each side, and two brought up the rear. In the centre, clothed in a peculiar miscellany of civilian clothes, walked the Italians from Grama Bay. They no longer wore battle-dress – God knows what had become of that – but there was no mistaking them.

One man dropped out from the centre of the group and bent down to fasten his boot-lace by the side of the road; the German guards paid no attention to him, but swung along unheedful. As the distance widened I thought I was going to witness an attempt at escape. But I was wrong. The man straightened himself, then went running after the others till he had caught them up.

I could not see the faces of the Italians clearly enough to make out their expressions, but I knew so well what they must be feeling that my stomach turned sick. And yet there was something so commonplace and matter-of-fact about the little cortege that I could hardly believe it was happening. I felt I needed to see some violent manifestation of their captivity; I needed to see them loaded with chains for my mind to accept the evidence of my eyes. It was incredible that there were Mikoli and Domenico – little Mikoli who had longed to see his wife in Bari, and Domenico who had sung his Neapolitan songs so gaily when we had been expecting a sortie – and that I had only to open the door and shout their names and they would hear me.

'Look!' I said to the others.

In silence, and taking turns at the narrow window, we watched the band as it passed into the distance, slowly growing smaller till it had disappeared.

Morat's family was numerous; they huddled at one end of the cottage, gazing earnestly at us and trying not to spoil their hospitality by any display of fear. They were clearly torn between a most natural terror of what would happen to them if the Germans were to raid their hut, and a devouring curiosity.

They followed every movement we made; if one of them had to leave the building for a minute he would come scurrying back, fearful of missing some never-to-be-forgotten antic of his strange guests.

To stay long in the house was impossible: we were exposing the family to too great danger. So that afternoon, in the still pouring rain, David and I sought a place where the party could shelter. Had it been any other time of year we could have lived in the open, but the torrential rain drove us to find some sort of roof.

It was a relief to be away from the rest of the party for a few hours. The continual intimacy with men of whom I was in command was beginning to be a strain: every hour of the day I was called upon to give decisions, and every process of thought that led to a decision had to be done through before their eyes. I was in the position of a conjuror who can never for a moment escape from his audience, or even distract their attention, while he prepares his next trick.

A few hundred feet above Morat's house, and still on the same inland side of the road, was a rough plateau. Here we found an abandoned goat-shed. One end of it had fallen in, but the rough thatch still held at the other and kept the rain out moderately well: we decided that it would have to serve.

When Chela returned in the morning there came with him two of the worst-looking scoundrels I have ever seen – unshaven, roughly clothed, hung about with weapons, and one of them with a truly awe-inspiring squint.

'Who are these two pretty fellows?' I asked him.

Chela looked shamefaced.

'They are the guards sent by the village to protect you,' he replied.

'I don't understand, Chela,' I said. 'Why can't we have some of our old guards? They were no earthly use, but at least I was not frightened of them.'

'These are the men you must accept, Major. So it is the will of the village. And I think perhaps it is good to be polite to them – no?'

We slipped cautiously out of Morat's house, covering our uniforms with pieces of Albanian garments, and with the two new guards walking in silence beside us, climbed up to the goatshed on the plateau.

Trotter surveyed the tumbled thatch and sodden floor.

'Ah!' he said. 'Just like Wolver'ampton.' And he gave a suck at his teeth.

'This plateau would be good for a dropping-ground,' Nigel suggested. 'Too many rocks about for men to parachute but it would be quite all right for stores.'

While some of us began to make the shed more habitable Nigel and David wandered off to examine the possibilities of the plateau. They had not gone far when there was an angry shout and a torrent of language from the guards.

Nervous and apologetic, Chela translated.

'They say that the officers are not to walk in that direction.'

David and Nigel were by now some four hundred yards off walking northwards.

'What on earth do you mean?' I said. 'They can walk where they please.'

'No, Major.' Chela's urgency lay in his voice; his face in front of the two guards betrayed nothing. 'I explain, but it is not good to say the words; otherwise these two may understand. The officers are walking towards a certain village where there are P-A-R-T-I-S-A-N-S. Do you understand?'

I nodded. He meant Trajas.

'These men are afraid that you will try to join these P-A-R-'

I cut in on him. 'I understand clearly. We are under arrest, eh?'

163

'Oh no, Major! But I think for a time it is wise to do what these dirty fellows want.'

When Nigel and David had been called back I collected everyone together. Uncomprehending, the two guards sat and watched us.

'I think I understand the form,' I said. 'Dukat is not quite sure at present whether we are a liability or an asset, so they've put us under arrest till they have made up their minds. They don't want to lose us to the Reds, so we're not allowed to make a move towards Trajas. If the Germans get on our trail and make things too hot for the village, they can always put themselves in the clear by betraying us. Hence the presence of these delightful Ugly Sisters.'

Nigel turned to one of them, smiling. The man stopped picking his teeth and took Nigel's offered hand, his yellow stumps showing in a grin.

'You slimy son-of-a-bitch,' said Nigel, with an air of ineffable charm. 'Instead of shaking your elegant hand I'd like to fetch you such a kick in the – ' And a stream of softly spoken abuse poured out.

Yellow-tooth grinned incomprehension.

'One thing,' I went on, 'which I think we must do at all costs is to make a pretence that we are still in wireless touch with H.Q. We'll have to do a great act of signalling our position and activities. It sounds rather theatrical and it will certainly be tedious to maintain, but if it prevents the Old Men of Dukat from making the wrong decision it will be worth it.'

'How can we pretend that when we've got no batteries?' asked Butch. 'These babes can't be so dumb as to think we can signal without a battery.'

'They may be,' I replied. 'Anyhow, let's try it on. Chela, get from these two men their exact names and let them understand that I have to signal them to our headquarters in London. Make it seem very important.'

The Ugly Sisters were visibly impressed: they spelled out their names to Chela, who wrote them down on a dirty piece of paper and handed it to me.

With great solemnity the radio operators set about rigging an aerial and preparing to transmit, while David, Nigel and I composed and enciphered a signal of gibberish.

When the mock enciphering was done Butch was for transmitting the signal at once. We explained to him that, to make the pretence a little more real, he ought to wait for the hour exactly before he could go on the air.

We all acted our heads off. Butch got so carried away that it took him fifteen minutes to 'transmit' the signal and another fifteen to 'receive' a supposedly incoming message: it was a tremendous performance and the two guards watched intently.

'They're swallowing it!' said Drake. 'Keep going, Butch. You're doing fine!'

Suddenly Swivel-Eye addressed a question to Chela in Albanian. Chela, with a very odd expression, turned to me.

'He wants to know,' he said, 'how you can signal without a battery?'

The question was so devastating that for a moment I could think of no way to answer it. David moved suavely into the breach.

'Very good question, that,' he replied, in the tone of a teacher answering questions at the end of a lecture. He moved to the set on which Butch, the lifeless ear-phones clapped over his head, was still rattling the key. 'See this?' He pointed to a small square object – part of the mechanism. 'Emergency battery. Splendid little job.'

Chela translated, and Swivel-Eye nodded with an air of sagacity.

'Mother of God!' said Nigel. 'I declare he's going to believe it!'

And he did. He had had something to do with signals years ago, Swivel-Eye explained, when he was in the Albanian Army, and he reckoned this emergency battery must be a fine thing.

Yellow-Tooth looked admiringly at his knowledgeable friend. Our story was believed. The crisis was passed.

As we lay down to sleep that night, David said: 'I thought Dripping Cave was the lowest we'd ever touch – but I was wrong.'

Certainly our fortunes were at a very low ebb, and the days that followed were a series of laborious efforts to re-establish ourselves.

Our main object was to make wireless contact with Italy, and to this end we sent an expedition with mules, provided by Chela, to try to cross the snow-covered mountain and recover from their hiding-places at Grama our petrol, batteries and charging engines.

When the expedition had departed Nigel came to me.

'I must push off south,' he said. 'I don't want to leave you, but after all this is not my area, and I don't feel that I'm being very useful here.'

'You'll have no wireless,' I told him.

He laughed. 'Neither have you now. So what's the odds? I'll go and find Harvey,' he went on, 'and use his set till I can get another of my own.' As an after-thought he added: 'I hope he's not on the run too!'

I was sorry to see Nigel go, but he was right. Dukat was not his area and I had no right to try and keep him. I was worried, though, about his wireless operator. Cooper was the best educated of the operators, a quiet, well-mannered boy of twenty-three, and he had seemed promising when he first arrived. But he was soft-fibred, and in the last ten days had fast disintegrated. He was filthy dirty; there were no laces or even string in his boots; he had torn the seat of his trousers on a rock and had left the rent unpatched, so that the tail of his shirt hung out; he had ceased to say 'sir' to his officers. Nor could either kindness or firmness pull him together; he had become apathetic.

Nigel shrugged his shoulders. 'There's nothing to be done about him. I can't ask to have him changed now!'

The Ugly Sisters showed great interest in the departure.

'What are we to tell them?' asked Chela. 'If they know he is going to help the Partisans they will have him stopped. They might try to kill him.'

'Tell them,' I said, 'that we have had a signal ordering the captain down to the Greek frontier. He is going down there to prevent the Greeks from trying to grab any of the South of Albania when the Germans withdraw. That should satisfy them.'

It did: so much so that Nigel could hardly avoid their embraces.

'There's one thing about losing all your kit,' said Nigel, as he stood ready to leave. 'You have no trouble in deciding what you're going to take.'

Apart from his gun, all his possessions would now go into his raincoat pockets.

'If you meet Harvey and get on the air quickly,' I said, 'you might tell H.Q. that we're all right. They may be worrying about us.'

Good-bye was said very casually.

'So long,' Nigel said.

'Good luck,' we replied.

Then he walked off in the rain with Cooper trailing behind him.

For all that our hut was abandoned and half-ruined, we soon discovered that, like everything else in this part of Albania, it had its price. One day, egged on no doubt by the Ugly Sisters, there appeared an ancient crone: the hut, she claimed, was hers; she wanted rent for it.

Chela knew the old witch, and told us her history.

Years ago, when she was still a young bride, her husband had been murdered by another man. Neither she nor her dead husband had a single male relative to avenge his death: the duty fell to her. For years she had lived alone in the mountain, nursing her revenge, until at last one day she had acquired a pistol. She descended from the mountain; she went into Valona – only to find that the man she sought, her husband's murderer, had long been dead. Undeterred, she had found substitutes. Two male members of the family still lived: she shot them both dead. Then she returned to her hovel in the mountain. Her life's mission was completed.

I looked with wonder at the old hag: love, passion, sorrow, hatred – all these she had known. And now she sat gazing at us with her sad, blank face, solemnly picking her nose.

I paid her the rent she asked.

A furious outbreak of firing one morning brought us running to the edge of our plateau to look down into the valley. We thought the war had really come at last to Dukat, but it turned out to be nothing but a *feu de joie*. Gani had been released by the Partisans and had made his way back to Dukat. Every man in the valley must have loosed off a dozen rounds that morning; some were even firing machine-guns into the air.

'Where the hell do they get all that ammunition to waste?' asked David.

'Stolen from our dump, no doubt,' I answered.

I thought to what use the Partisans could put those bullets, and cursed the Balli for their fecklessness.

'But why have the Partisans set Gani free?' I asked Chela.

'I do not know,' he replied. 'But it is good for Dukat. He has an influence in the village.' Then his face fell. 'They have also freed Misli,' he said.

'In God's name,' I asked, 'why?'

'I do not know. We shall find out.'

That night David, Munzi and I were bidden to a feast which Chela gave in Gani's honour. The meeting was held in Chela's own house, as it was thought that such a domestic festivity would be safe from German interruption. All the important men of the village were gathered to welcome Gani from the jaws of death, to wolf as much of Chela's food as they could cram into their bellies, and to hear what I had to say to them.

At last the toasts were ended, the goat bones had been picked clean and the debris removed. Then I spoke, with Munzi translating. I was not in a very strong position, so I decided to attack.

'I have some hard words to say,' I began. 'And since we are friends, I will be honest and not try to soften them.' Then I reminded them of their assurances about the guards, and I complained that at the first sign of danger the guards had vanished – only to return, insisting on their payment, when the danger was past. One of their villagers, instead of helping us, had stolen our gold; nor had he yet been apprehended.

'This,' I declared, 'is not the conduct of the brave men that I know you to be.'

'Sssst! Listen!' The little man in the neat white cap, who had been the spokesman when first I met the village elders, raised a warning finger and looked towards the roof. As we sat listening we could hear the sound of a plane.

'Whose is that plane?' he asked portentously.

'How should I know?' I replied.

'It is a German plane,' he stated. 'Above us at this very moment lies a German plane, sent perhaps to bomb our village for helping you, and yet you accuse us of not being brave...'

There was a murmur of assent in the smoke-filled, crowded room.

'That is ridiculous,' I replied. 'The Germans could destroy your village in a far easier way than by sending a plane, at night, to bomb it. That plane,' I went on, pausing a moment to make a show of listening to the engine note, 'is a British bomber: I can tell now by the sound of it. Perhaps it is flying overhead to see if it can pick up a signal from me. The Allied Headquarters are very interested in what happens to this mission. Apart from obvious military reasons, we are the only mission in Albania that is in friendly contact with your party, the Balli.'

I gave them a minute to take in that point; and all the time the plane went circling round and round overhead. I had no idea if it was an Allied plane or not, but if it was I heartily wished I could speak to the pilot a thousand feet or so above my head.

'Fly off, old man,' I wanted to say. 'You're doing me no good here at all.'

Their fears seemed a little allayed by this explanation. They even apologised for the behaviour of the guards, and assured me that Ali would be caught and the gold restored. I was asked to proceed.

'Victoria', 'Operation Victoria', was drumming in my mind. Dukat controlled the coast-road up which the German divisions would be forced to come. Here we could effect a tremendous slaughter when the withdrawal from Greece began. Somehow I had to persuade these men to play their part in the battle.

'A fortnight ago,' I said, 'I talked with Mucho. He spoke to me in his capacity as the leader of the Balli party and he made me certain promises: since then I have had no word from him and none of the promises have been fulfilled. So it seems that the Allies cannot depend upon the Balli as a party. Now I speak to you simply as the leaders of Dukat, as the head men of this village.'

My words went through the double process of interpretation, from English into Italian, from Italian into Albanian. The men became silent, listening intently. Now, I thought, was the time to hit them where it would hurt.

'You men of Dukat,' I said, 'have been for a long time in the midst of two wars, a great international war and a lesser civil war, and yet you have thought that you could avoid fighting and so preserve your homes and your flocks. That was a foolish policy, but so long as you took no aggressive step you still had a chance. But what have you done now? You have gone out to fight against the Partisans. You have fought shoulder to shoulder with the Germans. That was a grave fault – but you have made a worse one yet: you have not succeeded. The Partisans have not been destroyed. All you have done is to incur their bitter enmity, and also the enmity of the Allies who were supporting them.'

I had Munzi translate so far before I went on.

'This war,' I continued, 'is going to end in an Allied victory. You know that as well as I do. If a single man in this valley doubted it I should be betrayed to the Germans tomorrow. And what will become of you when the war is over, as it soon will be? What position will your village be in then?... Surrounded by your Partisan enemies, and with no sympathy or support from the Allies.'

Babel broke out when this was translated, but we managed to get them quiet again.

'You have one chance,' I said, 'and only one, to show where your sympathies really lie and save yourselves. A German withdrawal from Greece is expected shortly to take place.'

'When?' asked the spokesman quickly.

'I cannot tell you exactly, but soon. When that happens, Dukat must fight. Your houses and your flocks and your families may be destroyed, but better that way than in fighting your own countrymen: and that, I am convinced, will soon be your alternative.'

This speech ended in a dispute between them all, so violent that I thought someone was going to get knifed. I sat quietly in a corner of the room hoping that that 'someone' would not be me, and thinking that this was hardly a peaceful homecoming for the newly liberated Gani.

Yet in spite of the dissension some result was achieved. The Old Men of Dukat decided that they would collaborate as a community with the Allies, and a committee of six was appointed to work with me.

When at last the guests had put on their shoes, shouldered their guns and dispersed to their homes, still arguing, I had a chance to ask Gani his story. It was quite simple, he said. When the bus was ambushed he had been captured and dragged off into the mountains, but when at last he was brought for trial before Petchi and Besnik, the Partisan leaders had found no charge to bring against him – he had never fought against them, he had never collaborated with the Germans – and so he had been released.

'And Misli?' I asked. 'Why did they let him go?'

'Because he killed Ismail Carapizzi.'

'What!' I cried.

'Yes.' Gani gave a wry smile. 'They were going to shoot him because he had fought against them, but when it was pointed out that he had murdered Carapizzi they let him go.'

'But why, will you tell me? Why?'

'Because they said that Carapizzi was a renegade communist and deserved to be killed, and that therefore Misli had done a very good deed for which he should be rewarded.'

David and I looked at each other. There was nothing to say.

Gani could, or would, give little information as to the present condition of the Partisans. He believed they had taken a severe beating, but he stated that, apart from sporadic actions, the main German drive against them seemed to be over.

There was something in Gani's manner which I could not quite understand. He seemed to be concealing something, and I had a strong suspicion that he had come to terms with the Partisans. Possibly, in return for his life, the little man had agreed to act as an agent for them in Dukat.

There ensued days of endless talking, in which we discussed where, and how, and under whose command, our machine-gun positions should be placed; we discussed the evacuation from the village of the women and children; we discussed every possible aspect of our part in 'Victoria'. But, since the committee was composed of the representatives of each warring and mutually suspicious faction in the village, we got exactly nowhere. In a climax of ineptitude the committee was abolished and another one set up.

'God damn these Old Men of Dukat!' said Butch one day, in one of his rare moods of loquaciousness. 'I tell you, Major, they're playing us for suckers; they don't mean business. This committee meets to discuss plans with you, and I'll bet my life that every time they make you a promise they run straight home and form another committee to see how they can get out of keeping it.'

'You may be right,' I replied.

'I'm damn sure I'm right,' he insisted. 'And it just burns me up. Sons of bitches!' he added.

The party returned that had made the expedition to Grama. On the first attempt they had struggled to within a hundred feet of the summit when the animals, up to their bellies in snow, could go no farther. One of them fell down a cleft that was concealed by a deep drift and had to be shot. Two days later they had tried again, and this time they had got across. But they brought back with them only the batteries and charging engines; all the petrol had been stolen.

'There were a lot of empty tins with German labels lying around the old camp,' Drake reported. 'I should reckon a company must have come up from Vuno and camped there for a day or two.'

'It may have been they who took the petrol,' David suggested.

'I should hardly think so, sir,' said Drake. 'Else why would they leave the batteries and charging engines? No, sir, it's these – Albs that's done it.'

But Chela obtained petrol for us, stopping a German truck on the road and offering the driver eggs in exchange for a litre of petrol. He was delighted with himself, and came running up the mountain to give us the bottle and regale us with the story of his craftiness. The din of the charging-motor was like music, and when that evening Drake received a reply to his call sign, we let out a shout of joy and danced about. After fifteen days off the air we had regained contact.

As though to expiate his desertion of us on the first day of the 'run', Chela was now indefatigable on our behalf. Every day he brought us food from his house in the valley – black bread, dry goats' cheese, hard-boiled eggs. Without him I think we should have starved, though Butch did manage one day to shot an old, stray rooster with his revolver. He brought it back, blown almost to pieces, after a tremendous chase through the bushes.

All this while a great search for Old Ali had been going on. The recovery of the gold was a matter which the village had taken deeply to heart: no doubt they were horrified to think that the whole of what they considered to be their own legitimate loot was in danger of being scooped by the village reprobate. It was our daily pastime to watch through the field-glasses the progress of the hunt in the valley below, and I was continually amused by the irony of the situation. Little did the Germans know, as they drove up and down the road, that the posse of black-jacketed Albanians to whom they had just waved were engaged in a desperate hunt for five hundred pieces of British gold.

And one morning they caught Old Ali. Days and nights he had passed in holes on the mountain-side, but at last the need for food and warmth had driven him to his sister's house. He had been surrounded while he slept.

When he was hauled before me he fell on his knees, clutching me round the legs and trying to kiss my boots in token of repentance. His coat was lost, his shirt was torn, his cheeks and temples were sunken in, and his once jaunty moustache hung forlornly down.

I could not find it in me to be angry. I could only shake my head at him as at a naughty child and say: 'Oh, Ali, Ali!' And like a naughty child the old man pulled a face of pitiful remorse and sorrowfully shook his head too from side to side.

'Does he say why he took it?' I asked.

Chela replied. For all his talk of revenge and killing he now could scarcely conceal his smiles. 'He says he thought you were going to be killed, so he took the gold to save it from falling into the Germans' hands.'

We stood round Ali while he counted the money out in piles of ten. There were forty-eight little piles.

'Where are the other twenty sovereigns?' I asked.

With an air of injury at the imputation that he might have kept them, Ali set about counting the lot again. But half-way through he decided to come out with the truth – or something near it.

Two he had spent; eight he had given to a man as a bribe to keep silent... Might he be allowed, he asked, to keep the other ten as a reward for his honesty in returning the four hundred and eighty?

I told him that he could.

I was asked what punishment I wished given to the old man.

'None,' I said. 'There are some in Dukat more in need of punishment than Ali.'

He was led away, still wagging his head in sorrow at his own misdeeds.

Then David fell ill. One morning he complained of a fever and within forty-eight hours he was delirious. There was no way of telling what was wrong with him, and even if we had known it wouldn't have helped us, for we had no medicine – not even aspirin or a thermometer. We kept him warm and made him drink quantities of weak tea. I thought he was going to die.

The village chose this opportune moment to require of us that we moved our base. Our position, they pointed out, was known to all the villagers and shepherds, and might at any time become known to the Germans. Dukat had been able to disclaim knowledge of the base at Grama, but they would have no excuse if we were discovered on the plateau immediately above the village. Their complicity would be obvious.

'And how,' I asked the deputation, 'do you expect me to move? You can see for yourselves what state the captain is in.'

The deputation remained obstinate. The captain could be put on a mule.

I would have refused to budge had it not been for the arrival of a signal: 'Expect sortie containing your Victoria stores night 14th or following three nights. Boat will come Sea View.'

As this meant that several of us would have to cross Dukat mountain in any case, in order to arrange the reception, I decided that we might as well move the main body of the party at once.

Butch, Alpino and Lieutenant Tallei were sent off to Sea View. Manzitti and Drake were told to establish a base – a kind of half-way house – at the bivouac in Dukat mountain where Chela had come to meet us after the episode of the Dripping Cave. The litre of petrol obtained by Chela had soon been exhausted and no more had been forthcoming from the village, so both operators were told that they would have to rely on themselves somehow to get the petrol with which to run their charging engines. They were to do their utmost to maintain contact with Italy.

Trotter and I stayed behind with David, while the Ugly Sisters remained our all too close attendants, sleeping by our side in the hut at night, never more than a dozen paces distant by day. David was a good patient; he was conscious a lot of the time, and then he would lie quite still combating the fever. His delirium usually took the form of protest against some impossible task that had been allotted to him. 'I'm sorry,' he would say in a decisive voice, 'I'm really very sorry, but I simply can't do it.' It was a symptom, I think, of his feeling of oppression.

I left him one night to descend to Chela's house where Mucho had arrived. I went eagerly, hoping that he had come to bring news of effective Balli support. But he had nothing to say beyond pointing out that his life was in danger now from the Germans as well as from the Partisans.

'Somehow they learned of my visit to you in Grama,' he said, 'and now they are trying to catch me.'

No doubt the Germans had obtained this information from one of our Italians whom they had taken prisoner. The Italians had seen all that went on at Grama, and their interrogation was not likely to have been gentle.

Mucho sat cross-legged, staring into the fire. He looked downcast, but he smiled when he saw me stretch my legs out on the floor.

'Why do you smile?' I asked.

'Because we two, sitting here, are like symbols. You belong to a great people: you stretch out your legs and plant one foot in India and the other in Canada. I am a member of the smallest nation in Europe: it is fitting that I keep my legs tucked under me.'

He fell silent again, his fingers playing abstractedly with a string of amber, Mussulman beads. Though he would not admit it to me, I think he knew that his gamble had failed. The Partisans had not been destroyed; instead, his own party was more than ever implicated with the Germans.

Mucho left for Valona in the morning, and when he had gone Gani sidled up to me. He was always in and out of Chela's house.

'A letter has arrived for you,' he said, taking from his wallet a small screw of paper. It was typewritten, and from Besnik.

'Major,' it read, 'come to Gumenitza on day twentieth March. We have much to discuss.'

So Gani was acting for the Partisans. I looked at him, but his face revealed nothing.

'How am I to get away?' I asked. 'I have two guards with me day and night to prevent my making a move towards the Partisans. You know that.'

'They will let you go,' said Gani. His tone was assured. 'Your words the other night made an impression on the village. Now they think that through you they may reach a better understanding with the Partisans.'

'Then I had better tell the latest committee, whoever they are now, that I intend to go to Gumenitza on the twentieth.'

'The committee already know that you have been asked,' replied Gani quietly, 'and they have decided to let you go.'

Trotter met me outside the hut on my return. 'I think the captain's better, sir,' he said hopefully.

In the dark hut David lay on the floor. His face was waxen but cooler, definitely cooler. As I touched it I felt a flood of relief: he was not going to die.

'You're better,' I said.

'I am.' He gave a weak laugh. 'I'll live to be a major yet.'

'David,' I said, 'I'm going to leave you tomorrow night. Now that you're through the worst I think my job is to go over to Sea View and receive this sortie. Half the village is going to be there to stow the guns away quickly in the mountain, and there'll be hell's own mess if the Germans catch them at it.'

I went on to tell him of the invitation from the Partisans. He asked what date it was for.

'March the twentieth.'

'And what is it now?'

'The twelfth.'

'That gives me eight days. I'll come with you to Gumenitza.'

'You won't be strong enough.'

'Yes, I will. You see: I'll walk better than you can.'

Ever since Old Ali had returned the gold to me, I had been worried about its safety. The sovereigns he brought back I had put together with those I carried round my waist, as I thought it only right to be responsible for the stuff myself. But its weight was now too great to carry about. I had often thought of hiding it in a rock or hollow tree, but as I was under the constant surveillance of the Ugly Sisters I never found this possible. Even if I were to wander out of the hut during the night they would watch what I was doing and follow me. So when I left for Sea View I thought the only thing to do with the gold was to leave it in David's keeping. I pushed it under the pile of coats that served him as a pillow, and told him to mind it well.

On the night of March the thirteenth I crossed the main road and, with Chela, started up the mountain of Dukat. Snow was deep on the hill and it was not until the evening of the fourteenth that we reached the old cave at Sea View.

Butch and the two Italians were delighted to see us. They were existing with few blankets and little food, surrounded by the mournful debris of the camp. Sea View had not been tenanted since the Italians had left it in a hurry that night to come down to Grama, and the local shepherds had torn the place to bits. Everything they could carry they had looted, and what they could not carry they had wantonly smashed. The very floor of the cave had been grubbed up – no doubt in the search for gold that we might have left buried.

I asked Butch if he was in radio contact.

'I am now, but I shan't be much longer,' he replied. 'My battery is nearly flat, and I can't get petrol.'

'How did you get enough to charge your battery in the first place?'

He gave a short laugh. 'I bought back a litre of our own petrol from the shepherd who had stolen it from Grama. Now he says he's got no more left. Jesus!' he exploded. 'How I hate Albanians! Ignorant, yellow bastards!'

'Any sign of German patrols?' I asked.

'The shepherds are always screaming alarms,' said Butch. 'They come running, on an average, three times a day. But that's just their line of bull and we pay no attention. The truth is that a patrol comes down twice a week from the north. Luckily for us they always stop about a mile short of Sea View. Can't think why they don't come on a bit farther.'

He ruminated the point. The Germans' failure to walk that extra mile was clearly causing him a lot of thought.

'I shouldn't lose any sleep over it,' I said.

'No, sir!' He gave his abrupt laugh. 'But it don't seem natural somehow. They certainly oughter walk a bit farther and find this place.'

Alpino had found a baby rabbit, a fluffy ball of a thing no bigger than a child's fist, and on this rabbit they all doted. Butch in particular was quite jealous of it, and would begin to scowl if anyone but himself fondled it overlong.

One Albanian was in the camp, a messenger who was to go hot-foot to Dukat and call the villagers as soon as the ship arrived with the material.

The wind blew strong from the south that night and the sea was rough. It did not surprise me that there was no sortie.

On the fifteenth the wind dropped and the sea calmed, but still there was no sortie.

On the sixteenth Butch got a signal to say that a boat *had* come the previous night – but in error it had gone to Grama Bay. My temper that day was not improved by the demands of the shepherd who claimed to own the cave. He appeared and presented his bill for the rent of the cave during the weeks we had been absent from it. The occasional visitations of the German patrols from the north induced me to pay the bribe.

On the seventeenth Butch's battery was quite flat and he could not make contact, but though we had no way of knowing if the boat would come or not, we signalled for five hours both that night and the next. It was in vain.

On the morning of the nineteenth I left Sea View; I could wait no longer. As it was, I should have to do some hard walking to be in Gumenitza by the twentieth.

David and Trotter were sound asleep when I reached the hut on the plateau round about midnight. All had been quiet during my absence, they reported. David looked miraculously recovered.

'Do you really feel fit enough to make the walk tomorrow?' I asked him.

'I'll make it all right,' he said.

'Hallo! Where are the Ugly Sisters?' I had suddenly noticed that they were missing.

'Don't know,' David replied. 'I woke up one morning, soon after you left, and found they'd gone; they've never been back since. And I certainly haven't asked for them,' he added.

Whatever had caused their removal, after so long and so close a watch over us, I could not think. Anyhow, it solved any difficulties we might have had in departing for Trajas in the morning.

I rolled myself up in a blanket and lay down by the fire. My lice and fleas usually kept me awake for a time, but not that night, and I was almost asleep when I heard David say:

'Why on earth did you take the gold with you? It must have weighed a ton.'

'Don't be a fool,' I answered drowsily. 'It's under your head.'

I heard David sit up.

'Under my head?' he repeated slowly.

'Certainly. I put it there when I left. Don't you remember?'

David was silent. I sat up too.

'Christ! Don't tell me it's gone.'

David said with an effort: 'I was a bit vague about things when you left. I thought you'd put it under my head, but when I found it wasn't there one morning I thought I must have dreamt the whole thing, and that you had surely taken it with you.'

A sudden idea struck him. 'Our guards! It was after they'd gone that I found it was missing. Do you think...?'

'I have no doubt of it,' I said. 'The Ugly Sisters have come in to money.'

ELEVEN

IN TRAJAS we collected a guide – a solid, sullen-looking man.

David was still very weak and pale; although we climbed slowly the sweat poured from his face. But he managed to keep going.

Somewhere on the top of Gumenitza mountain we sat down and ate the hard-boiled eggs and bread that we carried.

David said: 'I suppose some people would envy us sitting here eating our lunch. After the war they will even pay to come to this country.' Then he asked abruptly: 'What would be the flying time from here to England?'

'Eight hours, perhaps,' I answered.

'Eight hours,' he repeated, pulling at his beard, and with an expression that was the nearest approach to perplexity that I ever saw in his face. 'You know,' he said, 'when I came to Albania I thought this was going to be a straightforward job of fighting, for ends which I understood. And now...'

'And now?' I prompted.

'And now I'm losing my way,' he said indignantly. 'I know why I'm fighting this war...'

Yes, I thought, you're fighting it because of those blue eyes and that fair hair. You're fighting it for the English wife you love, and for the English meadows that are your heritage.

'...but if I stay here much longer,' he continued, 'I shall get confused. This place is like another world.'

'It is another world,' I said. 'And London may be only eight hours distant, but this still remains another world.'

'A damned unattractive world,' said David.

'Agreed,' I said. 'A most unattractive other world – but still, don't forget, only eight hours distant from London.'

David gave me a look, then turned to gaze at the tumbled mountain-tops, at the valley of Dukat below where, in the far distance, we could see the Germans busy installing an anti-aircraft gun.

'I never want to see it again,' he said. 'It gives me a feeling of foreboding. Everything here is a grey colour: the skies are grey, the mountains are grey, even the people are grey – with fear. I hope I don't die here.'

'You're getting morbid,' I said. 'Come on. Let's move.'

From a distance Gumenitza appeared to be deserted, but as we drew closer we could make out through the glasses a group of men standing outside a building, which I took to be the village school. The dissimilarity of their clothes showed that they were not Germans, so they must be Partisans: we pushed on.

I thought there was less sign of life in the village since I had last seen it – less cattle, less dogs, less men. By one of the outlying huts a tiny girl raised her fist and squeaked: 'Death to Fascism!' at us. She looked dismayed when we only replied: 'Hallo!'

In the centre of the village we met two Partisan girls, both rather shapeless and greasy, dressed in breeches, and with rifles slung over their shoulders. We asked if Besnik were there and they replied that he was... 'and would we wait a minute while they spoke of our arrival'. We were not kept waiting long, for in a minute there came clattering out of a near-by house Besnik, Petchi and a crowd of followers. There was a great deal of enthusiastic hand-shaking – enthusiastic and as far as Besnik was concerned, quite sincere, I felt. Certainly I was very glad to see him, and as we walked down the tiny street with the others in a wedge behind us I was very conscious of the last words he had spoken to me – 'You too are young, and the young do not fail each other' – and I was troubled; for though the failure had been unintentional, unavoidable even, still it had been failure. Besnik, however, showed no sign but of the warmest friendship, and smiled, and laughed, and took my arm as we walked. Soon we were seated on the floor in the room where I had slept on my first visit to Gumenitza, the fire burning and glasses of raki in our hands.

'Dinner will not be ready for half an hour,' said Besnik. 'Let us not talk of serious things till we have eaten. Do you agree?'

I did, for I was glad of the opportunity to feel my way into the atmosphere before the arrival of the battle which I felt must be imminent. The raki slipped down, our feet steamed in front of the fire, and all the while Besnik teased us about our recent misfortunes, translating from French into Albanian for the benefit of Petchi. The commander seemed changed, I thought, quieter and more thoughtful.

David did not speak: indeed he could not. But he looked knowing, and very English, and occasionally said: '*Si, si*,' when an answer was obviously in the affirmative.

I avoided mention of the Partisans' own experience as I thought I should be hearing plenty of that before long, and the conversation had reached Winston Churchill – how incongruous his name sounded in that room! – when the inevitable goat made its appearance. As usual also, the plate was emptied and the bones gnawed clean in under five minutes; then, with a few belches and a general loosening of belts we settled down for the evening's business.

After agreeing that we would dispense with an interpreter as we could each understand the other's French, Besnik began. He spoke very quietly, with great deliberation, looking into the fire for the most part, but occasionally raising his eyes to mine.

'When we last met, Major, you promised us help. Since then we have never seen you, and we have received no help: none, absolutely none: This has made a great impression on us. Still, I do not now wish to speak reproaches for the past. That is over: let us forget it. I speak now of the present. As you know, the Brigade has withstood a very strong attack during the last weeks. We have now reached a stage where, if we do not receive help quickly, we shall cease to exist. I speak very frankly; we must, I repeat we must, have help.'

I translated the speech to David, who grunted and pulled at his beard. Petchi gazed moodily into the fire. Besnik and another Partisan officer, a good-looking man in civilian clothes, sat cross-legged waiting for me to reply. The room was very quiet.

'I can imagine that you need help, and Captain Marson and I are here now to bring it to you. In a minute we will discuss it. First, although you say you do not wish to discuss the past, I want to explain why you have never received the help I promised you. Without doing that we shall not understand each other now.'

Whenever I paused Besnik translated to his two friends. Now they all turned to me, their faces already set in unbelief.

'I made you my promise of help on January the ninth. On the sixteenth I arrived at Vuno, and discussed the method of off-loading and transport of stores. I left my soldier, Black, to establish a base at the monastery, and a few days later I sent Doctor Georgie to join him. If you do not believe in this evidence of good faith I cannot help you. Incidentally, I wrote a long letter to you from Vuno, but you never replied, though Black was there to act as messenger.

'Now, I told you when we met that I would try to ship you the first load of stores by the beginning of February. By the beginning of February the boat which was to bring those stores from Italy was loaded and ready to sail, but by that time the Germans had started their drive against your Brigade and we had lost contact with each other. I sent an officer to Vuno to reconnoitre, but he could not get through. He came back and reported to me that the whole area was overrun by the Germans, that the Partisans in those villages had left for the mountains, and that those who were left were hostile. There was nothing to be done but to cancel the sailing of the boat.

'Next came a period during which I could have come inland and looked for you. But where was I to look? Your own men seldom know where you are when a German drive is on. It might have taken me a fortnight to find you; I might have been unable to find you at all. Further, on the third of February the Germans moved into Dukat, thereby threatening the security of the one base I had. Finally, since the twenty-third of February, when the Germans discovered our base, we have been fully occupied with maintaining ourselves and have had small facilities for giving help to others. This has been the first chance I have had to make contact; I came at once.'

'Major,' said Besnik, 'I have told you we do not wish to speak of the past. That we were out of touch in the time of our greatest need was your fault, in that you made your base with the Balli in Dukat and not with us, where you should have been from the start.'

'I did not make a base there: I inherited a base. I also belong to the British Army and am under orders. Perhaps I should have been with you, but my orders were that I should keep open a sea base. Had the Partisans controlled the valley of Dukat the situation would have been simplified: but you didn't.'

In the firelight Besnik's face looked pale with emotion, but he still tried to keep an outburst under control.

'We only know one thing: we were promised help and it did not come; the reasons do not matter. And even if you could have brought no material help, you should have been with us yourself to give us moral support. We did not have even that. We were alone.'

There was a bitterness in his voice which could only have been caused by personal feelings. Besnik had believed personally in my good faith; he felt the more keenly what he considered to be a betrayal. In response to his anger I could feel my own rising. I felt a need to make them realise what my situation had been, yet as the arguments leapt to my mind I knew the futility of producing them. If the talk was not to end in a violent quarrel I must leave them with their conviction of my bad faith.

'All right,' I replied. 'I see that explanation is useless; you could never understand. We will speak only of the present. Firstly, you need help: you shall have it, and we will discuss that presently. Secondly, I have orders from my Headquarters to put a plan before you and to obtain your reply.'

Perhaps it was a mistake not to clinch the assistance first, but I was afraid that once that matter was decided they would discuss nothing else, and I needed to know their reactions to 'Victoria'.

'The Supreme Allied Commander in the Mediterranean, General Wilson' – by their faces I could see that they had never heard of him – 'has reason to believe that a German withdrawal from Greece may shortly take place. An operation is planned for the destruction of those German divisions. For its success it is essential that it be controlled from a central headquarters receiving information from all over the Southern Balkans. The questions which I am instructed to put to you are these: are you in principle willing to take part in this action, and, so that your part in it may be the more effective, are you willing to accept a British Liaison Officer through whom the orders of the Supreme Command will be transmitted to you?'

After a consultation with Petchi, Besnik replied: 'The Brigade is under discipline and can only accept orders from its own superior formation – that is, from the Central Partisan Committee. Whatever the Central Committee orders us to do, we carry out. We cannot accept orders from a British officer.'

'Let me put it this way then,' I answered. 'If the Central Committee agrees to take part in the operation, under the instructions of Allied Headquarters, are you, as a Brigade, willing to accept those instructions through a British Liaison Officer?'

There followed the usual discussion at the end of which Besnik turned to me and said with some impatience: 'In general we accept your plan, but all such discussion is a waste of time. It is academic to discuss how we shall fight the Germans when, if you do not immediately bring us help, we shall be unable to fight them at all.'

There was a pause and then, with deliberation, Besnik said: 'Listen, Major: we can continue as we are for ten more days; after that, as a Brigade, we shall cease to exist. We shall have no more ammunition. We can throw rocks at the enemy, and we shall, but that is not very effective.'

There were tears in his eyes as he finished speaking. It was the shortness of time that worried me. I felt confident enough that I could get an air sortie, but could I get one in ten days? I tried to work it out in my mind. Today was Monday, the twentieth. However early in the morning I started for the base I could not reach it in time to go on the air with a message that evening – even supposing Trotter's battery had any life in it, which I doubted, or that he had sufficient petrol to work the charging engine, which I was sure he had not. To get off a signal I would therefore have to go on to Drake, who was up in Dukat mountain. With steady walking I could reach him by the twenty-second, and get a signal off at latest by the morning of the twenty-third. By the twenty-fourth H.Q. should begin to act on it. That left six days for the organisation of the flight – six days at the very best. And I had no idea what present commitments were like: if there was a German push going on in Jugoslavia, most of our air-lift would be going there. Even the time of year was against us: it was winter and moonless, and in such conditions pilots were reluctant to venture for the first time into these savage valleys.

The atmosphere in the room was becoming very emotional, so I tried to bring it back to normal by speaking quietly and factually.

'You will get supplies dropped by air; that I promise. I cannot, however, promise that they will be here within ten days.'

Besnik took up my words at once. 'You cannot promise within ten days? Why not? Why not?'

'For one reason because I do not know if there will be planes available.'

'But the Allies have thousands of planes.'

'We have not thousands adapted for this special work.'

'Then send ordinary planes, by daylight if you wish, and let them throw the material out. We will get it.'

'I have told you I will do my best.'

Now Besnik's emotion ran away with him. 'There are some men in this Brigade who have done their best too.' The pulse of his anger was beating through his words. 'Come with me tomorrow, Major, and I will show you men dying of pneumonia – but we have no medicine for them. And how did they get pneumonia? Through fighting in the snow, and sleeping in the snow for weeks with neither coat nor blanket. Come and see them, Major. Come and see the food we give them – hard, black bread. I will show you other men who have gone barefoot in the mountains, absolutely barefoot; and they have got frost-bitten, and the frost-bite has turned to gangrene because we have no medicine. Come and see their feet tomorrow, Major.'

I turned to David. 'I am so cross,' I said, 'that if I make a reply now this party is going to end in tears. I shall stop talking and count up to twenty in my mind before I open my mouth again.'

It was the emotional approach which made me so furious; the implication that it was my callousness to the suffering of these men that restrained me from helping them.

When I had counted up to twenty I said to Besnik: 'I know that you have suffered. That does not affect my ability to bring you help. I refuse to commit myself to any date when help will arrive; you have already accused me of bad faith on that score and I do not wish to give you another opportunity. I refuse to say that you will have help inside ten days: that depends on factors quite outside of my control. All that I will say, and do say, is that I will bring you help and that I will do my utmost to bring it within ten days.'

Besnik translated to Petchi, who shrugged his shoulders. During the whole conversation he had scarcely spoken. They were silent.

'I have nothing more to say. I think we should go to bed,' I said.

We rose in silence, wrapped ourselves in the blankets which were brought, and in silence lay down again upon the floor. A Partisan put his head in round the door and received orders for calling us in the morning. The fire had died down; the room was cold and dark.

'Good night, David,' I called.

'Good night, old boy.'

I pulled my blanket round my ears and slept.

With first light the room, the house, the village outside, all came to life: the Partisans were moving off early. In our room 'Good mornings' were formally exchanged. For breakfast there was some black bread and a jug of water, and while we ate it I talked to David.

'What do you think of these Partisans?' I asked him.

'I rather like 'em. They seem a more straightforward lot than ours.'

'I'm glad you like them, because I think I'm going to have to leave you behind with them.'

'Sort of hostage, eh?'

'Yes, sort of,' I replied. 'One of us has got to stay to give them assurance of our good faith, and also to receive the sortie when it comes. They can't receive it alone. They'll not know when the plane is coming, or what signals to make, or anything.'

'All right,' David said, 'I'll stay with 'em.'

'I'm afraid it's got to be you, David. We could either of us stay and do this job, but I think I'm the only one at the moment who can cope with the Dukat situation.'

In my mind I also thought it would be good for David to have his own independent command, instead of acting as number two all the time.

He seemed quite happy about it, and we settled down to discuss plans. As soon as I got back to the plateau I would try to get off a signal on Trotter's set, but if his battery was flat, then I would go on and send one by Drake as quickly as I could.

'In any case,' I said, 'try and get hold of a litre or two of petrol through the Partisans. They may be able to lay hands on a little. And

I'll send Trotter inland to join you at once: he shouldn't take more than twenty-four hours to catch up with you.'

The Partisans, when they heard that David was staying, were delighted. They realised that we meant business. The emotional outburst of the night before was not referred to.

There was little else to do beyond arrange a code: we would need to exchange letters without them being read by every Albanian on the way.

As we were putting on our boots, David's lace broke. I saw it happen. He didn't say anything, he didn't even look up, but started to tie the broken ends together. I found that it cost a small effort to remove from my own boots the laces that he had given me, and offer them to him. He didn't want to accept them at first, but I told him not to be a fool.

I had quite a different feeling as I threaded his broken laces into my boots, and pulled them tight. I no longer felt surefooted, but it was something other than that. Those laces had held more than my boots together: they had given me assurance.

At seven o'clock we stepped out of the house into a light rain. It was a dismal morning with heavy clouds shrouding the mountains. The narrow street was full of Partisans moving towards the southern end of the village. I walked with Besnik, and I noticed the number of villagers who ran out to salute him, or shake his hand, or embrace him as he went by.

There was an open, muddy space at the end of the village, and here two horses stood. They were good-looking animals – once, no doubt, the property of some Italian officer. The Brigade Commander and his Commissar, however, did not mount, perhaps out of deference to the British Captain who was on foot.

The serious-faced little girl appeared in the crowd: I had not seen her previously on this visit. On Besnik's instructions she wrote me out a pass which would carry me through the Partisan lines – all done very efficiently, on a kind of field message-pad. I looked at her as she wrote; she was bare-headed in the rain, and the light overcoat she wore was utterly threadbare. When she handed me the pass I thanked her and smiled, but there was no response: her face remained set.

My ruffian of a guide from Trajas was there, and two Partisans were detailed to escort us to Trajas and then guide Trotter back the following day. I said good-bye to Petchi and he moved off with a group of Partisans, his horse led.

'Good-bye, David. Good luck.'

'Good luck to you.'

'Afraid you're going to get rather wet with no raincoat.'

'I'll be all right. So long.'

And with no covering but his sodden battle-dress, speaking no word of any language but his native English, towering head and shoulders above the ragged troop that surrounded him, Captain the Honourable David Marson moved off through the rain with the Fifth Partisan Brigade.

There remained Besnik.

'*Au revoir, mon commandant.*'

'*Au revoir.*'

He took my hand.

'Help will come,' I said.

'Thank you,' he replied, smiled, and without another word turned and followed quickly after his men.

The walk back seemed unending.

As we climbed higher, the rain gave place first to sleet and then to hail. The snow had been hard and crisp when David and I had crossed the previous day; now it had thawed so that the surface held for a moment, then suddenly collapsed beneath my weight and I plunged through knee-deep.

The physical present was boring – the tedious planting of alternate feet hour after hour – and I was also mentally depressed. During my early days in Albania I had been lit by the belief that I had the possibility to influence events: each journey had seemed to mark some progress. But now I no longer held the initiative: I was only adapting and disposing to counter the moves of a more powerful destiny.

Deliberately, as an escape from the present, I let myself slide into a day-dream: it was a habit I had acquired on these long walks.

First, words came singly, glancing and glinting through my mind. Then the words formed a rhythm, became sentences, poetry. Half-remembered snatches approached inconsequently:

'And his Aunt Jobiska made him drink
Lavender water tinged with pink.'

And the doggerel would refuse to go, but stay coursing in my brain... Lavender water tinged with pink... tinged with pink... tinged with pink...

And then Ann is there. She is never very far away, living always in my brain, in my blood. Dukat, the Partisans, the Germans, they all revolve around me – and at the centre of me is Ann. So they are all revolving round Ann. And they don't know it: that's the funny part of it!

But I don't want to think of the present. A small effort now and I can drift away into a world composed only of past and future, a magical world all of my own ordering... and so...

...And so I am in the theatre, seated expectant before the red-glowing curtain, and all the audience darkened, expectant, hushed. I can put a hand out and touch Ann beside me. The play is over. It's pouring with rain outside: lights are shining across the wet streets, and the taxis are in a block all the way down to Piccadilly. But it doesn't matter; we've got a car. Oh yes! You didn't know that, did you? Well, we have: a car or a carpet – it makes no difference. And a house... Where?... Wherever you like. Choose; name your place. This is my dream and I can steer it where I will.

So I'll steer it to a London house, a small house where the closing door shuts out the world, and supper is laid by a blazing fire, and upstairs there is a nursery with a fender where clothes are drying, and there is the crumby, milky smell of children. And Ann, always Ann – the touch, the sound, the scent of you. 'Oh thou weed that art so fair, and smell'st so sweet that the sense aches at thee.'

'I'm not a weed.' She's mock-indignant, half-laughing. 'I'm a woman.'

Indeed, my love, you are: indeed.

Indeed a weed. Widow's weeds. Are you a weed or a woman?... A woman, a woman.

'The price of flour has gone up twenty *leks* a quintal in Valona.' The guide is speaking to me, but I don't want to talk: I want to stay in my dream with Ann.

'I said the price of flour in Valona has gone up twenty *leks* a quintal.'

'Uh-huh.' I must make some sound. If I don't, the man will keep up this reiteration for ever.

'It's all the fault of the Balli. Traitors, that's what they are worse than the Germans. What do you say?'

I don't want to say anything. Pretend not to understand his Italian, that's best. And in my mind cling to that nursery fender, and the firelight, and the Ann that could be, might be.

...Now she is walking up the stairs: now turn her round on the step above me and her face is level with mine and her arms are round my neck... 'Sir, she can turn and turn and yet go on...' Poor Othello, poor Desdemona, poor Ann, poor me... 'the pity of it, Iago! O! Iago, the pity of it, Iago!'

The brute is stumbling through the snow close behind me now. He is determined to make me talk. 'Worse than the Germans, I say. Don't you agree?'

And if I agree, then another question, and another, and my dream will go, and I shall be back in the intolerable present.

'*Non capisco*,' I said. 'I don't understand.'

'Hein?'

I turn and shout at him, furious. 'I don't understand. I don't understand.'

He grunts, and as he falls back I can hear him mutter: 'You can understand well enough when you want to.'

191

TWELVE

IN THE LITTLE BOTHY on Dukat mountain, Drake, Manzitti and I were finishing enciphering a signal. It was the signal to Headquarters, requesting an air sortie for David.

'C over J,' Manzitti read out.

I ran my eye down the small piece of silk on which our cipher chart was printed.

'R – Robert,' I said.

Drake wrote down the letter.

'P over M,' said Manzitti.

He lifted the flap that covered the entrance and peered out; a flurry of snow blew in from out of the darkness. Manzitti let the flap drop and pulled his blanket closer round him.

'These blankets have warmth,' he said, 'but they have also many lice.'

'Have you many?' I asked.

'I am c-r-rawling,' he replied.

''Scuse me,' Drake broke in. 'I've got as far as R. What comes after R?'

Manzitti turned his attention back to the piece of paper in his hand.

'C over J,' he read out.

'R – Robert,' I said. 'That's it: that's where we got to. Go on from there.'

'P over M.'

'V – Vick.'

'L over R.'

'A – Able.'

'And that's the end,' declared Manzitti.

I handed the square of silk back to Drake.

'Now move your bottom a bit,' I said, 'because I want to stretch my legs out. I'm getting cramp.'

Drake gave a laugh, and the leaves that covered the floor rustled as he moved a few inches.

'That better?' he asked.

'Much,' I replied, and stretched out flat. 'No, it's not!' I cried. 'Now my feet are getting snowed on.'

'Of course they are,' said Drake, 'if you will stick them out through the door.'

I pulled my feet back in again.

'Midgets,' I said. 'Pygmies – that's whom this hut was built for.'

'Now then, sir,' said Drake, smiling. 'Can't have you being rude to our 'ouse. Munzi and me are very partial to it.'

'It's a very nice house,' I agreed. 'And I'm very glad to be with you both in it. It's like coming home.'

'Here's something that'll really make it seem like coming home,' said Drake. 'Have a Player's.'

He held out a round tin of cigarettes.

'Where did these come from?' I asked as I took one. 'Oh! of course – the sortie,' I went on before he had time to answer. 'I keep forgetting that the boat has been. Tell me more about it. Did it look to you as if they were getting the stores hidden away quickly?'

'Well, it was going all right when I was there yesterday,' said Drake. 'Of course, it was a bit confused, as there's such a hell of a lot came ashore. Must be twenty tons, I shouldn't wonder: mines, mortars, machine-guns – you never saw such a sight. '

'Have they sent us any Vickers?'

'Six!'

'No!'

'Yes, they have. Six lovely new Mark Fives. Oh, sir!' Drake leant forward with a look of entreaty. 'If you leave me stuck on this mountain-top with my radio when the fun begins, I'll... I'll... I don't know what I won't do. I've been buggered about by Jerry long enough now, and the sight of them Mark Fives... Oh boy! What a dream!'

'You'll get a fight, Drake, I promise. Now tell me, how many men were there from Dukat?'

'About forty. Gani's in charge of them. And they've got mules, and women, and...'

'Women?' I repeated.

'That's right. I reckon there's more women there than men. And they're carrying heavier loads than the mules! And there's mail come,' Drake rattled on, 'bags of mail, and food – you should see the food that's arrived! I brought these back with me yesterday.'

He pointed to some tins of condensed milk that lay in a corner with a bag of sugar. Suddenly a look of consternation came over his face.

'The tea! Where's the tea gone?'

He began to grub about among the leaves.

'Is this it?' asked Munzi, producing a small sack from behind his back.

'Yes, that's it,' said Drake. 'And just because you had it for a pillow last night there's no need for you to sit on it by day as well.'

Munzi apologised.

'Never mind,' said Drake. 'Now then...'

He looked round, mentally licking his lips, and both Manzitti and I knew what was coming.

'Munzi...'

'Yes?'

'Aren't you cold?'

It was Drake's never-varying ritual of which he would not miss a word.

'Very cold,' answered Munzi correctly.

'Major, aren't you feelin' low?'

I would not have dared deny it.

'Very low,' I replied.

'I knew it!' exclaimed the corporal. 'Then don't you think...' the words came now in a gradual crescendo, '...don't you think we might have a nice little...'

'Brew-up!' we all three shouted.

During the pause while the corporal busied himself with his tea-making I was thinking of the mail which he had said was at Sea View.

Mail... That meant that there might be a letter from Ann. Save for the message she had written on the back of the photograph it was three months since I had seen her writing. Now there must surely be a letter from her, there must. In the cave at Sea View, just the other side of this mountain, separated from me by so small a distance, there must be lying at this moment a letter that her hand had written. A few more hours and I should be reading it.

'Did you say there was some mail at Sea View?' I asked.

'That's right, sir: bags of it. Er – Munzi, pass that tin of milk, will you?'

'Was there any for me?'

'Yessir. I'm sure there was: several letters.'

And lying there among that several was one from Ann. The hours that separated me from it lay like a yoke across my neck. And then, with sudden revulsion, I cursed myself for allowing my hope so to leap up. There's no letter, I told myself. There is no letter, none, none. Don't for ever lay your heart open to these barbs.

'What about you, Munzi?' I asked. 'Were there any letters for you?'

Munzi smiled and shook his head.

'No. I'm afraid my family does not know if I am alive. They are all in Genoa, under the Germans. I hope they are safe.'

There was a moment's silence, and then came the sound of Drake smacking his lips as he tasted the tea. It was the delicate sound of a cat drinking milk.

'Not bad,' he said. 'Not bad at all... But I think just a *little* more sugar.'

He poured a handful into the mess-tin and stirred it with a twig. Then he sipped it again and gave a satisfied smile.

'Trotter himself couldn't find fault with this,' he said. 'I reckon this brew comes up even to Wolver'ampton standards.'

Munzi sighed. 'What a pity Trotter could not send this signal himself before he left; it would have saved a whole day.'

'His battery was dead flat and he hadn't a drop of petrol,' I said. 'Well, with luck he should catch up with David by tomorrow, and we must pray that the Partisans have managed to get hold of some petrol. Anyhow, Drake's signal will be going off in the morning. That'll give H.Q. six clear days to arrange the air sortie.'

Drake pulled a dubious face.

'I doubt if I'll get through before tomorrow afternoon,' he said. 'My battery's well charged – Chela sent me up a couple of litres yesterday – but I have terrible trouble contacting Italy in the mornings. I think some bit of this mountain must get in the way. For some reason the afternoon "sked" is better, but it's hard to maintain contact even then.'

'Well, do your best,' I said. 'Captain Marson's in a bit of a spot.'

'I should say he is!' The corporal gave a laugh. 'If those Partisans aren't sent some stores quickly, and they get to 'ear of what we've just given to Dukat, I'll bet the Captain won't half get some dirty looks.'

'If I thought,' I said, 'that it was only dirty looks that the Captain would get, I wouldn't be half so worried.'

We finished Drake's monumental brew, and stretched out on the leaves to sleep. But I did not fall asleep; I lay listening to the small rustlings in the roof just above my head, to the muffled protests of the twigs against the gradually increasing weight of the snow.

'Are you still awake?' Munzi spoke softly in the darkness.

Turning on my side I could dimly see his face in the last glow of the fire. He was lying propped on his elbow.

'What is it?' I asked.

'There is a man,' he said, 'who is on my conscience.'

'Oh! Who?'

'Doctor Georgie.'

Doctor Georgie had long been on my mind too, but I could not think why Munzi should be worried about him.

'You never knew him, though,' I said.

'No; I never met him, but I have thought about him. Now I am ashamed of the things that I have thought.'

'Then you don't believe, either, that it was Georgie leading that German patrol?'

'I thought so at the time,' said Munzi, 'but now I am sure that it could not have been him. Why should Georgie betray one thing and not another? Why should he lead the Germans to our base in Grama but keep from them the names of our Balli friends in Dukat? – Chela, for example. It would be very simple for the Germans to arrest Chela's family even if they could not catch Chela himself. No, I believe that Georgie has kept altogether silent.'

'I believe so too,' I replied. 'And yet of all the men I have met,

Georgie was the most frightened: he was really a coward.'

'Perhaps he had too much imagination,' said Munzi. 'Perhaps, when he was faced with the worst thing that he had imagined, he found that it was not so hard to endure.'

'Perhaps,' I said.

There was a pause, and into my mind came a picture of an old, discarded boot from which the upper had come away from the sole and whose Alpine nails stuck out sideways like a ragged moustache.

'I wonder if he is still alive,' I said.

'A month after his capture?'

The leaves stirred as Munzi lay down again, and I could hear him punching his tea-bag pillow into shape.

'No,' he said. 'Georgie is not alive. Good night.'

'Good night,' I said.

The morning broke radiant, and, as I climbed upwards through the woods, I saw that crocuses were breaking through the snow where it lay thin. Here and there violets gleamed from beneath the shelter of the undergrowth.

The spring was come at last. Winter had passed away overnight. On the mountain-top I stood with the morning sun warm on my back and looked out for miles over the Adriatic. The sea was as blue as the sky, and the snow no whiter than the small clouds. The beauty of the day was like a promise. Now I knew it!... There was a letter from my love!

This was no common day, no day for walking; it was a day on which to take wings. I began to run down the mountain, the snow flying up behind me in a cloud. I could not stumble, I could not tire; when I reached the snow line I could not stop: but went on running.

I passed mules struggling up the hill, heavily laden; women too were climbing upwards, great boxes of ammunition tied to their backs with cords: it made me wince to see them. And on I ran, over turf, over rocks, never faltering or stopping until I had reached Sea View.

Outside the cave Butch was opening a large wooden box.

'Hi there, Major!' he called out. 'Glad to see you.'

'What have you got there?' I asked.

'Oh, I guess it's some kind of a charger that my folks have sent me.'

He gave a kick at the box. 'And if it's the kind of a charger that I guess it is,' he said ominously. 'I'm going to smash the f – thing in pieces.'

'Where are Gani and his boys?' I asked.

'Down on the beach mostly, still sorting the stores. Jeez!' He gave a wag to his head. 'There's a hell of a lot of stuff come this sortie.'

'Any sign of the Germans?'

'We get six alarms a day, but they don't amount to anything. The Heinies always stop just short of here. I don't know why: it's getting me nervous.'

'Butch,' I said, 'the hell with everything else for a minute! Where's my mail?'

Butch led the way into the cave and pulled a bundle of letters from a crevice in the wall.

'These are yours, Major. I kept them separate for you.'

As I flicked through the bundle I could feel the old hollowness in my stomach, the constriction up the back of my neck, that came with the prospect of seeing Ann's writing.

But of Ann's writing there was no sign.

I looked through the bundle a second time, slowly. But it made no difference how slowly I looked: there was still no letter from Ann.

Butch had wandered out of the cave, and I could hear him banging away at his box outside.

'Butch,' I called.

The banging stopped, and the marine appeared in the entrance. 'Yeah?'

'Butch, are you sure there were no other letters for me?'

'Nothing else,' he said. 'Leastways, not unless I missed it.'

He dragged a big mail-bag out of a corner.

'All the mail came in this. I've bin through it real careful. What's left there now is for Captain Marson, and Trotter, and Black. 'Course,' he conceded, 'I might have missed something.'

'I don't expect you have,' I said, 'but I think I'll just make sure.'

Together we caught hold of the mail-bag and tipped its contents out on to the floor of the cave.

'Thanks, Butch,' I said. 'I'll sort through this. You get on with your own job.'

I sat down on a box and began to go through the pile. There were parcels, and packets, and letters, and papers, and periodicals. They were addressed to Trotter, to Marson, to Black, a few to Adams, and numerous copies of *The Scotsman* to one Gunner McCullough – of whom I had never heard. I went through them all with great care, examining the papers and periodicals to see if the letter could have become lodged in one of their folds, reading the address on each envelope in case the writing had become smudged and Butch had been unable to read it.

I sorted the entire pile. There was no letter from Ann.

– So she hadn't written. There it was. She just hadn't written. Perfectly clear: she hadn't written.

– She might have written, though, and the letter could have got lost. Air-mail was very erratic in war-time. Plane could get shot down. Mail could be burnt, or lost in the sea. Or she might have been forgetful and sent it by sea-mail. Sea-mail took months, literally months, to arrive.

– No, no, don't be fatuous. Face it, for Christ's sake, face it! There was no letter, and now there was no possibility of one till the boat came next – another month probably.

The yoke across my neck turned to lead.

Butch started to yell outside. I went to see what was the matter. He was kicking at the wooden box, from which he had now wrenched the lid, and letting out a string of curses.

'Look!' he shouted. 'Look what they've sent me!'

'What is it?'

There was a lot of flimsy metal scaffolding, and a thing like an aeroplane propeller.

'It looks like a windmill,' I said.

'That's just what it is,' said Butch bitterly. 'They've sent me a wind-charger. You set up this twelve-foot erection, and the wind blows the propeller round, and the propeller drives a dynamo, and the dynamo charges the batteries, and Jerry sees it from two miles away, and that's the end of that.'

'But didn't they send you petrol?' I asked.

'They sent just three jerricans, no more. And by the time they reached here that f – Jugoslav crew had stolen every drop. I could only tell by the smell of the cans what had been in them.'

'Well, Butch,' I said, 'you can't use this wind-charger. That's quite certain.'

Butch took the wooden propeller from the box and smashed it on the rocks. The small pieces he ground smaller with his heel. He took the metal scaffolding and tipped it into the ravine; it went rolling and clattering to the bottom. Then he gave a loud laugh.

'That relieves my feelings some,' he declared.

Down on the beach the Albanians were working furiously to remove and hide away the last of the stores before any Germans walked in. They were clearly delighted with their haul, and full of protestations of forthcoming prowess against the Germans. By dusk the work was completed: every gun and every bullet had been carried away and hidden in the mountain.

A gale arose at nightfall. It came shrieking down off the mountain, raising the dust and grit off the floor of the cave, preventing sleep. I was glad when the light came and I could leave Sea View to return to Drake and Manzitti.

It was a fight to get over the mountain that day. The snow on the summit had alternately thawed and then frozen, and the gale had pressed and polished it till the surface was like glass. The wind was lifting the soft snow from the lower levels and whipping it over the top in a stinging curtain. I scuttled over the summit on my hands and knees: it was impossible to stand. The descent to the base was punctuated by several falls into deep snow-drifts. In all it took six hours to arrive, and when I got there I was very tired.

The platform at the head of the gorge had an idyllic atmosphere. The snow was melting rapidly here, and I found Munzi gently mooning round amid a mass of snowdrops and crocuses.

But David's signal had not yet gone off.

While we crouched in the bothy and ate bread and goatcheese, Drake told me of his difficulties with the radio.

'This platform is too shut in, so I can't transmit from inside the shelter: I have to get out on the hill-side. It was snowing here yesterday, so I covered the set up with a ground-sheet. Then the ground-sheet got in the way of my operating the key, but I daren't take it off for fear the snow would get inside and ruin the set.'

Drake was making a terrible drama of his difficulties, but I liked him for it. He was an artist who put all his soul into his work, and without the temperament he would not have been such a fine operator.

'I was out there all morning,' he continued. 'Nothing doing. In the afternoon I made contact, but the silly sod at the other end insisted on *my* taking his message first. By the time 'is lordship was ready to take my message I'd lost contact with him. Christ!' Drake finished. 'I reckon yesterday afternoon near broke my 'eart. Leastways,' he corrected himself, 'it would 'ave done but for one thing – eh, Munzi?'

A look and a smile passed between the two.

'And the Major 'asn't noticed nothing,' Drake went on, looking at me shyly. 'Don't you see nothing, sir?'

'I don't know what on earth you're talking about,' I said.

Again Drake and Munzi caught each other's eye; this time they began to laugh. Still laughing, Drake leant forward and held out his arm.

'Look, sir!'

His sleeve was adorned with three brand-new chevrons.

'Sergeant Drake!' I cried.

'That's right, sir.' Drake's snub face was fairly beaming with pride. 'That was the incoming signal!'

I was delighted. No man deserved his promotion more fully.

'But tell me,' I asked, 'where did you get your stripes?'

Drake chuckled. 'Had 'em in my pack all the time, sir.'

'Well, you sly old...'

'No, sir: not sly. Just prepared. I've been sweatin' on this promotion a long time, and I'm an old enough soldier to know that it was bound to come at some damn silly time... and it did!' he added. He looked at his watch. 'Time I was getting ready: I'll be on the air again in fifteen minutes. Well, let's hope for better luck this time.' And he crawled out into the open.

There was a silence after Drake had left the hut, a silence broken by Manzitti.

'You are sad,' he said. 'Why are you sad?'

I never left Munzi without appreciating more and more, when I returned, his quietness and understanding. As he sat there now, his features were almost hidden in his black beard, but his eyes were full of expression even behind their glasses.

'You fall down in those spectacles of yours,' I said. 'You go to sleep in caves in them; when we first met, you were wading about in the sea in them. How do you manage never to break them?'

'You have not told me,' he insisted, 'why you are sad.'

It was not like Munzi to be so firm, it made me smile.

'All right then, Munzi, I'll tell you. I'm worried about this area. We have now received all this material for Dukat, but I'm not at all convinced that the weapons will be used against the Germans, and meanwhile it's only going to make David's position with the Partisans more difficult. I'm seriously wondering if we should not clear out of here entirely and have nothing more to do with the Balli. That means, in a way, that I shall have failed; and I had such hopes of making a success of this job. It was very important to me to do so.'

Manzitti drew a breath as though he were about to speak, but appeared to change his mind.

'Yes?' I queried.

'No.' He shook his head. 'It was something that would be silly to say. You know it already.'

'Perhaps I do. But never mind: go on.' Manzitti looked down at the ground. When he raised his head it was with an expression of extraordinary happiness.

'I am always finding that life is something...' He was so pent up with feeling that he could not find the words. '...something of wonderful. I love it,' he exploded. 'People I always see trying to be rich, and it has a good taste to be rich – but it has, too, a good taste to be poor. Neither is good and neither is bad: they are just different.' His tone became more serious, but the smile did not leave his face. 'I think it is the same with victory and defeat. You have won the war, and perhaps victory is sweet: I do not know. The taste in my mouth is salt, but it is in *my* taste: I welcome it: you cannot take it from me. And perhaps,' he finished quietly, 'perhaps I am not really defeated if I can say "welcome" to defeat.'

He blinked through his glasses. There was a silence.

'And so?' I said.

'And so,' Munzi said diffidently, 'I do not think that a small defeat in the valley of Dukat, in Albania, need make you sad. And I am sure that it is not making you sad. What other reason is there?'

I picked up a few dry leaves from the floor and fed them, one by one, into the fire. They spurted into white flame, then became as rapidly extinct.

'I am in love,' I said. 'That's as good a phrase to use as any. I wanted to make a gift to the woman I love of all that I did here, of all that happened to me. I wanted it to be a gift full of colour and warmth, like a jewel. Instead it has only been a rather dirty grey. And I am afraid she may not understand what I was trying to say.'

Munzi was silent.

'That is why I am sad,' I said. 'And since you do not like to answer, I will go on and tell you the answer that is in your mind... If a woman loves a man, the colour of his gift does not matter: she will take it to her heart. And if she does not love him, then still the colour does not matter: she will not see it however bright it be.'

Munzi gave a little smile.

'I know it,' I said. 'I need no friend to remind me of that. And I know in my heart which of those two is in my own case. And yet I cannot accept it. I cannot give up hoping.'

Munzi's smile broadened.

'That is why I like you,' he said.

Drake's body blocked the doorway.

'I made it! Got it off all right.' He blew out through his cheeks. 'Br-r-r, it's cold. Let's get by the fire a minute.'

We made way for him, and he sat rubbing his hands and passing them through the flames.

'Got an incoming too: Top Priority. Just get my hands a bit warmer arid we'll get crackin' on it. I can't hardly 'old a pencil now.'

We were half-way through the deciphering when Zechir appeared. He crawled into the hut, seized my hand and kissed it, then explained that Mucho had arrived at Chela's house and was asking to see me.

'Oh God!' I said 'I don't want to climb down into the valley tonight. I feel much too tired. Well, let's get this signal finished first, and see what it says.'

'Personal for Overton,' it said. 'You will come out at once for conference on Victoria. Stand by for sortie night twenty-fifth March or following three nights.'

Drake gave a whistle. 'That's tomorrow night. Are you glad about that, sir?'

I didn't know if I was glad or not. I couldn't take it in.

'It doesn't really register at the moment,' I said.

'You must certainly go down and talk to Mucho,' Munzi said. 'It will be your last chance if you are going out tomorrow night.'

He was right. I pulled my boots on and set off with Zechir. I felt depressed as I climbed down: I was sure that a conversation with Mucho would only be futile. I was curiously tired too, but I put that down to the fact that I had been walking continuously for six days.

Chela met me in the court-yard of his house and led me to the familiar pink room with the blue net curtains. It had a more desolate, unlived in air than usual, and was bitterly cold. I huddled over the charcoal brazier which seemed to give out even less than its customary heat, and soon Mucho walked into the room. He was extremely friendly, but a reserve and a tendency to small talk made me think that he was not at ease.

Where had he been? ...Oh! he had been up north, attending this or that conference. I ought to know that a great fusion of the anti-communist parties was taking place, in which he would be the secretary and representative of the Balli.

'Oh, yes?' I said.

I would ask no more questions. If he had any explanations to give, or proposals to make, I was not going to put them into his mouth for him. As a result nothing pertinent had been discussed by the time dinner came in.

It was the usual good dinner that Chela always provided, but I felt too tired to eat and was shivering with cold. When the meal was finished I told Mucho that I was feeling stupid with tiredness, and asked him if he would object to postponing our talk till the morning.

He agreed at once.

But when morning came he still had nothing of importance to say. Chela joined us, and the three of us sat bunched round the brazier while the wind whistled round the building and a dog howled in the yard.

Once there were footsteps in the corridor outside. Both Chela and Mucho started and reached for their guns. How nervous they are! I thought, then realised that I had done the same myself. It proved to be only Zechir.

At last I said: 'Mucho, we have talked now for an hour and said nothing. It is time to say what is in our minds. I like you personally very much; therefore I shall speak frankly. It is probable that in a day or two I shall be returning to Italy for a conference, and I shall have to report on what has happened, and give my opinion as to what should be done. What am I to say? I can only tell them that you have not carried out a single one of the assurances that you gave me when you came to Grama last month.'

Mucho smiled ruefully. 'It has not been easy,' he said.

'I know it has not been easy, and I am not blaming you personally for the failure. But good will and the desire to help are not enough to impress a military headquarters. Actions are needed, and you have done exactly nothing.'

He was silent.

'Mucho,' I went on, 'I am neither communist nor anti-communist: I am an Englishman. And as an Englishman I am not telling you that you have set yourself to fight not only against the Partisans but also against the Allies. I am not blaming you; I am only saying that our support is going to those who fight against the Germans. If you fight with the Germans, no matter how good you may believe the reason to be, you set yourself against the Allies – and you will be defeated.'

Still he said nothing, and so again I went on.

'You are a clever man, but you have been outwitted by the Partisans. Since they are fighting against the Germans they can sell the idea to their followers that to fight for their country against the invader is synonymous with communism. Since you fight with the Germans you lose the sympathy of your own people, and that of the Allies also. That is all. You and your party are now in a position from which I do not see how you are to escape, but escape you must if either are to survive.'

In the silence I padded across the room, to where my boots lay, and began to put them on. No one said a word while I fastened the old broken laces, or while I crossed the room again, to pick up my revolver and belt.

When I stood ready to go Mucho rose and smiled.

'I have been glad to know you,' he said, speaking very quietly, and I am sorry that history has not permitted us to be friends. I only hope that when these troubles are over we may meet again; we have much to talk about.' He held out his hand. 'You will go back to Italy and make your report. I shall stay here and continue with my work...' The quiet smile did not leave his face, but there was the tiniest hesitation before he added: '...for as long as I can.'

'Good-bye, Mucho.'

'Do not speak of me too badly.'

'I am not likely to.'

'I don't think you are. *Au revoir*.'

The climb back to the base seemed very hard. I felt weak and sick, and thought that I must have been poisoned by the charcoal fumes which I had been breathing all morning. But the weakness did not pass off and I decided that perhaps I was just very weary.

My heart, too, was as heavy as my feet. For all this scurrying over the mountains I had achieved nothing. These people of Dukat were hopeless. The herd were worse than beasts, and their leaders were caught in a pit of their own digging. I pictured the tired, set face of Mucho as we had shaken hands, and I thought how like Besnik he had looked. How like him he was, in every way save one – and that one would likely cost him his life.

Something moved in the track before my feet. It was a huge spider, with widespread legs and a reddish body as big as a fat grape. I touched it with the end of my stick, and it ran to the edge of the track, then rounded on the offending stick as if to give fight. It looked the very distillation of things evil. I raised my stick, poised it, then brought it down so as to squash the creature.

There is something horrible in the utterly unexpected, as when you strike what you believe to be hard and find it soft, or when you touch what you believe to be dry and find it slimy.

It was so with this spider. Instead of the squashy pulp for which I was prepared, my blow produced a violent and unexpected release of life.

The sack-like body burst, and out of it there poured a countless swarm of tiny ant-like creatures. Released from the dead husk of the spider, they darted across the track and into the grass at the side; some clung to my stick and had to be brushed off.

I felt suddenly and violently sick. I put a few paces between myself and the remains of the spider, then sat down, my mind seeking some interpretation of this explosion from death into life. Were the tiny insects its young, which the spider was about to spawn? Or were they parasites, preying on and slowly devouring the body of the larger insect? It seemed to be an occurrence full of meaning and yet meaningless. My thought sickened as I strained for the solution that lay just beyond my grasp.

On Gumenitza mountain the clouds hung low and heavy; it must be snowing hard up there. Behind the mountain and behind the snow-clouds was David with his Partisans. Was he going to receive his stores in time? And how would he fare alone?

Below me in the valley lay Chela's house. I thought of all the paths that had led through that house; and they seemed to me like the red lines marking the shipping routes on an atlas, converging and squeezing into a port. I could see the whole valley covered with straight red lines all leading to Chela's house. They converged on one side of the house, then poured out the other in a solid stream leading over the mountain to Sea View. They were so plain to see that I could not think how the Germans could be such fools as to miss them.

Some distance from the house stood a small black car – Mucho's: so he had not departed yet. Probably the Albanians were holding a post-mortem on the morning's conversation. There they were, in that pink and blue room, arguing it out, losing their tempers, taking heroic decisions, and all to no purpose; because they were trapped. Mucho could go running all over the mountains, hiding, scheming, intriguing, but he was doomed. He would never make another trip to Paris. Somewhere here in these mountains a German or an Albanian bullet would put an end to his fevered life. I felt quite sure of it, looking down on the house that contained him; and I found myself hoping for his sake that death would come to him quickly, and that he would not first have to endure imprisonment, when the days would move slowly towards inevitable execution and each one bring the lonely knowledge that when his body slumped lifeless the world would be quite indifferent – indifferent to his life, to his ideals, to his fight, and to his death. The world would never have heard of him.

Three months ago I had looked on Dukat valley for the first time. The sun had poured down on it, and the sound of kids bleating had risen up; it had seemed a green valley, promising adventure. Now, beneath the leaden skies, it looked desolate and hostile; its people, with few exceptions, were mean and ignorant, their lives ugly and unkind, and instead of adventure there had only been a long tale of effort, and discomfort, and I had to admit – failure. I was tired, and I was sick at heart.

I rose to my feet and began to climb again.

THIRTEEN

'YOU MUST BE FEELING lousy,' said the doctor.

'I am,' I replied.

'Never mind.' The doctor turned away. 'You'll feel a lot better when we've got you into bed.' A thought struck him and he turned back to me. 'Lousy?' he repeated. 'Do you mean literally?'

'Literally,' I said.

So an orderly was detailed to put me in a bath and shave off all my hair. As he clipped away I kept thinking that he was Zechir. That was because Zechir had shaved off my beard while I lay in the grotto; I had not wanted to return to Italy with a beard. But of course he wasn't Zechir, and I wasn't in Albania: he was a British medical orderly, and I was in Italy, in Bari, in a hospital, in a hot bath.

The man was half-way through clipping my head went the doctor returned.

'No, you idiot!' the doctor exclaimed. Not his head; that doesn't matter.'

But it was too late by then. Half my hair was off and half was on, and the bath water was going cold, and I felt I was going to be sick again, so I told the orderly to leave my hair as it was.

They put me in a small ward; there were only three other men in it. When I was in bed I began to laugh.

'What's the matter?' said the man in the bed next to me. 'What are you laughing at?'

It would have been difficult to explain to him, so I said: 'I'm laughing at the sheets.'

'Are they so funny?' he asked.

'I find them so,' I said.

I lay on my back and looked at the ceiling. A long way up it was, and very white.

The trouble was to disentangle the past from the present. The present loomed so huge that I could hardly see it; the past was remote, but very clear, like looking through the wrong end of a telescope.

If I looked down the telescope I could see myself plainly – leaving the cave, walking down the track to the beach, stopping every five minutes to retch. And when the others at last gave up flashing, I couldn't climb back again, but stayed on the beach by the fire.

All the next day I lay there too, in the rain.

I couldn't understand why no one came to help me, because it was raining very hard. Perhaps they thought I naturally liked lying on the beach in the rain, and that it was no business of theirs to interfere. At all events, it was evening before Butch realised that I was ill; then they picked me off the beach and carried me into the grotto – the grotto where the Italian doctor had lain and fought for life.

Of course, that was why the ceiling looked so unnatural. It should be black, and just above my head, and sometimes dripping.

After that the past wasn't so clear. It was a long tunnel of nausea, and the realisation that night after night the boat didn't come, and there were no signals because the batteries were flat, and I had to plan what they were to do with me if the Germans came... But all that was vague.

And now there was this overwhelming feeling of relief and security. No need now to be left alone, hidden in the bushes, if the Germans came: the Germans would not come. No need now to haggle with a lying shepherd over the price of a goat: now food was cooked, and brought, and set before me. On the road from Brindisi there had been hundreds of trucks, but no need at all to hide from them; they were ours, *ours*. On every side were soldiers, thousands of soldiers, calmly, confidently making for the same goal as mine; if I asked their help they would give it: if they spoke I would understand. For they were men of Derby and of Durham, of Northumberland and Sussex, men of my own land, and every word they spoke would be native to my ear.

The door of the ward was pushed open and a nurse came in.

'Who wants Ovaltine?' she questioned brightly.

She had a strong Irish brogue.

'Sister,' I said, 'would you mind saying that again?'

'I'll not, either. You're a foin one! Just arrived in the hospital and already you're makin' fon of me.'

'I'm not making fun of you,' I said. 'I just wasn't sure what you said.'

'Who wants Ovaltine?' she repeated.

And when she had gone I turned on my side and laughed into the pillow.

'What on earth are you laughing at now?' asked the man in the next bed.

'Ovaltine!' I said, still laughing, though I could as easily have wept. 'She asked who wanted *Ovaltine*!'

I lay alone in the ward, eating an orange. The occupants of the other three beds were nearly recovered; at certain hours they were allowed to get up and leave the ward. I picked at the orange pith with my thumb-nail, wondering when I should get news from the office, calculating for the twentieth time when I might expect a reply to the letter I had written to Ann.

It was four days since I had been taken into the hospital, three since I had written the letter. It would take an air-mail letter ten days to go from Italy to London – and I ought to add three days to that in case she was in the country: thirteen. Naturally I couldn't expect her to answer it the same day she received it but possibly the next: fourteen. Ten more days for her letter to reach Bari: twenty-four. Then throw in six days to cover accidents and delays: thirty... Thirty days before I could allow myself to expect an answer. And only three of them were gone.

The door swung open and the Irish sister came in.

'How are you feelin'?' she enquired.

'Foin,' I said.

'Now listen to me, Major Overton. If you're well enough to make fon of a good Doblin accent you're well enough to keep yourself toidy. Look at all this orange-peel!'

She clicked her tongue at me, stuffing the peel into the cigarette-tin that served as an ash-tray.

'I came to tell you,' she said, 'that there's a noice-lookin' colonel come to see you. I don't know his name, but he looks like Gary

Cooper. D'you feel well enough to talk to him?'

'Let him in,' I said.

She pushed open the door and called: 'Come in!'

Geoffrey Cleaver came hurrying into the room.

'Hullo, old boy,' he said.

'Hullo, Geoffrey.'

Archly the sister put her head back round the door. 'Remember, Colonel, only fifteen minutes.'

'Don't worry, Sister,' Cleaver called after her, 'I can only stay a moment.'

The door closed and Cleaver turned to me. 'It's good to see you back, John.' He'd lost none of his old intensity and confidence.

'It's good to be back,' I replied. ' – Though not like this. God! what a fool's thing to do!'

'You can't help getting ill,' said Cleaver. 'And from what the sister tells me, you seem to have made a proper job of it – malaria, jaundice, dysentery... And don't fret about the conference,' he ran on. 'It's never been held.'

He perched on the edge of the next bed and lit a cigarette.

'What's funny?' I questioned: I could see that he was holding back his laughter.

'Well, it's your hair!' He let out a guffaw. 'What have they done to you?'

'I ran my hand over my head. 'That's part of the disease,' I said. 'You'd better keep your distance.'

Cleaver assumed a sympathetic air.

'I'm very sorry not to have been to see you before,' he said, 'but it's just impossible to get away from the office.' He glanced at his watch. 'I really ought to be back there now.'

'Geoffrey,' I said, 'there's one thing badly on my mind. Tell me if David got his stores.'

Cleaver smiled. 'David got two plane-loads within four days of our receiving your signal. Trotter has joined him and we're in good radio contact with them. Relieved?'

'Very,' I said. 'And now what news from Sea View?'

The colonel pulled a face. 'You got out just in time,' he said.

'Both Drake and the American – what's his name? Butcher – went off the air the very next day.'

'No!'

He nodded. 'There's been not a sound from either of them for four days.'

'Lack of petrol,' I suggested. 'Their batteries may be flat.'

'Impossible.' Cleaver was emphatic. 'The sortie that brought you out took in gallons of petrol.'

There was a silence. Then I said: 'Well, I hope to God they're all right. If anything happens to that party you can be sure of one thing: as far as the valley of Dukat is concerned, there'll be no Operation Victoria.'

'Oh, but "Victoria" is off,' said Cleaver. 'Didn't you know?'

He was looking round, holding his cigarette in the air. 'Where can I put this out?'

I pushed the tin towards him. 'Here you are.'

'Yes,' he continued. 'I thought you knew that. I sent a signal – oh, seven days ago. But maybe you never received it.'

'Maybe,' I said. 'Anyhow, I wasn't taking much in seven days ago.'

'Yes,' he said, glancing again at his watch, 'they called the whole thing off... Most disappointing.' He got to his feet. 'Now, old boy I really must fly. Don't worry about your chaps: they've been all right before and they'll be all right again. Just you hurry up and get better.'

He patted my feet and was gone.

Stale smoke rose from the tin in which Cleaver's cigarette still smouldered beneath the orange-peel: I stubbed it out. It was very quiet; the only sound was of rattling glasses as a trolley was wheeled down the corridor outside. The afternoon sunlight poured through the window; it revealed the dust in the air and the pieces of bed-fluff that rolled about on the floor, blown by the draught that came under the door.

So 'Victoria' was off. And while I lay here in hospital the chase was on in Dukat mountain, this time perhaps in earnest. Where were they hiding now, I wondered?... Or were they fighting?... Or killed?... Or, worse, captured? I thought of Munzi's words as we had said good-bye:

'If I am caught I shall keep such a silence that they will not understand if I am English, French or Chinese.'

The nurse entered briskly.

'Oh, he's gone!' She sounded disappointed. 'He didn't stay long, did he?' She began to straighten my bed. 'Now that's what I call a real noice-lookin' fellow. Don't you see what I mean? – Don't you think he looks loike Gary Cooper?'

'Yes,' I said. 'Just.'

Ten days elapsed, and then came the news of Nigel's death. It came in a long signal from Harvey.

A week after leaving me, Nigel and Cooper had been travelling south with a Partisan escort when the party had been attacked by a band of Balli. Cooper had been killed outright; Nigel had escaped into the mountains. When the news reached Harvey he set out at once to the scene of the action; he found Cooper's body, and after a further search he at last found Nigel in a hut, alone, his feet badly frost-bitten. When Harvey arrived Nigel was still alive, but he died shortly afterwards of gangrene.

It was just a month after my return to Italy, and I was still on convalescent leave, when Cleaver called me to the office.

'You'll be glad to know,' he said, 'that your boys are all right. I've heard from the Americans that Butcher came on the air this morning. It seems they've had a whole brigade after them these last four weeks... Though that's a compliment which I doubt if they've appreciated.'

'Where are they now?' I questioned.

'At Sea View.'

'Is the chase over?'

'The signal doesn't say.'

'Anything from Drake?'

Cleaver shook his head. 'Nothing.'

Then he rose and began to walk about the room. "Victoria" is off. Our policy now is to support only the Partisans. David Marson is doing very well with the Fifth Brigade, and I don't intend to move him. But I don't think it would be fair, or useful to send you back to that Dukat area.' He stopped in front of me. 'If you agree I propose to pull your mission out.'

'How soon?' I asked.

'Tonight. The Italian navy can provide a Mas.'

'What's that?' I asked.

'M-A-S,' he spelled it out. 'Pronounced Marss. A thing like our M.T.B., but faster.'

'What's wrong with the old *Sea Maid*?' I asked.

'Too slow. This may have to be a quick in-and-out job.'

'I take it,' I said, 'that I may go and fish them out?'

'That's why I sent for you,' Cleaver replied. 'I want you to make your final decision when you get there.'

'Thanks,' I said. 'I'd hate anyone else to do it.'

As I left his office Cleaver picked up the telephone. 'I'll get on to the Americans,' he said. 'You'll need someone to help you and they'd probably like to send an officer.'

In the orderly-room I made out a signal. 'Personal from Overton. Definitely repeat definitely coming for you tonight Stop Stand by 2000 hours.' Butch should receive that during the afternoon.

The orderly-sergeant entered the room, and I handed him the signal.

'Get that off, Top Priority,' I said.

'Right, sir... Just a minute, sir,' He called after me as I was leaving the room. 'Got some mail in this morning: I think there's some for you at last.'

He pulled open a drawer and searched through a pile of letters.

'Yes, 'ere you are, sir.' He gave a knowing leer. 'This is for you.'

My hospital calculation had been accurate. Thirty days exactly it had taken to get Ann's reply.

I tore open the envelope and read:

'Dearest John,

'I was so glad to get your letter and to hear that you were safe, even if not well. I have not written for a long time as I did not want to upset you while you were on your job, and

215

now that you are safely in Italy I only hope that my letter will not arrive too late.

'My news, I know, will hurt you, but I had sooner you heard it from me than from anyone else. I am going to be married very soon.

'I know that this will be a blow to you, and there is no way in which I can soften it. I can only thank you from my heart for all the love you offered and which I was unable to accept.

'Ann.'

FOURTEEN

THE LAST LIGHT had faded from the sky before the Italian mainland was five miles astern. The Mas hurled itself eastwards through the darkness.

In the flush deck the Italian crew, in leather coats and oilskins, were at action stations. For a while I clung to the rail by one of the torpedo-tubes, but I decided that I was getting cold and drenched to no purpose: till we had arrived at the pin-point I was nothing but a passenger. I groped my way towards the companion-ladder and went below.

At once I exchanged the external noises of wind and spray and exhaust for the internal and deafening roar of the engines. I passed through the outer cabin, full of aluminium tubes and control-panels, and entered the tiny inner cabin. The Italian wireless operator was bowed over his work, a small bulb glowing green above his head. On the bunk lay the American officer; he sat up and made room for me beside him. His lips moved, but I could not hear what he said: the din of the engines was too great. He leaned forward and put his mouth close to my ear.

'Plenty of spray top-sides?'

I nodded my head emphatically.

He gave an amiable grin. He was a great bull of a boy.

I leaned forward in turn. 'You'll have quite a bit of paddling to do tonight. Feeling strong?'

In reply he held out his slab of a hand and clenched it. Then he leaned towards me and shouted one word: 'Terrific.'

We spoke no more but sat wedged into the bunk, occasionally putting out a hand to prevent ourselves from being thrown on to the floor.

Seven o'clock, my watch read. Now they would be leaving the cave, looking round to see if they had forgotten anything, taking farewell of the place for the last time. Did they know it was for the last time? Had they received my signal? And, having received it, had they believed it? Were they saying: 'If he says he's coming then he'll come'? Or did they think that tonight would be just another of those many nights that they had spent vainly flashing. I hoped that they had confidence in me, and I rejoiced that, barring a disaster, I would not fail them.

Seven hours the *Sea Maid* had taken to cross the Adriatic: the young Italian captain of the Mas expected to be across in an hour and a half. At eight o'clock I clambered up the companionway.

We must have been about three miles off-shore, for the mass of mountains loomed dark ahead. As on New Year's Eve, there was no moon and but little starlight, and on the starboard bow I could see the twinkling lights of Vuno.

We were still travelling at speed, leaping and bouncing from the waves. The wind, though not strong, was fresh from the south. That old South Wind! How well I remembered it, and how when it had sprung up in the past we had said: 'No sortie to-night!' ...Well, tonight there would be a sortie.

Surely by now we ought to see their signal. About a mile offshore we reduced speed and crept silently in on the auxiliary motor. Slowly, slowly we came on. Still there was no signal. I peered at the vague skyline ahead and tried to recall how it had looked when last I had approached the coast. The bearded lieutenant had gone forward and was standing in the bows.

'Are we right?' I asked in French.

'I think so,' he replied. I did not like to bother him again so I kept silent.

Then suddenly we saw their signal, a feeble yellow flicker – their torch battery must be flat, I thought – but unmistakably the signal.

'Shall we reply?' the lieutenant asked me.

'Yes,' I said. 'Then close in quickly.'

We flashed our letter, and back came the weak response. I laughed inside myself to think of Butch standing there now on the cliff, flashing like a madman with excitement and dancing up and down.

But God! how slowly we were coming in.

'Ahead!' the lieutenant would call.

'Ahead!' from the captain.

A tinkle from the engine-room.

Then, before we had edged forward a hundred yards: 'Stop!' called the lieutenant.

'Stop!' cried the captain.

Another tinkle from the engine-room, and we stopped.

Again the process repeated itself; then again. I began to grow exasperated. I could make out now where we were and I knew there was no need for this excessive caution.

The flashing from the shore ceased. Perhaps they were afraid that they had made a mistake and that we were a German patrol. They would never understand how we could take so long to close in.

'Ahead!'

'Stop!'

Tinkle, tinkle.

Damn these Italians! What was wrong with them?

The lieutenant spoke: 'Here we stop.'

'But man, you're eight hundred yards from the shore!'

'We can come no closer,' he answered. 'There may be rocks.'

'There are no rocks, I assure you. I know this coast backwards.'

'We come no farther.' He was adamant. 'We wait here.'

'Oh! all right.' Their timidity infuriated me. 'Launch the rubber boats then.'

The Carley floats, tied together, flopped into the water. The American officer and I climbed down into one of them.

'How long will you be?' called the Italian.

'Two hours perhaps,' I called back, and we paddled out towards the shore, towing behind us the spare boat.

It was hard going, but preferable to the pathetic progress of the Italians. The wind sliced the tops off the waves and lopped them into the rubber boat, but twenty minutes' paddling brought us to the bay: I could recognise the outline of the cliffs. For a long time there had been no flashing from the shore, and now I hesitated to call out in case the enemy was near. But all at once we heard a voice.

'Hey, there!' it called. 'Hallo!'

It was Drake shouting... So there were no Germans about.

'Drake!' I called back. 'It's me – Major Overton. Are you all right?'

'O.K.,' the answer returned. 'Come on in.'

Inside the bay the water was calmer and the wind bore to my nostrils the nostalgic scent of wood smoke. In a moment, I thought, I shall be seeing them, speaking to them. Now we were at the entrance to the creek; a moment later we had turned into its still, narrow water, and as I saw the dancing light from the fire leaping on the rock face ahead I caught my breath; it was all so familiar that I could not believe I had ever left the place. We turned the last corner – and there before me was the very scene that had met my eyes on New Year's Eve... the beach, the cliffs, the overhanging trees, the blazing fire, the men standing round it.

We stopped paddling, the boats drifting gently forward. Silently we drew nearer to the beach, and silently the figures, silhouetted against the firelight, moved towards the water's edge. I wanted to call out to them, but I could not: I could not break the silence. In the shallow water we climbed out, and still no word was spoken as we waded ashore, pulling the boats behind us.

Suddenly the spell was shattered and a clamour of greeting broke out. The Albanians rushed forward – Chela, Morat, and, with the tears in his eyes, little Zechir. They kissed me, they wrung my hands. 'Oh, Major! Major!' they cried, again and again.

And there was Alpino – heavens! how thin the man had got – nodding his head, and smiling, and patting me on the back.

'Drake! Hallo! How are you?'

'Fine, sir.' And his forthright, vigorous hand-shake.

Chela was half excited, half shy. He took my hand and kissed me on both cheeks.

Butch was sitting on the beach, lying back against the rocks as though he were unable to get up. 'Hi there, Major!' he called. His voice was weak and his smile flickered out.

But where was Munzi? I looked round and saw him standing quietly in the shadows. I went to him and took his hand.

'Munzi!'

There was a little silence. Then he said: 'I am glad to see you.'

His beard was half down his chest and his hair was long and matted, but even through his great thick glasses I could see the look in his eyes.

'I am very glad to see you, Munzi.'

Thank God he was safe! I had more feeling of responsibility for him than for any of them.

'Gather round, will you?' I said. 'We've a lot to decide quickly.'

As their feet crunched across the beach I glanced again at Butch: he alone did not move. Something was very wrong with him; under the tangled beard his face was sunken and thin. He would lie back as though asleep, then for a moment spring feverishly to life – laugh, and speak in a loud voice. A minute later he would have sunk back into his torpor. All the time his hand rested on his battered wireless set; occasionally he gripped it and hugged it closer.

'Are there any Germans near?' I asked.

There were none, it seemed, within two miles of Sea View. The main body of German troops had withdrawn from the mountain; only patrols were left.

Then I told them of the decision to withdraw the mission.

'Do any of you think it's possible to stay on?' I finished.

For a moment they were silent, then Drake said: 'I'm afraid it would be impossible. You can't trust Dukat no longer. How we've managed to escape this time is a miracle.'

'Chela?'

'You cannot stay in this area. You will be betrayed. I cannot control Dukat any longer.'

I looked round the ring of weary, unkempt men.

'All right,' I said. 'Then we'll embark at once... Who are these?' I nodded to a group of scarecrows who stood huddled together. 'Italians?'

'Italian soldiers,' said Munzi. 'Can we take them with us?'

'Of course we can,' I answered. Then a thought struck me. 'In fact,' I went on, 'they can help a lot.'

If the captain of the Mas continued to be so nervous for his ship, the evacuation was going to take a long time. If he knew that there were some fellow Italians to be taken off he would probably be more co-operative.

'Have you got a canvas boat?' I asked.

They had: it had been well hidden and had escaped the Germans' search.

'Good. Now listen, Munzi. There's an Italian Mas lying outside the bay. The captain won't bring her close in because he's afraid of the rocks. I want you to go out there now in the canvas boat – take as many of these Italians as you can – and tell the captain that it's perfectly safe to enter the bay. Tell him that he must do so. He won't believe me, but he'll believe his own countryman... And you'd better take the heavy gear with you,' I went on. 'The canvas boat has a solid bottom.'

We were loading the gear into the boat when there was a loud shout. I turned to see Butch, on his feet, looking through his pack.

'My boots have gone! My spare boots!' His voice was hysterical.

I went up to him. 'What boots? I asked. Nobody would take your boots.'

'But they have, I tell you. It's these filthy Albanians. They'd steal anything from you. Jesus! I'll shoot the man that's taken my boots.'

He drew his revolver and advanced on Morat.

'It's you,' he threatened. 'You've stolen them. Give 'em back.'

'Listen, Butch.' I went and stood close to him. 'Don't worry about your boots. Even if they are stolen, what of it? Tomorrow you'll be able to get a dozen pairs.'

He stared at me, slowly realising the meaning of my words.

'Yeah, that's right: so I will.' He lowered the revolver and walked away, mumbling to himself.

Drake caught my eye and touched his forehead. 'He's been getting that way for days,' he said.

The sooner that Butch was off the beach, I thought, the better.

'Butch,' I called.

He turned back, smiling. The outburst might never have been.

'Butch, I'd like you to go out with Munzi. We'll need an English-speaking signaller out there on the ship.'

'Sure,' he replied easily. 'I'll do that. I'll put my stuff in the boat.'

Beside Munzi and Butch there was room for four of the Italian soldiers. Four were left on the beach.

'You may find the Mas has drifted northwards,' I called as we pushed them off. 'You should find them easily, though.'

We settled round the fire, and while we waited, Drake and

Chela told me of the happenings of the last month. How they had escaped was indeed a miracle. The Germans had placed posts all along Dukat valley, and a second line of pickets along the summit of Dukat mountain. When these were in position and escape routes blocked, a battalion had driven up the coast from Vuno, combing every inch of the ground as they came. Shepherds had been shot and their flocks driven off. Dukat itself had been terrorised, and nothing had saved the mission from betrayal but the secrecy with which they had covered their movements. Chela, Zechir and Morat had been the only Albanians to know their whereabouts. They had lived in holes, eating little, moving every night to a different hiding-place. Often the Germans had passed within a few paces of where they lay.

'Chela,' I said, when the story was done, 'in a little while the Partisans will control Albania. Will your life be safe then?'

He shrugged. 'No.'

'Do you want to come to Italy with me? I can promise you little future, but at least your life will be safe.'

'I wish to come with you,' he said simply. He spoke a few words to Morat and Zechir, then he turned back to me. 'They wish to come too. Will you take them?'

I hesitated: it was against my orders to take them out. Then I looked at their eager faces.

'Yes,' I said. 'I'll take them.'

Drake asked what time it was. I looked at my watch: it was eleven. Munzi had been gone an hour.

Drake gave a laugh. 'Do you know, sir, what would put the lid on this?... For that Iti boat to go off and leave us 'ere! We've no radio: Butch took his with 'im.'

'What about yours?'

'Mine's useless. The power pack is busted. Butch has the only radio set.'

We all laughed. 'Don't worry,' I said. 'Munzi will have the Mas inside the bay in half an hour.'

But as the half-hour lengthened into an hour I began to grow alarmed. Could Drake have been right? Could the Italians, for some reason or other, have turned back? Had the canvas boat come to grief on its way out? Certainly, now that I noticed it, the sea was rising: sheltered though we were from the wind, there was an unmistakable swell in the creek. The water was slapping and booming against the overhanging walls of rock, and on the beach, where previously there had been only the gentle lapping of the ripples, small waves were now breaking with a steady suck at the pebbles.

At midnight I got to my feet.

'Looks like they're not coming for us,' I said. 'We'll have to go and look for them.'

We untied the rubber floats and piled into them. I took charge of one, the American officer of the other. We divided the Italians between the two boats, and I kept Drake with me in case we needed to signal. There were six of us in each float – uncomfortable but not, I hoped, too dangerous. We pushed off.

It had been a mistake to untie the boats, for once in the bay the wind struck us fairly and in a moment the two boats were yards apart. We managed to bring them together, and then, so that we should not get separated, I lashed them together again so that we formed a giant cuff-link. Now one rubber boat would be swung round by the sea till the paddlers faced the land again; now the two boats would be hurled together so that we had to fend each other off; next moment the cord which linked us would be stretched violently as the two boats plunged in opposite directions. Sometimes we became so entangled that the cord passed underneath one boat and drew us together till we were in danger of capsizing. Yet all the time we pushed slowly out across the bay till we had reached its mouth; ahead lay pitch darkness and the open sea.

'Now flash,' I said to Drake. 'Flash all round.' There was no advantage in caution now. If an inquisitive German patrol investigated in the morning they would find that the birds were flown. 'Signal – "Where are you?"'

Drake flashed out the message, but there came no answering blink out of the darkness.

'Try to the north,' I told him. 'They've probably drifted.'

'If Butch and Munzi never got there,' Drake called back above the noise of sea and wind, 'there'll be no one on the boat can read English.'

'If they see any flashing they must know it's us,' I shouted. 'Go on. Flash.'

Once again he began to signal, this time northwards, and he had not spelt out five letters before there came what seemed to be a reply out of the darkness. But God! how faint and distant.

'Paddle towards the light,' I ordered. 'Hard as you can. And Drake – '

'Sir?'

'Signal – "Come and fetch us".'

Lunging and ploughing the boats turned northwards while Drake sent his message. No doubt it was hard to read, for sometimes the light must have disappeared into the trough of a wave and sometimes, when the boats spun round, Drake found himself signalling in the opposite direction. At all events, no reply came from the Mas.

Perhaps they had missed our signals. Perhaps that one flash had been their last attempt to make contact with us before they turned and headed for Italy.

'Shall I send it again?' Drake asked.

'No,' I said. 'Sit down and paddle.'

Drake was a strong paddler whom we couldn't afford to waste on fruitless signalling. From the one faint signal we had received from the Mas I judged that the boat was more than half a mile away, and that it would take us three-quarters of an hour to reach her.

Our situation was probably precarious to say the least, but somehow I found it only exhilarating. Through the thin rubber floor of the boat I could feel the very shape of the sea. Here now was the last test, a simple test, uncomplicated by mental scruples; our lives depended on the strength of our arms, just that, and though my sinews ached, I could have shouted aloud for joy in the simplicity of the struggle.

I think we all shared this feeling of elation. Of the dozen men bobbing on the sea probably only three could swim and certainly many had never been even in a rowing-boat before, but though the spray broke over them and into the rubber floats I believe not one of them was frightened. When I called to them, a cheerful babel of tongues called back out of the night.

'Drake!' I yelled.

'Sir?'

'Give them another flash now. Show them we're on our way.' The torch shone out, but from the darkness ahead there came no response.

Half an hour must have passed, and slowly the men became quiet as their strength grew less and the realisation of their position was borne in upon them. Only Drake was vociferous, yelling curses at the Italians for not daring to bring their boat nearer.

'Bastards!' he shouted as he drove his paddle into the sea. 'Cowardly bastards!'

'Flash again. Keep flashing,' I cried; and again and again his torch shone out into the dark.

Then, suddenly, there she was right ahead of us in the murkiness, turning almost on her side as she rolled and wallowed in the sea. Dim lights shone. A line was heaved to us, but we missed it. Again it fell through the air, and this time Drake had it fast. Now we were alongside, clawing and grabbing our way on board, then lying there panting; unable to get to our feet.

On the narrow deck it was chaos. Every man was too spent to speak or understand any language but his own. While the crew of the Mas tried to secure and pull on board the waterlogged Carley floats, the men who had come aboard continually impeded them as they lurched towards the companion-way.

Someone caught my arms and gripped them. It was Manzitti. He seemed to be beside himself and was sobbing; he could speak no words. When I got him below he said: 'They... they...' then his mouth moved soundlessly and he rolled his head about.

'What is it? What's happened?' I caught his shoulders. He made an effort to control himself. 'They would not come any nearer. I told them it was safe, but they would not believe me.'

'Never mind, Munzi. It's over now. We're here.'

'You don't understand,' he said. 'We waited two hours.' Again he turned his head about as though he were going through the ordeal of waiting. His glasses were streaked with tears and salt water, and all the time his lips kept moving through his thick beard. 'Then they said you must be drowned. They were going without you. They would not wait... I begged them. I went down on my knees to them...'

'Don't, Munzi, don't.'

'And we had the wireless set. We knew you had no radio if you were left behind.' The words were coming quicker now. 'Butch and I, we wanted to go back to the shore, but they would not let us... Then we flashed to you, and we thought we saw a reply... But then they stopped us flashing. They said it was too dangerous... And then, just before you came, the captain said that it would soon be light; that we must go.'

'Munzi!'

'I cannot tell you what I have been through.' He made a little strangled noise. 'You see... they are Italians... Italians. And... and...' He could not go on, but sank back against the wall.

Wet bodies were pushing through into the inner cabin. The young captain came down the steps to ask if there was any reason why he should not open the engines up immediately... Did the noise matter? He looked strained and tired. I told him he could make all the noise he liked. He disappeared up the stairs again.

The telegraph rang, and we began to move under the auxiliary engine. Slowly we gathered way; the rolling eased; we moved faster, faster. Again the telegraph rang with a roar like thunder the main engines burst into life and the Mas leaped forward over the waves.

I wedged myself into a corner of the outer cabin and fell into a doze.

It was still dark when I woke, and still the boat thundered along. Steadying myself by the aluminium rail I moved to the door of the inner cabin and looked in. Under the light of the green bulb sleeping bodies lay about the puddled floor like dead fish in a basket. There was Drake, soldierly and neat even in his dilapidation. Chela slept sitting and, close to him, Morat and Zechir... What new life awaited those three? I noticed how deadly pale Butch was, and how, even in sleep, he still clutched his precious wireless set. Manzitti's head, with its black matted hair and beard, hung on his chest, jolting with the movement of the ship. There they all were – all except Black. I wished that I had not lost Black. This, then, was the end. Now the last rites had been performed; soon I should have no more part in the lives of these men whom I had grown to love.

As I returned to my seat in the corner I put my hand into my pocket and pulled out what I thought was my handkerchief. But it was not: it was Ann's letter. The blue writing-paper had gone pulpy; the writing had smeared and wriggled across the page. Not a word was now legible.

I sat and gazed at this sodden symbol of my double failure. And, to my surprise, I could feel no sorrow: I could only feel content – a great, lonely content that filled my heart. The tale was complete. If this was the end, then it was the ordained end and I accepted it. I smoothed the letter as best I could and put it back in my pocket.

I pulled back the covering from the window and looked out; it was still black. I could not see the spray, but water was trickling down the pane, streaking it as Manzitti's glasses had been streaked.

I passed my hand over my face: salt was caked in my hair and in my eyebrows. I moistened my lips, and there was a sharp taste in my mouth, the taste of salt... But it had a living savour. It could not be taken from me. I could welcome it.

When next I looked up, the dawn was breaking and the spray was hurtling past the window. Soon we should be there. Soon we should be on land again. Soon we must again take up our lives and move forward.

Heedless, like a stone skimming over a pond, the Mas thundered on.